No Fair, No Problem

Longarm leaped out of the darkness, tackling the outlaw and driving him out of the saddle. The man yelped in surprise and alarm as he fell, but Longarm didn't know if the sound would be enough to warn the others. He hoped not. He and the outlaw hit the ground, the impact knocking them apart.

Longarm rolled over and came up onto his feet first. His fist lashed out and caught the other man, who was just starting to rise. Longarm followed the blow with a kick, figuring that at the moment he couldn't afford such niceties as not kicking a man while he was down.

As far as he was concerned, that was the best time to kick an outlaw.

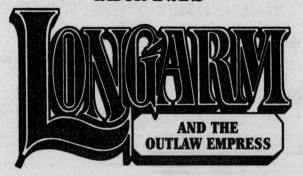

TABOR EVANS

LONGARM

AND THE OUTLAW EMPRESS

JOVE BOOKS, NEW YORK

THE BERKLEY PUBLISHING GROUP
Published by the Penguin Group
Penguin Group (USA) Inc.
375 Hudson Street, New York, New York 10014, USA
Penguin Group (Canada), 90 Eglinton Avenue East, Suite 700, Toronto, Ontario M4P 2Y3, Canada
(a division of Pearson Penguin Canada Inc.)
Penguin Books Ltd., 80 Strand, London WC2R 0RL, England
Penguin Group Ireland, 25 St. Stephen's Green, Dublin 2, Ireland (a division of Penguin Books Ltd.)
Penguin Group (Australia), 250 Camberwell Road, Camberwell, Victoria 3124, Australia
(a division of Pearson Australia Group Pty. Ltd.)
Penguin Books India Pvt. Ltd., 11 Community Centre, Panchsheel Park, New Delhi—110 017, India
Penguin Group (NZ), Cnr. Airborne and Rosedale Roads, Albany, Auckland 1310, New Zealand
(a division of Pearson New Zealand Ltd.)
Penguin Books (South Africa) (Pty.) Ltd., 24 Sturdee Avenue, Rosebank, Johannesburg 2196,
South Africa

Penguin Books Ltd., Registered Offices: 80 Strand, London WC2R 0RL, England

This is a work of fiction. Names, characters, places, and incidents either are the product of the author's imagination or are used fictitiously, and any resemblance to actual persons, living or dead, business establishments, events, or locales is entirely coincidental.

LONGARM AND THE OUTLAW EMPRESS

A Jove Book / published by arrangement with the author

PRINTING HISTORY
Jove edition / November 2006

ISBN: 0-515-14235-2

JOVE®
Jove Books are published by The Berkley Publishing Group,
a division of Penguin Group (USA) Inc.,
375 Hudson Street, New York, New York 10014.
JOVE is a registered trademark of Penguin Group (USA) Inc.
The "J" design is a trademark belonging to Penguin Group (USA) Inc.

PRINTED IN THE UNITED STATES OF AMERICA

10 9 8 7 6 5 4 3 2 1

Chapter 1

Longarm leaned back against the hard wooden seat, tried to ignore the dust blowing in through the windows of the bouncing, jolting stagecoach, and wondered whether the gal sitting across from him really wanted to do the deed with him or if she was just entertaining herself during a boring trip by making eyes at a stranger.

She wasn't bad-looking. In her late twenties, Longarm judged, with thick brown hair and a figure that bordered on being opulent without quite getting there. Her bosom was especially impressive as it thrust against the dark blue traveling outfit she wore. Her eyes were green and daring as they wandered over Longarm. From time to time her tongue slipped out of her mouth and lightly touched her full red lips.

If things had been different, Longarm probably would have tried to find out if she was serious or just teasing. But she had a wedding ring on her finger and a forty-year-old hombre dozing against her shoulder, so that sort of put a hitch in any plans Longarm might have made.

That and the fact that somebody might well be shooting at him before the stage got to where it was going.

The woman and her husband had gotten on the stage back in Gila Wells, Arizona Territory, the same place Longarm had boarded. The fella looked like some sort of businessman—a banker or a store owner, maybe. He had dozed off before the stage was five miles out of town on the Phoenix road. A few minutes later—Longarm supposed the woman waited until she was sure her husband was good and asleep—her gaze had grown bold.

He was the only other passenger. He had thrown his saddle on top of the coach and tied it down, then climbed inside, bringing his Winchester with him. He was dressed in range clothes—denim trousers and jacket and a butternut shirt. The Stetson that sat square on his head was flat-crowned and snuff-brown. He had been told in the past that he looked a little like an Indian because of his high cheekbones and his skin that was tanned to the color of old saddle leather. But no Indian had ever sported such a sweeping, luxurious, dark brown longhorn mustache.

Riding backward in the coach's front seat, he stretched his long legs as much as he could in the cramped confines of the bouncing Concord. His hand slipped inside his jacket and took one of his favorite three-for-a-nickel cheroots from his shirt pocket. He held it up and raised his eyebrows inquiringly at the woman. She smiled and made a motion with an elegantly manicured hand, indicating that he should go ahead and light up.

Longarm fished a lucifer out of the same pocket and snapped the match into life on an iron-hard thumbnail. He put the cheroot in his mouth, held the flame to the end of it, and puffed until the tightly rolled cylinder of tobacco was burning evenly. Then he shook out the match and dropped it on the floor of the coach. He drew smoke into his lungs and then blew it out. The dusty wind whipped it away, ruining any thought of blowing smoke rings.

"My name is Lucy," the woman said. "Lucy Clemenson."

On her shoulder, her husband let out a soft snore.

Longarm knew she was waiting for him to supply his name. "Custis Parker," he said, giving her the alias that he often used when he didn't want folks to know that he was really Deputy United States Marshal Custis Long, working for Chief Marshal Billy Vail out of the Denver office. It wasn't really a phony handle, since Parker was the middle name his ma had given him when he was born back in West-by-God Virginia.

"Are you traveling to Phoenix on business, Mr. Parker . . . or pleasure?" She managed to put a meaningful edge on the question.

Longarm said, "Well, I don't rightly know yet. I've been prospecting down around Gila Wells for a spell, but since I didn't have much luck at that I thought I'd head back up to ranching country and try to find a riding job. I expect to stop in Phoenix for a day or two first, though, and I figure I'll have a little fun while I'm there."

"Are you a cowboy, Mr. Parker?" Lucy Clemenson's tongue came out and touched her lips briefly. "I like cowboys."

"I've done my share of chousing those ornery critters." Again, not a total lie. Longarm had cowboyed for a while after coming west, following the end of the Late Unpleasantness some fifteen years earlier. But then he had pinned on a badge and hadn't followed any other line of work since.

3

"Where are you planning to stay in Phoenix?" Without waiting for him to answer, Lucy Clemenson went on, "We'll be staying at the Abernathy Hotel. That's one of the finest hotels in Phoenix, you know. Of course, I'll be stuck there by myself most of the time because Arthur is going up there to meet with several suppliers who furnish goods for his store in Gila Wells."

Arthur Clemenson continued snoring softly.

"Since Fate has cast us together in this bouncing contraption, perhaps we can continue our friendship in Phoenix," Lucy suggested.

Longarm wondered fleetingly if she was going to come right out and suggest that he drop by the hotel and screw her brains out while her husband was off at his business meetings. Seemed like ol' Arthur was one hell of a sound sleeper. The way those big breasts of Lucy's were rapidly rising and falling under her dress, she had to be excited by the flirting she was doing with this handsome stranger right under her husband's nose.

Longarm didn't answer right away, just puffed on the cheroot a couple of times instead. He didn't want to lead the woman on. He was in this stagecoach because of his job, not to make the acquaintance of some frustrated married woman with an itch in her drawers.

But before he could figure out exactly what he wanted to say, the coach hit a particularly rough rut in the trail and lurched violently on its broad leather thorough-braces. Longarm was jolted forward, and for a second he found himself inadvertently looking at the crotch of Arthur Clemenson's tweed trousers.

The son of a bitch was hard!

Longarm leaned back against the seat again and clenched his teeth on the cheroot. Across from him, Lucy

Clemenson was still smiling seductively at him and doing that touching-her-lips-with-her-tongue trick. She had no idea Longarm had spotted her husband's erection.

Either Arthur was having a mighty nice dream, or he was really awake and just pretending to doze on his wife's shoulder while she practically hiked her petticoat up and opened her legs to a stranger. Longarm figured it was the latter. He had a pretty good idea, too, that if he had gone to the Abernathy Hotel in Phoenix to look her up—which he never would have—Lucy wouldn't have been there. She and ol' Art would've been in some other hotel bedroom, pounding away at each other, all hot and bothered by the way she had acted like such a slut in the stagecoach.

Or else she *would* have been there, and her husband would be, too, and Longarm was damned if he was even going to *think* about that.

Luckily he didn't have to, because at that moment the stage lurched again and began to skid to a sudden, unexpected halt. Up on the box, the driver called out sharply to the six-horse hitch as he hauled back on the leathers.

This time there was no way Arthur Clemenson could pretend to still be asleep, because he and his wife were almost thrown off the seat onto the floor of the coach by the violent stop. "Oh, my God!" cried Lucy. "What's happening? What's wrong?"

Longarm leaned over and looked out the window. The trail had just made a bend around a large boulder, and a log lay across it. The driver hadn't been able to see the obstacle until the coach was almost on top of it.

A swift rataplan of hoofbeats made Longarm look toward a nearby arroyo, and he wasn't the least bit surprised to see four riders come boiling out of it. They were masked, with bandannas tied around the lower halves of their faces and their hat brims pulled low to further obscure their features.

And of course, they had guns in their hands.

"Looks like the stage is being held up," drawled Longarm.

Lucy Clemenson clapped her hands to her mouth, but that didn't do much to muffle the terrified shriek she let out.

Her husband, now wide awake if he hadn't been all along, grabbed her arm and said, "Lucy! Stop that! Screaming won't do any good."

That was true, thought Longarm, and it might even do some harm if all the caterwauling made those gunmen nervous. A nervous owlhoot was often a trigger-happy owlhoot. Longarm said firmly, "You'll be just fine, ma'am. If you settle down and cooperate, I don't reckon anybody will hurt you."

Arthur Clemenson gave him a hard-eyed glance. "Are you part of this, mister?" he demanded.

"Not hardly. But I know how these road agents operate. Chances are they won't start shooting unless they're forced to."

Lucy's scream had died away into a bubbling sob. Clemenson said, "Listen to the man, Lucy. You'll just make things worse by carrying on."

She sniffed and made a visible effort to control her fear. It wasn't helped by the sudden blasts as the robbers fired a couple of shots in the air. They surrounded the coach, two on each side of the stopped vehicle.

"Driver, throw down that scattergun!"

The order came from one of the masked men in a harsh voice. Longarm felt the coach shift a little on its thoroughbraces as the elderly jehu moved on the box.

"Take it easy, mister," the old-timer said in a querulous voice. "I'm throwin' it down. I ain't plannin' to cause you any trouble."

"That's a good idea," said the spokesman for the gang. Longarm heard the driver's shotgun strike the ground. "Now the hogleg."

A pistol thudded to the trail beside the greener.

"Stay where you are and keep your hands up," ordered the boss outlaw. Then he turned his attention to the passengers. "You there, in the coach! Climb out slow and easy, and don't try anything! If you do, we'll fill you full of lead!"

Lucy sobbed again and clutched at her husband. "Oh, Arthur, I can't, I just can't!"

"You have to, dear," he told her. "If we don't do what they tell us, they're liable to kill us. They're desperados. They don't have anything to lose."

He was right about that. This bunch didn't have a history of harming their victims, but Longarm didn't doubt that they would shoot if they felt they had to. Keeping his voice calm and steady, he said to Lucy, "Listen to your husband, ma'am. We'll all get through this." He reached for the door handle. "I'll go first, and you folks just follow me, nice and easy like the man said."

He swung the door back and moved slowly into the opening, holding his hands up and out in front of him where the outlaws on that side of the coach could plainly see them.

"That's good, that's good," the leader said as Longarm stepped out. The man jerked the Colt in his hand, indicating that Longarm was to move to his right. The big lawman did so, keeping his hands up.

It was tempting to reach for his own Colt, which was

holstered on his left hip in a cross-draw rig. But in the first place, it was damned difficult to outdraw an already-drawn gun, mighty near impossible, in fact, and Longarm knew it. And in the second place, to even try it would ruin all his carefully laid plans.

As soon as Longarm was clear of the door, Arthur Clemenson moved into it. He climbed out, slightly awkwardly, and then turned back to reach up into the coach. "Come on, Lucy," he urged. "You have to do this."

Sniffling, she descended from the coach with her husband's help. As the outlaws got their first good look at her, the one next to the leader grunted in appreciation. The leader glanced sharply at him, as if in warning.

Longarm caught the little byplay between the two owlhoots. This gang didn't have any record of molesting female passengers during their stage holdups. Out here on the frontier, laying an unwanted hand on a decent woman would get a man hunted down and killed faster than just about anything except maybe stealing a horse. And then it would probably depend on the horse.

Once the three passengers were out of the coach, the pair of outlaws on the other side of the vehicle dismounted while the two on this side covered Longarm and the Clemensons. They went to the boot at the rear of the stagecoach and began untying the canvas cover.

The boss outlaw looked at Longarm and said, "All right, you, big fella . . . take that gun out left-handed and toss it in the brush."

"Sure," said Longarm. It went against the grain for him to give up his gun, but he had to play along. Besides, he still had a little two-shot derringer in his jacket pocket and another Colt Peacemaker tucked behind his belt at the small of his back, if it really came down to a need for gunplay. Riding in the coach with the gun behind him hadn't been very comfortable, but the weight of it was mighty reassuring right about now.

"You got a gun, mister?" the leader of the gang asked Clemenson.

"No, I don't carry a weapon. I'm a businessman, not a . . . a shootist."

"Really?" The owlhoot chuckled sarcastically. "And here I'd mistook you for Wild Bill Hickok, come back to life."

Clemenson flushed angrily. "If you're going to rob us, then go ahead and rob us," he snapped. "There's no need to be insulting."

"All right, empty your pockets," ordered the leader. "Lady, let's have what's in your bag."

Lucy sniffled but complied with the command, opening her bag and taking out a small coin purse. Her husband handed over a fat wallet. The wallet that Longarm slipped out of his pocket contained only a couple of greenbacks. The rest of his money, along with the folder that held his badge and bona fides, was hidden in a secret pocket on his saddle, on top of the coach.

"Now your rings and watches and all your other jewelry."

Longarm wasn't carrying the turnip watch that usually rode in his pocket. He had left it in Gila Wells with the local sheriff, who was going to mail it to Billy Vail back in Denver. Longarm could reclaim it when this job was over and he returned home. He turned empty palms toward the leader of the gang and said, "It wasn't much, but you've cleaned me out, pard."

"You sure about that?" Even in the shadow of the pulled-down hat brim, Longarm could see the shrewdness in the man's eyes. "You look like a saddle tramp, but maybe you've got a money belt strapped under those duds."

Longarm forced his muscles not to tense. If the owl-hoots searched him, they would find the derringer and the gun hidden at his back. Instead he laughed and said, "I damn sure wish I *did* have a money belt, and something to put in it!"

He didn't know if that would deflect their attention from him, but the next moment something else did. One of the outlaws rummaging through the boot at the rear of the coach suddenly said, "It ain't here!"

The boss's head jerked toward him. "What?"

"It ain't here, I said! We've looked all through the boot. He lied to us, T—"

The man stopped himself before he accidentally called the boss by name. Even that near-slip was enough to make the leader scowl darkly. He was also angry about whatever they had expected to find in the boot not being there.

Swinging his gun toward the driver, he demanded, "Are you carrying anything else?"

The jehu had his hands up like Longarm and the others. He was a white-bearded old-timer who wore a dust-covered, concho-studded buckskin vest over a flannel shirt. An ancient, battered hat with the brim pushed up in front was jammed down on a tangled thatch of white hair. As the boss outlaw barked the question at him, he licked his lips nervously and then said, "Not a blessed thing, mister, not even a mail pouch on this run. You can look up here under the seat if you want. There ain't no strongbox."

"I can see that from here," growled the leader.

"What was it you was lookin' for?"

"Never mind about that." Anger and frustration drew

the man's words taut. He jerked his gun barrel at Long-arm and the Clemensons. "Get back in there. Old man, climb down and get in with them. If any of you so much as poke your nose out in the next half-hour, I swear it'll get shot off!"

The driver clambered down from the box while Arthur and Lucy Clemenson got back into the coach. Longarm went next, and finally the driver joined them.

"Cut the leaders!" the boss outlaw ordered one of the other men. Longarm had hoped they wouldn't do that, but he was prepared for the eventuality. After one of the out-laws had cut loose the first two horses in the team, he yelled at them and fired his gun into the air, sending the animals running.

Then the man swung up into his saddle and joined his three companions. They fired several shots just above the coach to reinforce the warning they had given the people inside. Lucy Clemenson screamed again and ducked, even though the bullets hadn't come anywhere near her. Her husband put his arms around her to comfort her.

Outside the coach, the outlaws wheeled their horses and galloped off toward the arroyo. Longarm heard the hoofbeats receding in the distance. He looked over at the stagecoach driver, who had sat down beside him. The two men exchanged satisfied grins.

"Well," said Longarm, "that worked out just fine."

Chapter 2

"Just fine!" exploded Arthur Clemenson. "Are you insane? Those men just *robbed* us! They threatened to kill us!"

"Yeah, but they didn't get the silver shipment they was expectin' to find," said the driver. He chortled. "I reckon that tells us what we need to know, Custis. There's sure enough somebody back in Gila Wells workin' hand in glove with them scallywags."

Longarm nodded. "We'll figure out who it is once the gang's rounded up. Shouldn't be too hard. Jeff Walters planned to let different things slip to different folks in the mining syndicate's office, so once he knows that the gang stopped this particular coach, that'll tell him who the inside man is."

Clemenson stared back and forth between Longarm and the old-timer in amazement. Even Lucy, in her upset state, was beginning to realize that not everything was as she had believed it to be. She sniffled, blinked away some tears, and said, "You . . . you're not a cowboy!"

Longarm smiled. "No, ma'am. Deputy U.S. Marshal Custis Long, at your service." He reached up and gave a polite tug on the brim of his Stetson, then inclined his head toward the man beside him. "And this scruffy old pelican is Salty Stevens. We've worked together before on a few cases, so I asked him to give me a hand on this one."

"You . . . you're a lawman?" stammered Clemenson in astonishment.

"That's right."

"Well, then, why the hell did you just stand there and let those outlaws rob us?" the businessman shouted furiously.

Longarm felt a surge of anger and reined in his own temper. He didn't really blame Clemenson for being mad. For all he had known, the outlaws were going to rape his wife and then kill them all. Of course, if Longarm had seen that things were going bad, he would have dropped the ruse and done his best to defend the couple. But Clemenson hadn't had any way of knowing that.

"You weren't in as much danger as you thought you were," Longarm told them. "That bunch has held up several stagecoaches in these parts lately. That's why my boss, the chief marshal for the Western Region, sent me and a couple more deputies down here. We figured the gang has an inside man and we've been trying to nab him. Now that we've found out what we need to know, Salty can take that information on to Phoenix while I go after the robbers."

"You're going after them?" asked Clemenson. "How?"

Longarm didn't answer the question directly. He reached for the door handle instead. "I reckon it's been long enough now to get out again."

Clemenson yelped in alarm. "Don't! That man said he'd shoot us if we tried to get out of the coach."

14

"Him and the other three are probably a mile away by now," Longarm explained patiently. "That was just a threat to scare us, so they could get a bigger lead. That's the way they usually operate. I told you they've pulled jobs like this before, so we know what they do. That was how I knew there was a good chance they wouldn't hurt any of us unless something happened to spook them."

"You're a liar," Lucy said. "You told me you were a cowboy." That falsehood seemed to bother her more than anything else.

Clemenson said, "You still haven't told me how you're going to go after them. You don't have a horse, and you can't chase them in this stagecoach."

"I've got a horse," said Longarm as he swung the door open. He stepped out. Salty followed him.

Longarm looked around. He didn't see any sign of the holdup men and couldn't hear their horses anymore. They had lit a shuck out of here, just as he expected. Still, the hair on the back of his neck stood up a little as he thought that one of them could be perched on a hill somewhere, maybe a thousand yards away, watching the stagecoach through field glasses. A shot from a Sharps buffalo gun could carry that far. None of the outlaws had been carrying such a weapon during the holdup, but they could have had one stashed somewhere nearby just for the occasion.

He couldn't worry about that possibility. Instead he went to the team and began unhitching the big bay gelding that was the off leader now that the first two horses in line had been run off. The bay was a little smaller than the other horses, but not enough so that the difference was too obvious. The outlaws hadn't noticed. Longarm had been counting on that.

"It'll take us a long time to get to Phoenix with only three horses pullin' this coach," said Salty.

"The other two won't have gone far. I'll round them up before I go after that bunch."

Salty frowned dubiously. "You don't want the trail gettin' cold."

"That chore won't take long enough to worry about. This will be the freshest trail anybody's tried to follow so far, since those varmints started raising hell down here."

The old-timer scratched his jutting white beard. "Yeah, that's true enough, I reckon. Lemme finish that unhitchin'. You fetch your saddle down."

Longarm climbed onto the driver's box and untied his McClellan saddle from the rail around the top of the coach. He lowered it to Salty, who had finished freeing the bay from its harness. Longarm vaulted lithely to the ground and took the saddle from the old jehu.

Arthur Clemenson got out of the coach while Longarm was getting the bay ready to ride. "This is your saddle horse?" he asked.

Longarm tightened the cinch. "Yep. Draft horses are a mite bigger and stronger, but he was able to pose as one for a while . . . like I posed as a drifting cowboy."

"And you're going to follow those outlaws?"

"That's the idea."

"Do you think you'll be able to recover my wallet and watch and my wife's jewelry?"

Longarm walked over to where he had tossed his six-gun and retrieved it. He slipped it back into the cross-draw rig as he said, "I'll try, Mr. Clemenson, but I can't make you any promises. My job is to round up the gang that's been stealing silver shipments. That falls under federal jurisdiction because of the contracts that the mining syndicate down at Gila Wells has with the U.S. government, and my first duty is to the Justice Department. But if I can lay hands on your goods without jeopardizing the case, I'll get 'em back for you."

"Thank you, Marshal. I understand." Clemenson's voice turned hard again. "But if you don't recover my property, I intend to file a complaint with your superior, based on the fact that you just stood there and let those men rob us. That seems to me to be an inappropriate way for a federal officer to behave."

Longarm wanted to tell Clemenson to go ahead and file his complaint and be damned, but he bit back the angry words. As Billy Vail liked to remind him from time to time, they worked for the government and the government was run by the people, at least in theory. So in a way Clemenson was one of Longarm's bosses—although he was damned if he was going to think of the man that way.

With his jaw tightly clenched, Longarm swung up into the saddle and rode down the trail in search of the two stampeded horses. He found them a few minutes later. They were cropping contently at the bunch grass beside the trail. Longarm hazed the horses back to the stagecoach.

"You go ahead after them varmints," Salty told him. "I'll have to do some patchin' on the harness where that bastard cut it, but I'll get those horses hitched back up after a while and we'll start on into Phoenix."

"I'll give you a hand if you need it, driver," offered Clemenson. "I may not look like it now, but when I was a boy I worked some in a stable."

"Much obliged," said Salty.

Longarm edged his horse over by the coach and said to Clemenson, "Hand me my rifle out of there, would you?"

The man reached inside, got the Winchester, and handed it up to Longarm. As he was sliding the rifle into the saddle boot, Lucy Clemenson looked out the window at him, an expression of cool disdain on her face. Obviously her feelings toward him had changed considerably in the past half-hour. That was just fine with Longarm. He gave her a polite nod anyway and then turned away from the coach.

Salty lifted a hand in farewell. "Be careful, Custis," he called.

"You, too, old-timer."

With that, Longarm heeled the bay into a trot toward the arroyo where the fleeing outlaws had disappeared.

This was rocky, semi-arid country south of Phoenix, the sort of terrain where a trail was difficult to follow. The hard ground didn't take hoofprints well except in the sandy stretches, and anybody who didn't want to be followed would take pains to avoid areas like that.

But to an experienced tracker and manhunter like Longarm, there were nearly always a few signs here and there to tell him which way his quarry had gone. The outlaws hadn't been trying to cover their trail when they descended into the arroyo, so Longarm had no trouble finding where they had ridden down a crumbled bank. The few hoofprints he could see indicated that the men had ridden north. He headed that way, too, moving slow and easy, his keen eyes always alert as he rode along the bottom of the defile.

There was only a limited number of places where they could get out of the arroyo. Longarm checked every one he came to and saw no sign that the men he was following had left the twisting gash in the earth. As the day went on the temperature grew warmer, and down here in this gully he didn't even get any breeze. He took his jacket off, rolled it up, and tied it behind his saddle. Taking his hat off for a moment, he sleeved sweat from his forehead.

The arroyo curved northwestward. Longarm knew there was a range of small mountains in that direction. He wouldn't be a bit surprised if the gang had their hideout up in those mountains.

After several miles, the floor of the arroyo gradually lifted and finally it petered out entirely and Longarm found himself riding once again on flat, brush-dotted plains. He had found some more tracks that indicated the riders had followed the arroyo all the way to its end and then headed off toward the mountains. Those gray, rounded peaks looked close in the crystal clear air, so close that it seemed almost like Longarm could reach out and touch them, but he knew that was an illusion. The mountains were still a good ten miles away.

A short distance farther on, he found some horse droppings that were fairly fresh. In this hot, dry air, it was difficult to judge exactly how much time had passed since the horse had left this pile behind, but Longarm knew the outlaws couldn't be more than an hour ahead of him.

The sun wheeled on to the west. Finally, in late afternoon, he reached the foothills of that little mountain range. The landscape grew more rugged and green.

He reined the bay to a stop and sat there in the saddle for a long moment, scanning the hills ahead of him, searching for movement, or the reflection of the lowering sun from some bit of metal. He didn't see anything, but that didn't mean the owlhoots weren't up there. By now, they probably knew that he was pursuing them. Men like that would check their back trail pretty often, and they had to have seen him riding across the open, almost desolate countryside.

Of course, they might not be sure it was him. As far as they knew, he didn't have a saddle horse and was stranded back there with the crippled stagecoach. Other men rode through this country. They might have seen him and decided that he didn't have anything to do with them.

Longarm didn't want to bet his life on that possibility, though. Lawbreakers, like lawmen, were just naturally suspicious hombres. They wouldn't be likely to ignore a potential threat.

That meant he could be riding straight into an ambush or some other sort of trouble. But it wouldn't be the first time, and anyway, he didn't see that he had much choice.

Some bent-down grass and a few more horse apples pointed him in the right direction. He followed a little valley between two hills that climbed to a rocky saddle of ground. As he drew within a couple of hundred yards, his eyes narrowed as he studied the rocks in that saddle. They were big enough to give a man, or even two, some cover. . . .

That thought had barely gone through his mind when his eyes caught a flicker of movement. Instantly, he kicked his feet free of the stirrups and dived off the bay's back, grabbing the stock of the Winchester and dragging it free as he fell.

Two shots cracked as he hit the ground and rolled fast to the side. One of the bullets struck a rock and whined off harmlessly. Longarm didn't know where the other one went, but since he wasn't hit and the horse wasn't, either, he considered that shot harmless, too. He came to a stop in a little depression behind a couple of scrubby but evidently hardy bushes. The thin growth wouldn't stop a bullet, but at least it screened him from the eyes of the bushwhackers.

Another shot sounded. The bullet kicked up dirt near the hooves of the bay. The bastards were trying to shoot his horse and set him a-foot!

"Shoo!" Longarm called to the horse as it danced around skittishly. He'd rather have it run off than shot down. At least if the animal bolted, Longarm would still have a chance of catching up with it later.

As another shot came too close for comfort, the bay turned and lunged off at right angles to the path Longarm had been following up to the saddle between the hills. Longarm was glad to see the horse go. Now he could concentrate on dealing with those blasted drygulchers.

Unfortunately, there was no cover around him. He couldn't really go anywhere. As long as the two riflemen stayed up there and took the occasional potshot at him to let him know they were still there, he was pinned down. He could return their fire, but they had better cover than he did. It would just be blind luck if he scored a hit on either of them.

There had been four members of the gang that held up the stagecoach, he mused as two more shots rang out and the bullets whistled over his head. Did that mean that two of them had stayed behind to ambush the man following them while the other two rode on ahead to the hideout?

Or were the other two somewhere nearby, waiting for him to be pinned down so that they could circle around and catch him in a crossfire?

No sooner had that thought gone through Longarm's mind than he heard the sudden rattle of stones somewhere behind him. He jerked around and rolled over. A bullet cut through the brush no more than a foot from his head.

But that wasn't the most immediate threat. The two men charging at him, their hands filled with guns, fit that description a whole lot better.

Chapter 3

Longarm wasn't sure where the outlaws had been lurking, but there were plenty of hiding places in these foothills. And it didn't really matter at the moment. What was important was that they began to fire at him, smoke and flame geysering from the muzzles of their guns.

He already had a round in the Winchester's chamber, and he squeezed the trigger. The rifle cracked as he fired it from his position lying on his back in the little depression. Luck as well as skill guided the shot, and the bullet caught one of the charging owlhoots in the throat. The slug angled up, slicing through the upper spine and severing arteries so that a crimson fountain suddenly spewed from the wound. The man flipped over backward like he had run into a stone wall.

But the other man was still alive and shooting, and the bullets flying from his gun thudded into the ground scant inches from Longarm. The big lawman worked the Winchester's lever and jackknifed up off the ground. A bullet fired by one of the hidden gunmen on the higher ground screamed past his ear from behind. He dived forward as more shots sizzled through the air over his head. As he landed on his belly, he triggered the rifle again, firing three times as fast as he could work the lever.

Only one of the bullets found its target, but that one bored into the belly of the charging outlaw, doubling him over in agony, his gun slipping from his fingers. Momentum pitched him forward, and as he landed on the ground, he curled up around the terrible pain in his midsection.

Longarm figured that man was out of the fight. He rolled again, well aware that he was still a target for the men hidden in the rocks. As he came to his feet he saw spurts of smoke up there, followed instantly by the crack of shots. He felt a tug on the side of his shirt and knew that one of the bullets had come that close to hitting him. Snapping the Winchester to his shoulder, he slammed four rounds at the bushwhackers, again triggering them off as fast as he could work the rifle's lever.

Hoping that might make them duck for cover, Longarm took off in a zigzagging run toward scrubby trees about twenty yards to his left. That seemed like a mighty long twenty yards, even though he covered the ground in less than a handful of heartbeats. A slug kicked up dust near his feet as he threw himself behind the trees. Another bullet chewed bark from one of the trunks.

His position wasn't perfect, but it was sure as hell an improvement. Not only that, but two members of the gang were down, one dead and the other mortally wounded and rapidly closing in on crossing the divide, to judge by the amount of blood. Longarm had cut the odds against him in half.

He lay there propped on his elbows, waiting for a shot

24

and trying to catch his breath. For many years, he had lived on the edge of danger, skirting death again and again, but each time still sent his heart racing. He reckoned that a man never really got used to nearly dying.

The guns fell silent. From this angle, the hidden riflemen didn't have a very good shot at Longarm. Of course, he didn't have a good shot at them, either. It was a standoff of sorts, but it couldn't last for very long. The sun would be down in less than an hour, Longarm reckoned, and once the fiery orb dropped below the horizon, darkness would follow quickly.

That's why Longarm wasn't surprised when he heard the sudden rattle of hoofbeats. The bushwhackers had seen their plans go awry, and two of them were dead—the second man Longarm had shot had stopped moving now. The surviving members of the gang couldn't be blamed for deciding to cut their losses and taking off for the tall and uncut.

Longarm heard something behind him and glanced over his shoulder. The bay had come back and was now standing just a few yards away, looking at him curiously. Longarm was about to stand up and reach for the reins when one last shot rang out above him. The horse jerked his head up but didn't make a sound before toppling over on its side. Blood welled darkly from the hole in the animal's head.

Longarm's deeply tanned face quirked in a grimace of anger and disgust, and he uttered a heartfelt "Shit!"

One of those outlaws had stayed behind just long enough to get in a final, lucky shot. Longarm couldn't continue chasing them without a horse, and right now he didn't have one.

He turned his head to glare up at the rocks where the

outlaws had hidden. He heard more hoofbeats. That would be the second man, the one who had killed the bay horse, following his partner.

Even though Longarm was convinced of that, he waited for several minutes before standing up and moving into the open. He walked around the bay and went toward the two men lying on the ground, each of them surrounded by a pool of blood. Longarm kept the Winchester trained on them as he approached, but neither man moved, nor was likely to ever again. He checked closer and made sure both men were dead.

They had been on foot when they attacked him, so they had to have left their mounts somewhere nearby. Longarm went in search of the horses and finally found them about twenty minutes later, in a gully that was screened by a stand of small trees.

Longarm picked the most likely looking of the pair and mounted it, then rode back to the site of the ambush leading the other horse. By now he had only ten or fifteen minutes of good light left, and he knew that wouldn't be enough to allow him to catch up to the other two outlaws. As bitter as the pill was to swallow, he would just have to wait until morning and hope he could pick up their trail. Even if he was able to do that, they would have a good long lead on him.

Since he couldn't do much of anything else, he searched the bodies of the two men he had killed. Neither of them had the meager loot from the stagecoach robbery, which meant that neither of them was the leader. That didn't surprise Longarm. He had figured that the boss outlaw would have been more likely to be one of the bushwhackers hidden behind the rocks.

One of the dead men was a burly hombre in his early

thirties, with a short, curly brown beard. The other man was a little younger, maybe in his late twenties, and Longarm frowned as he looked from one face to the other and saw the strong resemblance between them, despite the fact that one face was bearded and the other clean-shaven. The younger man had been considerably smaller, too. But Longarm had no doubt that they were brothers.

Their pockets held a little money and some ammunition, an elk's-tooth lucky piece, a medal from the Civil War—maybe earned, maybe stolen, it was hard to say; the older of the two outlaws might have served in the latter days of that war, lying about his age to get into the army—and a folded piece of paper. Longarm unfolded the paper and studied it in the rapidly fading light.

It was a map, he saw. Not a hand-drawn map, but a professionally printed one, and what it displayed was the state of Nevada. There was nothing unusual about that. However, someone had taken a pencil and drawn a circle around a spot in the rugged mountains south of the valley of the Humboldt River. Next to it in crudely printed letters was written the word *Zamora*.

Longarm frowned. Who or what the hell was Zamora? And what was located at the spot circled on the map? By and large, Nevada was one of the most desolate places west of the Mississippi, and the valley of the Humboldt was especially barren. Of course, there were mines in Nevada. Men with enough daring and luck had gotten rich off the silver and gold deposits to be found there. Maybe the circle on the map marked the location of a mine, and this fella Zamora owned it.

But what did that have to do with a gang of stagecoach robbers in Arizona Territory? Maybe the gang had been planning to head for Nevada when they got through robbing down here, thought Longarm. That was just a guess on his part, but it was worth pondering, especially if he couldn't get on the trail of the surviving owlhoots or locate their hideout. He wondered if Billy Vail would be willing to let him make a trip to Nevada.

He took the two horses and moved higher in the foothills, searching for a good place to make camp for the night. He didn't like leaving the bodies behind for scavengers, but the ground was hard and he didn't have a shovel. Besides, they had done their damnedest to kill him, and that didn't put him in an overly generous mood. He clucked to the horses and rode on.

"This arm hurts like blazes, Tom," said the younger of the two men riding through the night.

"The bullet barely grazed you," replied the older one. "You'll be fine."

That was easy for Tom to say, thought Brad Corrigan. He wasn't the one who'd been wounded. Brad muttered a curse under his breath. It had been a damned lucky shot. No way that bastard they had bushwhacked should have been able to hit him, hidden as he and Tom had been in those boulders.

Brad wondered, not for the first time today, just who that stubborn son of a bitch really was.

Tom didn't think he was just a saddle tramp, as he had appeared to be when the Corrigan brothers held up the stagecoach. A saddle tramp wouldn't have found a horse and come after them like this man had, Tom said. No drifting cowboy had that much ambition and determination. The man had to be a star packer of some sort. At least, that was the way Tom had it figured, and Brad had always known that his oldest brother was plenty smart.

Only brother now, thought Brad with a wrench of grief

28

in his guts. Asa and Logan were dead. That bastard had killed them.

Fighting back tears of grief as he thought about how he would never see his brothers again, Brad asked, "How long are we gonna ride? Are we gonna make camp sometime?"

"Damn it, Brad, do you have to whine so blasted much?" snapped Tom. "You're a man full-grown. Why don't you act like one for a change?"

The words stung, but Brad told himself that Tom didn't really mean them. Tom was just upset about Asa and Logan, too. With only a year between them in age, he and Asa had been close, even for brothers. They had come up with the idea of stealing the silver shipments that were usually carried by stagecoach from Gila Wells to Phoenix, and they had planned all the jobs together. Tom knew a fella who worked as a clerk in the office of Jeff Walters, superintendent of the Gila Wells Mining Syndicate; they had been acquaintances back in Kansas after the four Corrigan brothers had left the family farm in Illinois and started drifting west. This clerk had some sort of secret that he didn't want anybody to know about, so it had been easy for Tom to persuade him to tip them off every time a shipment of silver was going out, in return for keeping quiet about what he knew.

And for weeks now, everything had gone off without a hitch—until today. Until that tall, mustachioed son of a bitch, whoever he was, had come after them. Brad still couldn't quite bring himself to believe that Asa and Logan were gone. The ambush should have worked. That bastard should have been buzzard bait by now.

"If I ever line my sights on that hombre again, I'll kill him for sure," muttered Brad.

Tom didn't have to ask who his little brother was talking about. "You had your chances back there," he said.

"So did you," replied Brad. "In fact, you had more of them because I couldn't handle a rifle after he winged me."

The shot that had struck him had been a ricochet, so the bullet had lost some of its power. But it had still hurt something fierce as it burned across his upper left arm, ripping his shirt sleeve and leaving a bloody red welt on the flesh. Tom had cut a strip off the bottom of Brad's shirt and bound up the wound. When they got a chance, Tom had said, they would do a better job of cleaning and bandaging it.

"I'm the one who killed his horse," said Tom. "Better be thankful for that. If I hadn't, he'd still be dogging our trail."

"How do you know he's not? Maybe he got Asa's horse, or Logan's."

"It would have taken him a while to find them, and he can't trail us in the dark." Tom sounded confident. "If we push on all night, by morning we'll be back at the cabin and he'll never find us."

"You mean we're not gonna stop and make camp?"

Tom let out a snort of derision. "When we're already this close to the hideout? That'd be a damned stupid thing to do, Brad."

In other words, thought Brad, he's telling me that *I'm* damned stupid. Well, maybe he was, at least compared to Tom, but he didn't appreciate having that pointed out.

"Ewell's gonna be damned sorry if he double-crossed us," Tom went on. "I couldn't hardly believe it when Logan said the silver wasn't there on the stagecoach."

"He's been right about all the other shipments," Brad

pointed out. "Maybe he just made a mistake this time, or somebody told him wrong."

"Or somebody told him the wrong thing *on purpose*," mused Tom. He was silent for a few moments as he rocked along in the saddle, and Brad knew that meant he was thinking. Finally, he continued, "Walters must have figured out by now that somebody who works for the mining syndicate has been passing information to us. So he called in the law and worked out a plan to catch whoever the inside man was."

"Or Ewell just sold us out."

Tom shook his head. "He wouldn't do that. He's too scared of what I know about him."

"It must've been something pretty bad." Tom had never told Brad exactly what Ewell's secret was.

Tom laughed. "Bad enough to get him lynched. He killed a couple of women in Kansas. They were just whores, but still . . . He talked 'em into coming to his shack, and then he cut 'em up bad enough that they died. He buried the bodies so that nobody would ever know what had happened to them . . . not that anybody really cared about a pair of soiled doves. I never would have known about it if he hadn't gotten really drunk one night and started blubberin' about what he'd done. I reckon he felt guilty."

"I should think so!" said Brad, appalled by what he had just heard. "That's terrible."

Tom looked over at him and said, "Little brother, there's one thing you've got to learn about people: if they want to do something bad enough, they'll find a way to convince themselves that it's all right to go ahead and do it."

31

"Like holding up stagecoaches and stealing silver shipments? Ma and Pa didn't raise us to be outlaws, Tom."

"They didn't raise us to be anything except miserable, dirt-poor bastards like them," said Tom. "So don't start in on me about us being outlaws, Brad."

Both brothers fell silent again for a spell, each brooding on his own thoughts. Finally, Tom said, "The law will be looking for us more than ever now. And with Asa and Logan gone, maybe it's time for us to move on and get out of this part of the country with the loot we've already got stashed."

"You mean it? Give up bein' desperadoes?"

"I didn't say that. But we could find us a good place where we could lie low for a while, until that lawdog behind us and all his star-packing compadres get tired of looking for us. I've already got a place in mind."

"That sounds fine to me, Tom," said Brad. He was tired of being on edge all the time, constantly worrying about being hunted down and discovered by lawmen. He knew good and well that Tom wouldn't let himself be captured. He would fight to the death if anybody tried to arrest him, and that meant Brad would have to fight to the death, too. And Brad sure didn't want to die.

As Tom had predicted, they reached the little log cabin high in the hills before dawn. "We'll rest the horses for a couple of hours and get some sleep ourselves," Tom declared, "and then we'll pack up our gear and that silver and get out of here."

He unwrapped the crude bandage from Brad's arm, being a little rough about it so that it hurt when the dried blood came loose. More blood began to seep from the wound. It hurt even worse when Tom took a bottle of whiskey and poured it over the gash. But then he wrapped clean strips of cloth around Brad's arm and tied them tightly, and after a while the wound felt better and Brad was able to go to sleep.

He was jolted out of his slumber by Tom's angry curses. It felt to Brad like he had just closed his eyes, but the door of the cabin was open and he saw bright sunshine outside. At least a couple of hours must have gone by while he was asleep. He pushed himself up on an elbow on his rope bunk and watched Tom stomping furiously around the cabin and pawing through all their gear.

"What's wrong?" asked Brad. "Did you lose something?"

"The map!" raged Tom. "Where's that damned map?"

Brad's forehead creased in a frown. "What map? What are you talking about, Tom?"

"I had a map . . . It showed the place I figured we'd go to lie low, a place I heard about."

Brad could only shake his head. "I don't know a thing about it. Maybe Asa or Logan took it."

"They wouldn't have had any reason to." Tom frowned darkly. "Although Asa and I had talked about it. He might've gotten curious. Damn it! If one of them had the map, that means that lawdog's probably got it now!"

"Then maybe we'd better go someplace else," Brad suggested worriedly. "I don't want to run into that hombre again."

"That's the difference between you and me, little brother. I *want* to see him again. I want to be looking right into his eyes when I blow his damned brains out."

Brad swung his legs off the bunk and ran his hands through his brown hair. "Yeah," he mumbled. "Yeah, it'd be nice to settle the score. But we can't go to whatever place you were talking about if there's a chance that lawman will trail us there."

Tom thought it over for a second and then shook his head. "No," he said, "we're still going."

"But Tom—"

"If everything I've heard about this place is true"—an ugly smile tugged at Tom's mouth, turning his normally handsome face flat and vicious—"It won't make a damned bit of difference whether that star packer finds us or not. In fact, if he shows up there looking for us . . . he'll just be dead that much sooner."

Chapter 4

Ah, peace and quiet. It was wonderful.

But if that was strictly true, wondered Jessica Starbuck, then why did she sometimes feel like throwing her
head back and screaming out of sheer boredom?

Jessie stood on the porch of the big house at the head-
quarters of the Circle Star, the vast ranch she owned in
South Texas. She was a beautiful woman in her twenties,
slender and lithe but well-curved at breast and hip, as the
man's shirt and denim trousers she wore displayed quite
plainly without being too brazen about it. Thick reddish-
gold hair tumbled around her head and over her shoulders. She leaned on the porch railing and watched the two
men riding toward her. Jonas Gibson had come to the Circle Star to buy a bull—one particular, and particularly
fine, bull—and Ki had taken Gibson out to the pasture to
get a look at the animal.

This was how she spent her days now, thought Jessie,
carrying out the mundane business of running a ranch. It

was a huge ranch, of course, one of the best in Texas, and it had its own challenges, many of them, but nothing like what she and Ki had faced in the past. Not really all that long ago, in fact, but sometimes it seemed like an eternity.

Jessie's father, Alex Starbuck, had founded the Circle Star and built it into a successful spread. But the ranch had been only one of his far-flung business enterprises. He had been one of the wealthiest men in the country and had had interests that stretched all across the West. Around the world, actually—and that was what had brought him into conflict with a cartel of European businessmen who would stop at nothing to further their own ventures. Not even murder, as Alex had found out tragically when an attempt on his life by the cartel had resulted in the death of his beloved wife instead.

That tragedy intensified the war between Alex Starbuck and the cartel. Eventually, numbers had won out, and Alex had been killed. That left the Starbuck empire in the hands of his only child, his daughter Jessica. The members of the cartel must have been licking their chops at the prospect of having to deal only with an inexperienced young woman. They would crush her and take control of Alex Starbuck's holdings with no trouble.

But it hadn't worked out that way. Jessie had proven to be remarkably resourceful, as well as highly intelligent and able to ride and shoot as well as any man and better than most. Not only that, but she had a secret weapon as well—Ki, the half-American, half-Japanese protector and friend who had been devoted to Alex Starbuck. As Jessie's bodyguard since she was a little girl, Ki had become a willing and highly capable ally in her war against the cartel.

For several years, the two of them had done battle

against those wily foes and their minions, the epic conflict carrying them from one end of the frontier to the other. Finally, with the help of Jessie's friend Deputy U.S. Marshal Custis Long, they had succeeded in smashing the cartel once and for all.

Of course, that hadn't meant all their troubles were over. Jessie's wealth enabled her and Ki to travel from one end of the frontier to the other, so that they could handle the problems that inevitably cropped up in the running of the Starbuck empire. They had run across villainy of all sorts and lived an exciting life for quite a while. Jessie had gotten to the point that the scent of powder smoke was almost like perfume to her.

But lately, it had begun to seem like those days had drawn to a close. Everything was running smoothly, and she and Ki had been able to stay close to home instead of galloping off into excitement and danger.

And damned if she didn't really miss that time in her life, she thought now as Ki and Jonas Gibson reined their horses to a stop in front of the porch.

At least there was an occasional distraction—like Jonas.

He was a big man, tall and broad-shouldered, with dark brown hair and a handsome, open face. He wore an expensive suit and pearl-gray Stetson but didn't seem to care all that much that they had a fine layer of dust on them. Jessie liked a man who wasn't fussy about things, a man who didn't mind a little trail dust and hard work. Jonas Gibson definitely had that look about him.

Ki's black trousers and vest and collarless gray shirt had dust on them, too, as did the black hat he wore. The hat covered up the narrow band of cloth that he always wore around his head to hold back his long, thick, raven-dark hair. His eyes had a slight Asian cast, but he could have almost passed for an American cowhand if not for his habit of wearing rope-soled sandals instead of boots. Nor did he carry a gun as most cowboys did, but the pockets of his vest held a number of deadly weapons— the razor-sharp throwing stars known as *shuriken* and several little knives that were equally lethal in Ki's hands. In addition, his mastery of fighting skills was second to none, and he knew probably a hundred different ways to kill a man with his bare hands. Not that he had ever bothered to count them, as he was too much at peace with himself to do something like that.

Jessie smiled at Jonas Gibson as he dismounted. "Well, what did you think of Shorty?"

Gibson returned the smile. "He's certainly an impressive specimen. Seems like a fine bull like him would have a more highfalutin' name than Shorty, though."

"Oh, he does," said Jessie. "His real name is Bartholomew Remington Black the Third. But Shorty just seems to suit him better, because of those stumpy little legs of his."

Gibson raised his eyebrows. "Certain other portions of his anatomy aren't stumpy, though."

Jessie laughed. Having been raised on a ranch, she wasn't going to be embarrassed by the subject of a bull's pizzle. She said, "No, he's quite well-endowed in that area."

"And that's one reason I'm willing to pay you four thousand dollars for him."

"I believe the price we discussed was seven thousand, five hundred," Jessie returned without hesitation. She didn't mind a little haggling, if that was the way Gibson wanted to play this.

"I'm just a small rancher, Miss Starbuck," he said. "I can't afford to pay you that much. Besides, that bull *is* awfully short. I don't know if he can reach the cows. What about five thousand?"

"I was about to suggest six," said Jessie. "And he'll find a way to reach them, trust me."

"Five thousand, five hundred?"

Jessie thought about it. Shorty was worth more than that. But Gibson's ranch was just getting established up on the Brazos, and he probably *didn't* have a lot of ready cash. And Shorty was guaranteed to improve his herd. Jessie reached her decision.

"We have a deal," she said, "on one condition."

"What's that?"

"That you have dinner with me this evening."

She expected Gibson to agree without hesitation, but to her surprise he seemed to be thinking it over. And even more surprisingly, a moment later he shook his head.

"No deal," he said. "Not without one other condition."

"What's that?" Jessie asked with a slight frown.

"That you come to Fort Worth on the train with Shorty and let *me* take *you* to dinner when I pick him up. As well as dinner here tonight, of course."

It was Jessie's turn to hesitate and appear to be considering the proposition, but she was just pretending and from the twinkle in Gibson's eyes, she figured he knew it. She said, "All right, we have a deal." She put out a hand.

His large hand enfolded her smaller one. His clasp was firm and strong without being crushing. Jessie liked the feel of it.

When he let go of her hand, he said, "I ought to get cleaned up . . ."

"Of course. I'll show you to your room. You'll be stay-

39

ing the night, of course. It's too late in the day and too far back to town for you to do anything else."

"I appreciate the hospitality, Miss Starbuck."

"Call me Jessie," she told him. "If we're going to be doing business together, we don't have to be quite so formal."

"All right, Jessie, I like that. The name suits you."

Ki was still sitting on his horse in front of the porch. As Jessie started to turn away to show Gibson into the house, she caught her old friend's eye and saw his tolerant smile. Ki had sensed the sparks between Jessie and Gibson, and he knew her well enough to be aware that something might develop. Ki never judged her, even though she knew that in the eyes of frontier society her behavior was sometimes a mite bold. As a student of Eastern philosophy, Ki believed that the mind and the body should be kept in the proper balance, and one part of balancing the body was attending to its natural appetites. Since the relationship between Ki and Jessie had always been similar to that of older brother and younger sister, there had never been anything improper between them and never would be, but neither did they interfere with the other's affairs of the heart.

At this point, Jessie didn't know for sure what would happen between her and Jonas Gibson—but she was intrigued by him, that was for sure.

She took him up to the second floor of the big ranch house and showed him which room he would be using while he was on the Circle Star. Then she went to her own room to prepare for the evening.

When she came downstairs later, she found Gibson waiting for her in the parlor, sipping from a glass of wine that one of Jessie's Mexican servants had brought him. At her soft footstep, he turned to greet her. She saw his eyebrows go up and said, "Surprised, Jonas?"

"No, not really," he said. "I'd heard how beautiful you are, Jessie. But some things, a man just has to see for himself before he can fully appreciate them."

She smiled, pleased by his response. She had never been afflicted with false modesty and knew she looked good. That had been her intention. She wore a light blue gown that swooped low at the neck, leaving her shoulders bare and plunging deeply enough so that the upper swells of her full breasts were visible. The dress was cinched tight at the waist, however, Jessie didn't require a corset to give her an hourglass figure. She managed that all on her own, with nothing but what El Señor Dios had given her.

One of the servants appeared and handed her a glass of wine. She lifted it and said, "To Shorty. Without him, the two of us might not have ever met."

"I'll drink to that," Gibson said as he clinked his glass gently against hers. "To Shorty, with thanks!"

They drank, and then Jessie said, "Dinner should be ready. Shall we go into the dining room?"

Gibson extended his arm. "Allow me, Miss Starbuck."

Smiling, Jessie linked arms with him and said, "Thank you, Mr. Gibson."

The food was delicious, the wine flowed freely, and the company was more than pleasant as the evening passed. Gibson had an easy, charming manner about him. He provided some details about his life during their conversation, but unlike some men, he didn't want to talk only about himself. He was interested in everything that had happened to her, too. Of course, Jessie didn't even attempt to tell him about most of the adventures she and Ki had had. That would have taken the whole evening—and Jessie had other plans for the rest of the night.

So did Gibson. Jessie could tell that he was as attracted to her as she was to him. They were both adults, and she had never believed in being overly coy. After dinner they drank some brandy and Gibson smoked one of the fine cigars that Jessie kept on hand for visitors, and then she suggested that they step out onto the porch. Gibson agreed without hesitation.

It was a warm, moonlit night. A half-moon floated in the sable sky over South Texas. When Jessie said, "Beautiful, isn't it?", Gibson put a hand on her bare arm and said, "Yes, you are."

She turned toward him and tipped her head back slightly, and his mouth came down on hers in a gentle yet sensuous kiss. She lifted her arms and put them around his neck as his arms went around her waist. The kiss became harder, more urgent and passionate. Gibson pulled her tightly against him, her body molding itself to his.

"Jessie . . ." he said when they broke the kiss. "Please don't think that I'm too bold—"

"I'll think that you're not bold enough if you don't take me upstairs and make love to me," she whispered.

He kissed her again, and this time her lips parted so that his tongue could slide hotly into her mouth. Both of them were breathing hard when they finally stepped apart and turned to go into the house.

Jessie took Gibson's hand and led him upstairs. She took him to her bedroom, where only a single lamp burned with the flame turned low. Her hands were pulling off his string tie and unfastening the buttons of his shirt almost before the door was closed. He was just as eager, running his big hands over her body and cupping her breasts through her gown so that the valley between them deepened. He caressed her for a moment, then his arms went around her again and his hands found the buttons on the back of her gown. Deftly, he flipped them open as she slid her hands inside his now open shirt and clutched at his muscular chest with its thick mat of brown hair.

They undressed each other without rushing things, although each of them obviously felt a certain sense of urgency. But Jessie experienced a profound feeling of relief and anticipation when they were finally both nude and she sprawled back on the big four-poster bed with its thick, comfortable mattress. As Gibson leaned over her to kiss her, she closed both hands around his erect shaft, pleased at the length and heft of it. Her touch pleased him, too, judging by the groan that came from deep within him as she began to stroke him.

He lay beside her, bending his head to kiss her breasts. He licked and sucked each nipple in turn until they stood up prominently. While he was doing that, his hand strayed down over the flatness of her belly to the triangle of fine-spun hair that was the same shade of reddish-gold as the hair on her head. He stroked it, then his fingers stole between her thighs to find the soft, wet heat. Jessie's hands tightened reflexively on his manhood as he slipped a finger inside her and at the same time used his thumb to stroke the sensitive little nubbin of flesh at the top of her femininity. Her legs spread even wider and her hips began to pump slowly as she ground against his hand.

She felt his organ quiver and throb, and he whispered, "Jessie . . ." She knew he couldn't wait much longer to be inside her, and she couldn't wait for him to be there.

"Yes, Jonas," she said. "Yes!"

He moved into position above her. She guided the

head of his shaft to her opening. She was already so wet with arousal that he slid easily into her with a surge of his hips, sheathing himself fully inside her. Jessie drew her knees up and thrust back at him, drawing him even deeper inside her. Her arms went around his neck again, and she hung on for dear life as he began a steady, driving rhythm.

She felt herself rising higher and higher toward the peak, and when she reached it her culmination roared through her with earth-shattering force, shaking her to the very core of her being. At the same time, Jonas Gibson roared in pleasure as his own climax gripped him. He emptied himself in her, mixing his heated juices with her own.

Together they coasted down the far side of that mountain, their pulses hammering, their breath coming hard and fast, their bodies covered with a fine sheen of sweat. When Gibson's softening organ slipped out of her, both of them made little noises of disappointment. Jessie reached down and took the slick shaft in one hand while she used the other to cup the heavy sacs underneath it.

"I wouldn't mind doing that again," she said.

"Lord, woman," he grumbled, but the smile on his face took any sting out of the words, "I'm not a champion bull like Shorty, you know."

"Definitely not short . . . but I'm not sure about the champion part." She stroked his manhood and felt a throb go through it. "What's that?" She bent her head and licked one of his nipples, and his organ stirred even more. "Ah, you just need the right inspiration."

"If you . . . keep this up . . . you're liable to kill me before we conclude our business deal, Jessie."

"Some things are more important than business," she said.

A short time later, when he was hard again and she swung a leg over his hips and straddled him, sliding down onto the thick pole of male flesh, she knew she was right.

And she was thankful all over again for distractions like Jonas Gibson.

Chapter 5

Jessie came awake instantly at the light touch on her shoulder, her senses fully alert. Some habits were hard to break, and she had lived on the edge of danger for a long time.

As she sat up, the man who had awakened her said, "It's me, Jessie."

"I know that, Ki," she replied. Even in the darkness of her room, which was relieved only by faint light from the moon and stars that filtered in through the thin curtains over the window, she had instinctively recognized him right away. Although her bedroom was not off-limits to him—there were few limits between two such old, good friends—she knew something had to be wrong for him to have come in here to wake her like this. "What is it?"

"Jonas Gibson is gone."

Jessie frowned in the darkness. After she and Gibson had made love a second time, he had left her room and gone back to his own, pleading exhaustion.

"What do you mean, gone?" Ki wouldn't be referring to the fact that Gibson was no longer in her bed.

"He left the house a short time ago, went to the barn, saddled his horse, and rode off in the direction of the pasture where Shorty is kept."

Jessie's frown deepened. "Maybe he just wanted to take a look at the bull again," she suggested. She couldn't think of any other reason for such odd behavior on Gibson's part.

Ki shook his head and said, "It's the middle of the night, and his attitude was too furtive. He is up to no good, Jessie."

A flare of anger went through her. Ki had no right to suggest such a thing.

And yet he had every right, she reminded herself. They had been a team for too long, had saved each other's life too many times, for her to suddenly disregard his instincts.

"I'll get dressed and be downstairs in a minute."

Ki nodded and left the room. Without lighting the lamp, Jessie pulled on denim trousers and a man's shirt. She shoved her feet into her soft leather riding boots, then hesitated as her hand reached for the gunbelt that was looped over the back of a chair.

Her hesitation lasted only a second. Then she picked up the gun belt and strapped it around her hips. The weight of the holstered Colt, with its ivory grip specially fashioned to fit her hand, felt familiar and good.

Ki hadn't wasted his time while waiting for her. He had saddled a pair of horses for them and had the mounts ready in front of the porch. He was already in the saddle, wearing black silk trousers and the black vest that contained his *shuriken* and throwing knives over his bare

48

chest. Tonight he looked more like a Japanese warrior than an American cowboy.

Jessie took the reins of her horse from him and swung up into the saddle. They started toward Shorty's pasture, which was about a mile away from the big house.

"How did you happen to see Jonas sneaking out?" she asked.

"I was meditating when a slight noise intruded on my thoughts," explained Ki. "I attempted to ignore it at first, but something told me it might be important. So I slipped outside in time to see Gibson go into the barn. When he came out on his horse and rode away a few moments later, I went to let you know."

"So he's not very far ahead of us," mused Jessie.

"No," Ki agreed. "Not far."

Jessie tried not to jump to any conclusions. She liked Jonas Gibson, and because of that she wanted to give him the benefit of the doubt. She couldn't think of any legitimate reason for him to be riding around the Circle Star in the middle of the night like this, though.

Had he lied to her about wanting to buy the prize bull called Shorty?

Maybe he didn't even *have* a ranch up on the Brazos. Maybe he wanted to *steal* Shorty. The bull was easily worth the seventy-five-hundred dollars she had asked for him originally, and he wasn't even in his prime yet. That was enough money to tempt a lot of men.

But she had believed that Gibson was better than that, and she hated to think that she could have been so wrong about him. Jessie didn't want to accept that.

What they found when they got to Shorty's pasture might force her to change her mind.

"The shipping herd's not far from that pasture," she

said. "We've got somebody riding nighthawk out there, don't we?"

Ki nodded. "Russell Dobbs."

Jessie had to think for a second to remember who Russell Dobbs was. The Circle Star employed a lot of ranch hands. But then she recalled that Dobbs was a young man from over around Victoria. He was barely in his twenties, and the Circle Star was the first big ranch for which he had ridden. But he had demonstrated already that he was a good, reliable hand.

"If there's any trouble going on, Russell might be close enough to investigate it," she said. "I haven't heard any shots."

"Not yet," said Ki.

As if to prove his veiled prophecy accurate, a gun suddenly blasted somewhere up ahead in the darkness. A second shot followed quickly on the heels of the first one.

"Let's go!" called Jessie as she dug her heels into the flanks of her mount and sent the horse leaping forward in a gallop.

Ki was right behind her and quickly drew even with her as they raced toward the spot where Colt flame had bloomed in the darkness.

Whether she wanted to believe it or not, Jessie now knew that bad trouble was afoot on the Circle Star—and Jonas Gibson was right in the middle of it.

Gibson's conscience troubled him as he rode away from the ranch house. That came as a complete surprise to him.

"Damn it, Jonas," he said aloud to himself in a soft voice, "just because you went to bed with the woman doesn't mean that you have to abandon the plan."

In truth, bedding Jessie hadn't been part of the plan.

All he was supposed to do was come to the Circle Star, find out exactly where that bull was, and signal the location to the others. The gang had watchers posted so when he shone the bull's-eye lantern out the window and opened and closed its shutter to make the flashes of light form words in Morse code, they would see the signal and be able to decipher the directions he was passing on. Then he would slip out of the house, join the rest of the gang at the pasture, and together they would drive away the bull that was going to provide such a handsome payoff. That was all there was to it.

So why the hell was he wishing he had never gotten mixed up in this affair?

The answer was as simple as the plan—Jessie Starbuck.

Gibson had known many women during his career as a gambler, con man, and outlaw, but none of them had ever affected him so strongly. He was much too cynical to believe that he had fallen in love or anything like that, but it was true that the first time he'd laid eyes on her, he'd felt something deep in his gut, some instinctive reaction unlike any he had ever known.

It would have been nice to have the time to get to know her better, to maybe find out if what he felt was the real thing. But of course there was no time. The job would be done tonight, and by morning they would have driven the bull to the isolated siding where a locomotive and a private freight car waited. The boss *really* wanted that bull and wasn't afraid to spend the money necessary to get it. Jessie Starbuck would never see old Shorty again.

That prospect shouldn't have bothered him, Gibson knew, but it did. Silently, he cursed himself for giving in to temptation. If he hadn't taken Jessie to bed, he probably wouldn't feel this way now. It was too late to change anything, so he would just have to live with it.

He had no trouble finding the pasture again. Fenced off by barbed wire, it was a large area dotted with trees and carpeted by lush grass. Shorty had the place to himself, as befitted a champion.

The other five men were waiting for him. Nick Darrow was in charge of the job. Gibson had worked with him before, and so had the other men. They were a good bunch, steady and dependable and utterly ruthless when they had to be. Not that Gibson really expected any trouble. This was going to be the easiest money he had ever earned.

Darrow lifted a hand in greeting. He was around thirty-five, with a thatch of prematurely white hair under his black Stetson with its curled brim. He rested his hands on the saddle horn as he leaned forward and said, "Good job, Gibson. That bull's right where you said it would be."

Gibson saw the massive dark shape against the grass and knew that it was Shorty. The bull was grazing contentedly about a hundred yards on the other side of the fence. A few snips with some wire cutters, and all they'd have to do would be ride in and get him. Sonny Montoya, one of the other members of the gang, was mighty handy with a rope, having been a vaquero. He would dab a loop on Shorty and lead him out.

"Is the critter going to give us any trouble?" Darrow went on.

"I don't think so," said Gibson. "He seemed pretty gentle and good-natured when I was out here this afternoon."

"That's 'cause all he's interested in is them lady cows," drawled Blue Atkinson, another member of the gang.

"Let's go," said squat, dark Simon Jarvis. "I don't like bein' here. I've heard too many bad things about that Starbuck bitch and her Chinaman servant."

Gibson's jaw tightened angrily. He didn't like Jarvis all that much to start with, and the easy way he had called Jessie a bad name just now made Gibson like him even less. Plus Gibson knew that Ki wasn't a Chinaman, much less Jessie's "servant".

It wouldn't do any good to say anything to Jarvis. The man would just think he was crazy to be defending somebody they were about to rob, and so would the others. So Gibson kept his anger to himself.

The sixth and final member of the gang was narrow-faced Pete Mallory. He stepped down from his horse and took a pair of wire cutters from his pocket as he approached the barbed wire. "Want me to go ahead and cut the fence, Nick?" he asked.

"Yeah," said Darrow. "The sooner we get this done, the better."

"Wait a minute," said Gibson in a sharp voice, startling himself as much as he did the others. He hadn't known he was going to speak until the words were out of his mouth. He rushed on while the impulse had him in its grip. "Are you sure about this, Nick?"

"What the hell do you mean, am I sure?"

"You don't even know for certain who we're working for," Gibson pointed out. "How do you know he won't double-cross us?"

"He paid us two thousand dollars up front," said Darrow. "Nobody's going to back out of a deal after investing that much money in it."

"And he promised to pay us three thousand more once

we deliver the bull. That's five thousand. Hell, Nick, that's a big chunk of what the bull's worth! Where's the profit in that for him?"

Darrow shook his head stubbornly. "I don't care whether he makes any profit or not, as long as I get what was promised to me." He eased a hand down to the butt of the pistol on his hip. "And anybody who tries to double-cross me is going to be mighty sorry."

"I just don't like it," said Gibson. "I don't trust him. Maybe what we should do is leave the bull here and go meet the boss at that siding. We could tell him that he has to let us in on what's really going on, or there's no deal. If he cooperates, we can always come back and get the bull later."

"Except for the fact that if you disappear, the Starbuck woman's going to suspect that something's going on," snapped Darrow. "She's liable to move the bull or even ship it somewhere else entirely. Hell, she owns property all over the place, I've heard."

"Besides," said Blue Atkinson, "you've got her fooled now, Jonas. Why waste all your time and trouble, not to mention our time?" Blue chuckled. "Or maybe you plan on stayin' so you can spend more time with Miss Jessie whilst the rest of us are off talkin' to the boss. Can't say as I'd blame you for wantin' to do that. She is one *mighty* fine-lookin' woman."

"Jessie's got nothing to do with this. Like I said, I'm just not sure I trust the boss."

"But I do," said Darrow, his voice flat and hard. "So we're going through with it, right now. Pete, cut that barbwire."

Mallory raised the wire cutters and said, "Sure thing, Nick."

He snipped the top strand of the tightly strung wire with its sharp barbs. It sprang back as it parted, causing Mallory to step away from it quickly.

"Almost got me," he said. "I'll be a mite more careful next time . . ."

As he stretched out the hand holding the wire cutters toward the fence, the sound of hoofbeats came clearly to the ears of all six men. Darrow barked, "Hold it! Don't cut any more until we find out who that is."

The rider continued to approach the members of the gang. Gibson could tell by the sound of the hoofbeats that only one man was coming toward them. The direction from which the horsebacker approached—west— told Gibson that he was probably the cowboy assigned to ride night herd on the Circle Star stock. This was bad luck, damned bad luck.

"Let me deal with him," said Gibson. "Maybe it's somebody who saw me with Jessie earlier today. I can tell him that I'm a guest here on the ranch."

Darrow leaned over and spat. "That explains you, not us. But we'll give it a try."

Gibson could see the rider now, cantering his horse toward them, apparently curious but not really concerned. He drew rein about twenty feet away and lifted a hand in greeting, saying, "Howdy, fellas. What're y'all doin' out here in the middle of the night?"

Gibson knew that one of the secrets to telling a lie was to act as if the thought of not being believed never entered your mind. So he spoke up forthrightly and said, "Hello. I'm Jonas Gibson. I'm visiting the Circle Star on business. Are you one of Miss Starbuck's ranch hands?"

"Yep. Name of Russell Dobbs."

"Maybe you saw me out here this afternoon with Ki,"

Gibson went on. "He was showing me Shorty." Gibson gestured toward the bull, who had finally noticed the humans and their horses and was now lumbering toward them.

The cowboy shook his head. "No, can't say as I recollect you, mister. Who are these other fellas?"

"Friends of mine," said Gibson. "I was, ah, showing Shorty to them. I'm going to be buying him from Miss Starbuck."

"Hadn't heard a thing about it," said Dobbs. Evidently he wasn't overly bright, but even so, he was starting to get suspicious. Gibson could hear it in his voice as he went on. "Maybe you fellas better ride back to the ranch house with me. Miss Starbuck don't want folks wanderin' around the Circle Star, 'specially at night."

Damn it, thought Gibson, the boy must have ears like a bat to have heard them. That was just further proof, as if he needed it, that this job had gone south and ought to be called off.

"Oh, I don't think that's necessary," he went on, still trying to head off trouble. "We've seen the bull, so we'll just ride on—"

Russell Dobbs reached for the stock of the Winchester that rode in a saddle sheath under his right leg. "I don't think so," he said. "You're coming with—"

"The hell with this," said Nick Darrow. His draw was fast and smooth as he brought his Colt up and shot the young cowboy in the chest.

Gibson gasped in shock at the blast. The bullet rocked Dobbs back in his saddle but didn't knock him off his mount. As the cowboy's horse danced skittishly to the side, Dobbs tried again to grab his rifle.

Darrow shot him again, and this time Dobbs pitched

from the saddle and fell to the ground in a loose, limp sprawl that signified death.

"What the hell!" cried Gibson. "You killed him!"

"Damn right I did," growled Darrow. He swung his head toward Mallory and snapped, "Pete, finish cutting that fence. We're taking that bull *now*!"

Things had gone too far now for them to back out, Gibson realized. Whether he liked it or not, they had to go through with the job. That meant he would never see Jessie Starbuck again, and when she found out what had happened, she would remember him with hatred in her heart.

A second later things got even worse, because more hoofbeats sounded in the night and Jarvis said, "Somebody else is comin'!"

The next words out of Darrow's mouth sent a chill through Gibson.

"Whoever it is . . . kill 'em!"

Chapter 6

"Wait a minute!" Gibson burst out. "You can't—"

Darrow whirled on him. "Damn you, Gibson!" he flared. "I'm in charge here! If you've gone soft, get in there and help Sonny round up that bull!"

Gibson's horse moved nervously underneath him. He didn't know what to do. He didn't want any more of Jessie's hands to be hurt or killed. And for all he knew, one of the people now galloping toward Shorty's pasture could be Jessie herself—

Without thinking about what he was doing, he drew his gun and said, "It's over, Nick! You boys get out of here. I'll stay and stall whoever that is—"

"What the hell's wrong with you?" demanded Darrow. "Have you gone crazy?"

"No, I'm just not going to let you kill anybody else." Especially not Jessie Starbuck, thought Gibson.

"Well, that's just too bad," grated Darrow, "because now I'm gonna have to kill *you!*"

The move didn't take Gibson completely by surprise, but he wasn't fast enough to stop it. Darrow jumped his horse to the side as Gibson fired. The slug sizzled through the space where Darrow had been a second earlier.

In the next heartbeat, flame gouted from the muzzle of Darrow's gun and what felt like a giant fist slammed into Gibson's chest. The impact toppled him from his saddle and dropped him to the ground. A sob of mingled agony and frustration welled from him.

He had thought that if he could shoot Darrow, the others would be so shocked that they would go along with him and flee. But it hadn't worked . . . he hadn't been fast and accurate enough, and now Gibson knew with a sense of icy finality that he was dying. Blackness darker than the night ebbed and flowed around him, and as if from a million miles away, he heard Jessie shout, "Ki, look out!"

The next thing Gibson heard was a groan of despair. He realized it came from his own throat. Jessie and Ki were up against men who wouldn't hesitate to kill—and there wasn't a damned thing he could do about it.

Then the blackness closed in completely around him.

Jessie wasn't sure what was going on, but she suspected the men were trying to steal Shorty. As much as she hated to think it of him, it looked like Jonas Gibson was in on the theft, too. With the reins in her left hand, she drew her Colt with the right. As if they shared the same thought, she and Ki veered their mounts away from each other, splitting up so that they could come at the thieves from two different angles. Jessie went to the left and Ki to the right.

She heard the shouted order to kill them and called a warning to Ki. A second later several men opened fire, flame spouting from their guns. In this uncertain light, getting a good aim was difficult, and so far Jessie and Ki hadn't given the thieves anything to shoot at except the sound of their horses' hoofbeats.

The gunmen were making themselves targets, though, with their muzzle flashes. Jessie held her own fire until she was closer—then the ivory-handled revolver in her hand bucked against her palm as she triggered two fast shots.

Ki swooped in from the other direction, almost invisible in the darkness. His hand plucked two of the throwing stars from a pocket on his vest. With a snap of his wrist he sent them both flying toward a spot just above and to the right of one of the muzzle flashes. Over the pounding of his horse's hooves, he heard a man howl in pain and knew that at least one of the *shuriken* had found its mark.

On the other side of the fight, Jessie didn't know if either of her bullets had scored. The shots coming back at her intensified, so she leaned low over the neck of the running horse and fired again. This time she was rewarded by the sight of a muzzle blast daggering up at the sky. She knew the shot must have been an involuntary one after the gun-wielder's aim was thrown off by him being hit.

She had heard the cry of pain from one of the other men and figured that was Ki's doing. So at least two of the thieves were wounded. But they still outnumbered Jessie and Ki by a considerable margin.

The situation got even worse when Jessie's horse suddenly stumbled and went down. She was thrown violently from the saddle, and as she flew through the air she thought that the horse must have stepped in a hole. Pure bad luck.

Then she slammed into the ground and was too stunned to think for several moments. The impact knocked all the air out of her lungs and left her gasping for breath as she tried to recover her wits.

Hoofbeats pounded close by. She knew she was in great danger and needed to get up, but she couldn't force her muscles to obey the commands her brain was sending out. Somehow she had managed to hang on to the Colt when she fell, but now she felt the weapon plucked effortlessly from her fingers. Shots blasted, deafeningly close. At last she was able to move again and started to push herself up off the ground, determined to die fighting if that was the best she could do.

A hand on her shoulder held her down, again without any seeming effort. "Stay there," a voice said, and Jessie recognized it as Ki's. He had seen her fall and had rushed to her side to protect her. He had her gun, and as he knelt beside her he snapped another shot at the enemy.

Just because Ki preferred his traditional Japanese weapons and didn't carry a gun didn't mean he didn't know how to use one. He was an excellent shot, in fact, and his accuracy even under these difficult conditions had the unknown gunmen scurrying. "Let's go!" one of them shouted. Jessie thought it was the same man who had issued the order to kill them. So the leader was still alive.

Hoofbeats sounded loud and clear as the men fled. Ki pressed the gun into her hand again. "You had better reload," he told her. "I think it's empty."

Jessie sat up, thumbed fresh cartridges out of the loops on her gun belt, and started replacing the spent shells in the Colt's cylinder. Ki darted off on foot, vanishing in the darkness. Jessie knew he was going to check out the situation. The gunmen might have left some of their number behind, wounded but still dangerous.

Ki moved like he was part of the night. Though he thought of himself as a samurai, a warrior who served a master, Jessie knew he was skilled enough to have been a ninja, that special class of warrior who could travel through the darkness as if he wasn't even there and kill without ever being seen. He was, simply, the most dangerous man Jessie had ever known—and at the same time the kindest and gentlest.

When the Colt was reloaded she got to her feet and moved in a crouch to the side of her horse, who had gotten up from its fall. Jessie knelt and quickly checked the horse's legs. None of them seemed to be broken, but one of them was definitely lame. The horse would barely put any weight on that limb.

With the soft padding of his sandals on the grass, Ki came back and told her, "There are three men lying over there by the fence, two dead and one badly wounded." He paused. "The one who is still alive is Jonas Gibson."

Breath hissed between Jessie's teeth. She had been prepared for bad news concerning Gibson, but now she had the horrible thought that maybe it had been her bullet that had wounded him. "How bad is he hurt?" she asked.

"He will not live," said Ki bluntly. "He is unconscious and may not ever wake up."

Jessie closed her eyes for a moment. When she opened them, her tone was businesslike as she asked, "Do you know the other men?"

"One of them is Russell Dobbs."

Jessie didn't say anything. She had feared that the young cowboy might be dead, but that didn't soften the news any. She drew a deep breath, said a mental prayer for Russell's soul, and then asked Ki, "What about the other man?"

"I never saw him before."

Jessie turned toward the fence, but Ki stopped her with a hand on her arm. "Jessie, there is more," he said. "The fence is cut. Shorty is gone."

She nodded. "I figured as much. They were after him all along. The question now is whether or not Jonas was part of it."

"We may never know, if he doesn't regain consciousness. Are we going after the other men?"

"My horse is lame," said Jessie. "And you can't trail them at night by yourself."

"They cannot move too fast with that bull," Ki pointed out.

"I know. That's why I'm hoping we'll be able to catch up to them tomorrow."

She might have said something else, but at that moment the sound of a groan came to their ears. Startled, Jessie jerked her head toward it.

"Jonas," she whispered. She grasped Ki's arm. "Take me to him."

They hurried over to where Jonas Gibson had fallen with a bullet in his chest. Even though the moon was low in the sky by now, it still gave off enough light for Jessie to be able to see the dark stain on the breast of Gibson's shirt. She knelt beside him, touched his shoulder lightly, and said, "Jonas? Can you hear me? It's Jessie."

Gibson stirred slightly and his eyelids flickered open. "J-Jessie . . . ?" he said in a husky whisper.

"I'm right here," she told him.

"S-sorry . . . Jessie . . . I tried . . . to stop them."

She leaned over him. "You tried to stop them from stealing Shorty?"

"From . . . hurting you."

"You mean one of the thieves shot you?"

He didn't answer for a moment, and she thought he was gone. But then he sighed and said, "Darrow . . . N-Nick Darrow . . . shot me . . . shot . . . young cowboy . . . so sorry . . . Jessie . . . never meant to . . . to hurt you."

"You were part of it." She hated to accuse him at a time like this, when he was fading fast, but she had to know and there would never be another chance.

"Y-yeah . . . but I . . . changed my mind . . . after . . . met you." He found the strength to lift his hand, and his fingers closed hard around hers. "What I felt . . . for you . . . wasn't part of . . . the plan."

His fingers stiffened suddenly and then relaxed, and they slipped away from her hand as one last breath sighed from his body.

"Nick Darrow," said Jessie, her voice like ice. "Remember that name, Ki. Because sooner or later I'm going to find him—and kill him."

Blue Atkinson wasn't his usual genial self as the men rode through the night, driving the massive, short-legged bull. Montoya's rope was still around the bull's neck.

Blue cursed in a steady monotone instead of making jokes. He had been in a bad mood ever since something sharp had come flying out of the darkness to stick itself in his gun arm. At first he thought it was a knife, but when he went to pull it out, he cut the fingers of his other hand on some sort of star-shaped, razor-edged thing. It must have been that Chinaman who threw it at him, he'd thought as he dropped the odd weapon on the ground.

The thing sure as hell wasn't something an American would use.

So now his arm hurt like blazes and was getting stiff as blood dripped down it, and he wondered if the star-shaped thing had had some sort of poison on it. That seemed like the kind of thing a dirty Chinaman would do, he thought.

Nick Darrow listened to Blue's bitching for as long as he could stand it, then snapped, "Will you shut the hell up? We know your arm hurts. Better to have a hurt arm than to be layin' back there dead like Pete."

Darrow didn't really care that much about Mallory. Pete had been a dependable man, but he wasn't Darrow's friend or anything like that. Somebody in Darrow's line of work didn't need friends, just associates who could be counted on to back his play when trouble started. Pete Mallory had fit into that group just fine.

But now Mallory was dead and Darrow would find somebody to take his place on the next job. Simple as that. The only reason Darrow had brought up the subject of Mallory's death was in hopes of quieting Blue.

It seemed to be working. Blue muttered under his breath, but he stopped cursing and moaning about how that Chinaman had stuck something in his arm.

Simon Jarvis kept looking back over his shoulder. "They're gonna come after us," he said.

"Maybe not," said Darrow. "There were only a couple of them, and I think we got one. At least I saw one of them go down hard, like he'd been hit."

"I don't care. I've heard stories about that Starbuck bitch. She ain't the sort to take this lyin' down, Nick."

Despite the pain in his arm, Blue couldn't resist the

opportunity to crack wise. "I can think of something else I'd like for her to take lyin' down," he said with as jaunty a grin as he could manage under the circumstances.

"You can forget about that," Darrow told him. "I don't plan to come within a hundred miles of the Circle Star ever again."

"What *are* you going to do with your share of the money, Nick?" asked Jarvis.

"I was thinking I might go somewhere and lie low for a while," mused Darrow with uncharacteristic thoughtfulness. "Some place where I can play cards and drink some fine whiskey and dally with some even finer ladies, without havin' to worry about some damned star packer trying to arrest me."

"That sounds mighty nice," said Blue. "Don't know where you'd find a place like that, at least on this side of the border. You may have to head for old Mexico, Nick. Señoritas and tequila."

Darrow spat. "I don't like Mexico. Everything's too dirty, and the whole place stinks of chili peppers. I hate the smell of chili peppers." He looked over at Montoya. "No offense, Sonny."

The blank-faced former vaquero just shrugged. If anything ever offended him—or moved him to any sort of emotion at all—the others had never seen it.

Jarvis said, "Well, if you find a place like you were talkin' about, let me know. I'll go with you."

They pushed on through the night, and despite Darrow's belief that no serious pursuit of them would be mounted until the next morning, he looked back over his shoulder from time to time just like Jarvis. He had heard stories about Jessica Starbuck, too. She would want vengeance for the death of her ranch hand, and she would want that stumpy-legged bull back.

The sky in the east turned gray and then orange with the approach of dawn. Red streaks in the heavens heralded the rising of the sun. The men had been riding for a long time and their horses were worn out. The stolen bull, with its short legs, had been forced to take even more steps to cover the same amount of ground, and he was dragging, too. Sonny doubled the lead rope and slapped at Shorty's rump with it in an attempt to get the bull to move along a little faster. It was hard to rush a critter that weighed more than a thousand pounds.

Finally, Darrow raised an arm and pointed ahead of them, across the brush-dotted plains. "There it is," he said. "The siding."

The place didn't have a name. There were no houses or businesses, not even a flag stop and a water tank. Just the rail line with its row of telegraph poles beside it, and the siding where a short private train waited. The train was made up of engine, tender, cattle car, coach, and caboose. As the riders drew closer, Darrow saw the fancy brass and gold trim and fittings on the private coach and knew that it had to belong to a rich man—the man who had hired him and the others to steal Shorty.

To tell the truth, Darrow had never laid eyes on their employer. All the dealings had been carried out through intermediaries. But the cash he'd been promised had been delivered on schedule and that was all he really cared about. He didn't know if the boss was actually on that private train and would take possession of the stolen bull in person, but again it didn't matter. As long as the balance of the agreed-upon money was here, Darrow would be satisfied.

Someone must have been watching and waiting for them, because as they approached the siding, driving the bull, the door at the rear of the opulent coach opened. A couple of men in dark suits and bowler hats stepped out onto the railed platform. Each man carried a rifle and had twin Colts holstered at his hips. Their faces were hard and their eyes like flint as they watched Darrow and the others rein to a halt. Darrow could tell by looking at them that they were just hired guns and muscle, although they were top of the line in that area. Both of them looked like they could kill without batting an eyelash.

"Here you go, boys," he drawled as he looked up at the two men on the platform. "Tell your boss we brought that fancy prize bull from the Circle Star, just like we agreed to."

"Tell her yourself, Mr. Darrow," a woman's voice said, taking Darrow by surprise. She walked out of the coach behind the two hard-faced gunmen, who moved to the sides to let her step up between them. That was when Darrow really felt like he'd been punched in the gut. He'd had no idea that he and the others were really working for a woman.

And certainly not for the most beautiful woman he had ever seen in his life.

Chapter 7

She was tall and willowy, but there was nothing fragile about her. She radiated an aura of strength and determination and command that would have been unusual and compelling in a man, let alone in a woman. Darrow had ridden with Quantrill during the war, and the guerrilla leader was the last person he had known who possessed the same sort of qualities that this woman did.

At the same time, she was heart-stoppingly lovely, with thick blond curls that cascaded around her face and shoulders. She wore an expensive gown that was tight enough so that every curve, every sensuous line of her body was revealed. Darrow felt his pulse hammering in his head as he studied the enticing swell of her breasts. When he forced his gaze up to her face, he saw tolerant amusement lurking in her striking blue eyes.

"I take it you didn't know that your employer was a woman, Mr. Darrow?" she asked in a throaty voice that was like music to his ears.

He realized that he was gaping at her like a moonstruck boy. A glance at his companions told him that they were reacting to her the same way, even the normally impassive Sonny Montoya. If she could get to that stolid Mexican, she could get a rise out of a stone, thought Darrow.

He forced himself to sound steadier than he felt as he said, "No, but a woman's money spends just as good as a man's. You've got the rest of the price we agreed on for the bull?"

She nodded. "Three thousand dollars, in gold coins as specified." She moved closer to the railing around the platform and gripped it with slender hands. Her nails were long and painted a deep crimson. She looked at the bull and went on, "So this is the famous Bartholomew Remington Black the Third. The pride of the Circle Star Ranch." The woman glanced at Darrow. "Better known as Shorty?"

Darrow nodded. "That's right. I'm not sure why you wanted him, ma'am, but he's all yours . . . as soon as you cough up that three grand."

"I've never done anything so indelicate as to 'cough up' anything," she said coolly, "but if you'd like to come inside, I'll be glad to pay you the rest of your fee."

Darrow said, "Sure," and swung down from the saddle. He handed the reins to Jarvis.

"You want us to come with you, Nick?" asked the dark, stocky outlaw.

"No, I can handle this by myself," replied Darrow, and the other men looked disappointed but resigned to being left out of this part of the deal.

As Darrow climbed onto the platform, the woman said to one of her companions, "Have the animal loaded into the cattle car, Heinrich."

The man jerked his head in a nod and said in a guttural voice, *"Jawohl."*

Darrow frowned. He had been around settlements in central Texas like Fredericksburg and New Braunfels often enough to recognize German when he heard it.

"Come with us, Conrad," the woman said to the other bowler-hatted gunman. He followed her and Darrow into the train car, which was just as luxurious and finely appointed on the inside as it was outside, with heavy furniture, crystal lamps, an actual bar, and thick rugs on the floor.

The woman went to the sort of large, rolltop desk that looked more like it ought to be in a bank or an office than in a train car. She opened one of the drawers and took out a canvas bag. Turning to Darrow, she held it out and said, "Three thousand dollars."

He took the bag and opened it, peering inside and catching his breath a little as the light hit the coins it contained. The pile of double eagles had a mighty fine sheen to them. The bag was heavy, but the woman had handled it like it didn't weigh much at all. Beautiful *and* strong, he thought.

"That concludes our business," she said.

Darrow knew she was right, but he suddenly found himself not wanting to leave. He liked it here. This was the sort of fancy place—and fancy woman—he had always thought he deserved. He asked, "Is there anything else we can do for you, ma'am?"

She started to shake her head, but then she stopped and asked, "While you were on the Circle Star, did you see the woman called Jessica Starbuck?"

Darrow thought that maybe he had heard a woman's voice during the fracas the night before, and if that was the case it must have been the Starbuck woman. But he hadn't actually *seen* her, so he shook his head.

"No, I'm afraid not."

"A pity. I'm sure you would have enjoyed it. I'm told that she is very beautiful."

Darrow smiled. "She could be the prettiest woman in Texas and still not be half as beautiful as you, ma'am."

"You consider yourself a charming man, yes, Mr. Darrow?" she asked with a laugh.

He shrugged and said, "I'm just telling the truth as I see it." He glanced at the guard called Conrad. Surely there was a sleeping compartment somewhere in this luxurious coach. If that stone-faced yahoo would just go away for a while, the woman might be persuaded to give Darrow a little bonus. . . .

The door at the back of the car opened suddenly, and Heinrich hurried in. He spoke rapidly in German, and the look on the woman's face told Darrow that any plans for a rendezvous with her that might have been a-borning in his head were now ruined. She had completely lost interest in him. Instead she issued orders in German to the bowler-hatted hombres, then said to Darrow, "I'm sorry, but it is time for the train to leave."

"What's going on?" he asked stubbornly, not wanting to go. "Is something wrong?"

"Not really. I expected this to happen. At least the bull is already loaded."

She moved toward the open door at the rear of the car as she spoke, and Darrow had no choice but to follow. As they reached the platform, Blue Atkinson called to him, "Hey, Nick! Riders comin', and they're in a hurry!"

The woman smiled as her crimson-nailed hands gripped the railing again. "If I'm not mistaken, that will be Jessica Starbuck and some of her men now," she said, sounding pleased by the prospect.

Darrow didn't like it much. This was going to mean a fight. And judging by the way the locomotive was rumbling and hissing, it had steam up and was ready to roll.

The woman was going to leave them here to face the Circle Star's vengeance, damn her!

No, not damn her, he amended as she turned toward him. She was too beautiful to be damned. "Delay them until we're well away, and there will be an extra thousand dollars in it for you," she said.

"How do we collect?" he asked.

She tucked something in the pocket of his vest. "You'll have no trouble finding me." Then she stunned him by putting her hands on his shoulders and leaning in to kiss him. Her mouth was warm and sweet, and he felt lightning crackle along his veins as it clung to his for one long, maddening moment. When she pulled back, she said huskily, "Consider that . . . a down payment."

He took a deep breath, turned to his men, and bellowed, "Stop those riders . . . *now!*"

For a kiss like that, he would almost be willing to die—and consider it payment in full.

The group of riders had started out from the Starbuck ranch as soon as the eastern sky had lightened enough for them to see where they were going. Jessie and Ki were in the lead, and behind them rode eight members of her tough, gun-handy crew from the Circle Star. Jessie wore range clothes again, with a flat-crowned brown hat held on her head by a taut chin strap. Beside her Ki was dressed in black and gray. He had a Winchester in a saddle boot under his leg, but he still didn't carry a handgun.

As they left the site of the battle, Ki rode ahead of Jessie, his gaze locked on the ground as he followed the tracks left by Shorty and the men who had stolen the bull. They hadn't gone to any great pains to conceal their trail, noted Ki. He said as much to Jessie.

"They don't care whether or not we follow them," she said.

"They had to be aware that there would be pursuit," said Ki. "They killed two men."

Jessie frowned in thought. "Maybe they're not taking the bull very far. They can't plan on driving him all the way to San Antonio. What's in the direction they're going?"

"No large settlements for a long way," said Ki.

"But there *is* a rail line," Jessie said slowly. The Texas & New Orleans ran from San Antonio to Del Rio and then on to El Paso and points west. There were connections to other rail lines in San Antonio if somebody wanted to go in another direction. And if Jessie recalled correctly, there was a siding on the T&NO line at about the spot where the thieves' trail would intersect it if they kept going in the same direction—

"They're headed for the siding!" she exclaimed as those thoughts came together in her head. "Somebody must be meeting them there with a cattle car to pick up Shorty!"

"That *is* a reasonable explanation," admitted Ki, "but we have no way of knowing whether or not it is the *correct* explanation."

"It has to be," said Jessie, feeling it in her gut. "Otherwise why aren't they trying to hide their trail? They know they can reach the siding by mid-morning."

Ki couldn't argue with her logic. Instead he asked, "What do you suggest we do?"

Jessie took a deep breath. "We forget about following their trail and just ride for that siding as fast as we can. Maybe we can get there in time to stop them from turning Shorty over to whoever is waiting for him."

"And if they turn off in another direction and do not go to the siding?" asked Ki. "In that case we will probably lose their trail and may not be able to find it again."

"That's a chance we'll have to take," Jessie said grimly.

Ki inclined his head in acknowledgment of the decision. He trusted Jessie's instincts, just as she trusted his.

She reined her mount to a halt and hipped around in the saddle to address the punchers who followed her. "We're heading for that siding up on the Texas and New Orleans," she told them. "I think that's where those buzzards are taking Shorty."

The men nodded in agreement. They rode for the brand, and what Jessie said was what they would do.

"Let's go!" she called as she heeled her horse into a run.

They galloped on through the morning as the sun rose higher. Jessie glanced at Ki, who rode beside her, and then back over her shoulder at the men following them. She would be putting their lives at risk, too, but that was part of riding for the Circle Star. For that matter, it was part of living on the frontier, which, although maybe not as wild as it once had been, could still be a mighty dangerous place from time to time. She worried about the amount of dust billowing into the sky from the pounding hooves of their horses. That dust cloud would warn the men they were following that vengeance was closing in on them, but it couldn't be helped.

As Jessie peered ahead again over the mostly flat, brush-dotted terrain, she suddenly spotted a plume of smoke rising in the clear blue morning air. "Look!" she called to Ki and pointed at the smoke. "That's got to be from a locomotive!"

He nodded. "They have steam up!"

Jessie bit back a curse. They had pushed their horses as fast as they could without riding the animals into the ground, but the siding was still at least half a mile away. And from the looks of things, the train was getting ready to pull out. She could see it now, a short train, probably specially chartered for this job.

But she had no idea who could be responsible for it. She had wracked her brain, trying to figure out the reason behind the theft of the bull. Shorty was valuable, no doubt about that, but was he worth hiring gunmen and killing people? There was something else going on. Jessie didn't know what it was, but her instincts told her there was more beneath the surface.

They were within a quarter of a mile of the siding now, with their mounts flashing over the landscape at full speed.

With a chug and a whistle and a puff of black smoke from the diamond-shaped stack on the Baldwin locomotive, the train lurched into motion and began to roll west, jolting from the siding onto the main tracks.

At the same time, several men on horseback spurred to the far side of the tracks and hurriedly dismounted. They threw themselves down behind the slightly raised roadbed. Jessie wasn't surprised when smoke and flame spurted from rifle barrels poked over the steel rails. "Spread out!" she called to her men. "Don't stay bunched up where you're better targets!" She hauled on the reins and sent her horse veering to the left. To Ki, she shouted, "I'm going for the train!"

She knew that Shorty was on that train. She could see the cattle car now, hooked on behind the coal tender. Behind it was a passenger coach and then the caboose.

Ki's dun pounded along just behind Jessie's buckskin. If she was going to try to intercept the train, he was going with her. That left the Circle Star ranch hands to deal with the gunmen who had hunkered down behind the T&NO roadbed. Those men were probably the ones who had actually stolen Shorty and killed Gibson and Russell Dobbs, thought Jessie.

But the person truly responsible for what had happened was on that train along with Shorty. Jessie felt certain of that. The train was where the real showdown would take place.

But only if she could catch up to it. She urged the buckskin on, faster and faster. Two men appeared on the platform at the rear of the caboose. Jessie couldn't tell much about them except that they wore dark suits of some sort.

And they had rifles, she realized a moment later as she saw the puffs of smoke from the muzzles.

The men didn't seem to be trying to hit her and Ki, however. They were just firing in their general direction as if they were attempting to discourage pursuit without killing any of those giving chase. So Jessie disregarded any potential danger the men might represent and charged ahead heedlessly.

"Jessie, look out!" shouted Ki. "The arroyo!"

She saw what he was talking about. A deep streambed with jagged banks, dry most of the year, slashed across the landscape in front of them. The tracks crossed it on a trestle, but that was several hundred yards north of the path Jessie was following. She had charted a course running at an angle to the railroad tracks because she knew that represented her only chance of catching up to the train.

But now that arroyo was in the way. If she turned north and rode along the dry wash to cross it at the trestle, the delay would allow the train to get such a big lead that it would be impossible to catch as it built up speed. Even trying to intercept it at the angle Jessie was following was a long shot.

To have any chance at all, she and the buckskin galloping valiantly underneath her had to jump that arroyo.

It was a hundred yards away, fifty, twenty-five. Ki shouted, "Jessie, no! It's too wide!"

She ignored him. She could see the arroyo plainly now. They could make it, she told herself. She glanced at the train, which was just now rumbling across the trestle. All she had to do was leap that arroyo, and she would be able to catch up. They could make it. . . .

She hauled back sharply on the reins, crying, "Whoa! Whoa, damn it!" The buckskin practically sat on its haunches as it came to a sliding, skidding, dust-billowing halt that left both horse and rider trembling on the brink.

Ki was right. The damned dry wash was just too wide. They never would have made it, and Jessie knew it. All she would have accomplished if she had tried to make the jump would be to kill the horse and probably herself. That wouldn't get Shorty back, and it wouldn't avenge those deaths.

But by God, it was hard to just sit there and watch that train dwindling in the distance. "Another day," whispered Jessie between clenched teeth.

Ki rode up beside her and brought his horse to a stop.

"You did the right thing," he told her. "Killing yourself would accomplish nothing."

"I know," she said. She took a deep breath. "What about the others?"

Ki shook his head. "I don't know. We should ride back and see."

They turned their horses back to the east. During her pursuit of the train, Jessie had been vaguely aware of shooting going on behind her and knew that her cowboys were swapping lead with the outlaws.

But now silence hung over the flat, semi-arid landscape. She and Ki urged their horses into a trot. They covered the ground quickly and found the Circle Star men waiting beside the tracks, dismounted as they tended to the wounds that several of the punchers had suffered in the fight.

Jessie didn't see any sign of the outlaws.

"Where are they, Dave?" she asked one of the men.

Dave shook his head disgustedly. "They took off for the tall and uncut, Miss Jessie," he said. "I'm mighty sorry. But they were wicked shots, and they had that roadbed for protection so we couldn't get at 'em with our bullets. They knocked half of us out of our saddles and made us all go to ground, then lit a shuck out of here."

"How bad are the wounds?" asked Jessie, always concerned with the welfare of the men who rode for her.

"Mike's got a busted leg, Cotton's hit in both arms, and Phil and Barney are both drilled through the body. I don't *think* any of 'em are gonna die, but we ought to get 'em back to the ranch so we can get some real medical attention for them as soon as we can."

Jessie nodded. "You're right, of course. And don't

worry about those men getting away. I know you did the best you could." She added in a hard voice, "Anyway, they haven't gotten away for long."

"You're going after them?" asked Ki.

"Two men were killed on my land, and something that belongs to me was stolen," said Jessie. "Now four more men are hurt, Shorty's still gone, and the men responsible for all of it got away apparently without a scratch. What do you think I'm going to do, Ki?"

A faint smile tugged at the corners of his mouth under his mustache. "I think I'm going after them with you," he said.

She nodded. She wouldn't have it any other way.

And those bastards just *thought* they had gotten away. This wasn't over yet.

Not hardly.

Chapter 8

Henry, the four-eyed young gent who played the type-writer in Billy Vail's outer office, was pounding away at the keyboard when Longarm came in. The big deputy had a long-running feud with Henry, but deep down he didn't know whether to admire the hombre or pity him. Anybody who could spend his days *tap-tap-tap*ping away like that was either damned determined or just plain crazy. Maybe both.

Barely glancing up from the typewriter, Henry said, "Marshal Vail wants to see you. He's not happy."

Longarm was worn out, covered with dust, and not exactly in a pleasant frame of mind his own self. He dropped the saddle he was carrying, which made Henry look up with a glare, and said, "I just rode back into Denver less'n fifteen minutes ago. Ain't even been home yet. It ain't like I've kept Billy waiting all day."

"He's just anxious to hear your report." Henry jerked

his head toward the door of the inner office. "You'd better get in there."

Muttering under his breath, Longarm fished out a cheroot, clamped it unlit between his teeth, opened the door, and went in to beard the lion.

Billy Vail didn't look like a lion. In fact, with his round, cherubic face and pink, mostly bald scalp, he looked more like somebody's kindly ol' grandpa. Not many people would take him for the chief marshal of the Western District. Nor would they have guessed that in his earlier days, before he had gone to riding a desk, he had been a Texas Ranger, one of the most rip-roaring, hell-bending lawmen ever to fork a horse and chase down bandits in the Lone Star State.

Vail pushed his chair back from the desk, glowered at Longarm, and said, "Custis."

"Don't start in on me, Billy," said Longarm. "It ain't like them stagecoach bandits got away clean. Two of 'em are dead, and I got a lead on the other two." He took the folded map of Nevada out of his pocket and tossed it onto Vail's paper-littered desk.

Vail frowned at it like Longarm had just dropped a snake on his desk. He picked up the paper and unfolded it. "A map. What about it?"

"See the spot that's circled?"

"Yeah."

"I think that's where the two that got away are headed."

Vail's frown deepened. "That's pretty desolate country, up in those mountains. Why would anybody go there?"

"I don't know," said Longarm with a shake of his head. "But why else would one of those owlhoots have

84

been carrying around a map like that if he didn't intend to use it to get somewhere?"

"Who the hell knows? And who the hell is Zamora?"

Again, Longarm shook his head. "That's another one I can't answer, Billy, at least not just yet."

Vail glanced up at him. "Let me guess. You want to go traipsing off to Nevada—at the Justice Department's expense, mind you—to try to track down those robbers, find out who Zamora is, and discover what's in this place marked on the map." He poked the unfolded paper with a blunt fingertip.

Longarm sat down on the red leather chair in front of the desk and cocked his right ankle on his left knee. "That's about the size of it," he admitted.

Vail didn't say anything for several long moments. To fill the time, Longarm dug out a lucifer, lit the cheroot, and blew a smoke ring toward the banjo clock that was ticking away on the wall of the chief marshal's office.

Finally, Vail said, "If the two outlaws who are left have headed for this place in Nevada, the way you believe they have, Custis, then they don't represent a threat to the silver shipments between Gila Wells and Phoenix anymore. What about the inside man they had working for them at the mining syndicate?"

"Salty wired Jeff Walters in Gila Wells as soon as he got to Phoenix," explained Longarm. "The fact that the gang hit the coach Salty and I were on told Walters which of his clerks was mixed up with the outlaws. It was a fella named Ewell. The local law went to arrest the fella, but when he saw the sheriff coming, he yanked out a pistol, stuck it in his mouth, and pulled the trigger. Saved the sheriff a bullet, I guess, because when he saw that the hombre had an iron, he was about to throw down on him."

Vail grimaced in disgust. "Blew his own brains out, did he? Why in blazes would anybody do that?"

"My guess is that once he knew the law was on to him, he didn't want to face it."

"I reckon," said Vail.

Longarm nodded solemnly. "What about Nevada?"

"The case is over." Vail's voice was curt. "You broke up the gang and stopped the robberies. That's all we set out to do."

"What about all the loot those bastards stole before I got there?" asked Longarm. "They must've had a pretty good cache of it."

"It's already gone," said Vail with a shrug. "I'm sure the syndicate would like to have it back, but they're not expecting it."

"One of 'em shot and killed a pretty good horse."

"Hard to justify sending a deputy all the way to Nevada on account of one horse."

Longarm chewed angrily on the cheroot. He knew that his boss was right. Still, he didn't like being told the case was over. He supposed he was a little like a bulldog—once he got his teeth set in something, he didn't want to let go.

Sounding idly curious, Vail asked, "Were you able to trail the two jaspers who got away?"

Longarm nodded. "I followed them as far as Flagstaff. From there they headed off toward Utah, and I lost 'em in that Godforsaken wilderness northeast of the Grand Canyon o' the Colorado. I swear, that's got to be the ugliest country in all of God's creation. Nothing but rocks and vermilion cliffs and emptiness. But I rode through it for nigh on to a week before I finally gave up and headed back here."

"I'm surprised you didn't just keep going into Nevada then and there."

"I thought about it," admitted Longarm. "But neither of the horses I had was worth much. They had belonged to the two owlhoots I killed after the holdup. I was running mighty low on supplies, too, and I figured I could come back here and catch a train for Carson City, maybe come at the mountains from that direction."

"At government expense," said Vail dryly. "You know how Henry feels about all the expense vouchers you turn in, Custis. If it was up to him, he'd disallow most of them."

"Yeah, but if it was up to him, there'd never be any outlaws caught, the way he'd have us go about it," Longarm pointed out. He was too tired to restrain his impatience. Perhaps unwisely, he prodded, "What's it gonna be, Billy? Yea or nay? Do I go after those other two outlaws or not?"

Vail's normally pursed mouth narrowed to a thin line, and Longarm figured he had gone too far. But then the chief marshal said, "There's something else going on here, isn't there, Custis? Why are you so insistent on going after those two?"

Longarm grimaced. "I don't know, Billy, I honestly don't. But something inside me tells me that I ought to. That I need to go to Nevada and try to find the place marked on that map. Call it a hunch, I reckon. I can't explain it any better than that."

"That's good enough for me," said Vail with a nod. "You've been working for me for a long time. If I don't know by now to trust your hunches, I damned sure ought to, as many times as they've paid off."

A grin stretched across Longarm's tanned face.

"Thanks, Billy. I'd promise you that you won't regret it, but hell, who knows? Maybe this is the time when I'm just pure-dee wrong about things."

"If you are," said Vail, "you're the one who's going to have to justify all the expense vouchers to Henry."

Longarm carried his saddle back to his rented room on the other side of Cherry Creek, dropped it off there, and then headed for a nearby bathhouse with some clean clothes tucked under his arm. He wanted to get the weeks of trail dust off him, not to mention soak away some of the weariness.

He spent an hour in a tub of hot water, the proprietor of the place heating it up from time to time with fresh, steaming buckets. When Longarm finally felt clean again, he dried off and dressed in the brown tweed suit he had brought with him. From the bathhouse he walked down the street to the barbershop he usually patronized and sat in the chair while the Italian barber put hot towels on his face and then gave him a nice, close shave. Smelling of bay rum, Longarm felt like a new man when he left the place. His tiredness was gone, and new energy had taken its place.

Instead of turning his steps toward one of Denver's many saloons, dance halls, or out-and-out whorehouses, he walked briskly toward the public library instead.

His steps echoed from the high ceiling as he entered the big cavernous building. He spotted a familiar face at the main desk and was pleased to see that Miss Lorna Hammett was working today. Lorna was short and amply rounded, with thick brown hair and beautiful blue eyes. She was also one of the smartest people Longarm had ever known, male or female, and read so much that she seemed to know at least a little about almost any subject you could name.

A happy smile appeared on her face as she saw Longarm striding toward her. She came out from behind the desk and said, "Hello, Marshal Long. I didn't know you were back in Denver."

"Just got in earlier today," he told her. "How are you, Miss Hammett?"

"Fine, but I've missed seeing you around here her for the past few weeks."

"Wasn't my idea to be gone that long. Some owlhoots led me on a not-so-merry chase."

"But you caught them, I'm sure," she said.

Longarm frowned and shook his head. "Not all of them. A couple got away. That's why I'm here today. I need to know if you've got any books that have recent maps in them."

"Government and military topographic and survey maps?" suggested Lorna.

Longarm nodded. "That'd do mighty fine, I think."

"Come with me up to the third floor. We'll see what we can find." As they walked toward the staircase, she went on, "Does this mean that you'll be leaving again soon, so that you can track down the men who got away?"

"That's the plan," said Longarm. "I'll be on the train to Nevada tomorrow."

"In that case," Lorna began, lowering her voice as they started up the stairs so that only Longarm could hear her, "you have to come to my room tonight and make love to me at least three or four times."

Longarm grinned as he glanced at her in surprise. She didn't usually make such bold comments here in the library, although she could say some pretty amazing things once they were alone and she was caught in the grip of passion.

"I expect I can do that," he said.

"You're not expecting it any more than I am, Custis."

They climbed the stairs to the third floor, which was filled with high shelves arranged close together, so that they almost seemed to be leaning toward one another. Not many folks ever came up here. As Longarm and Lorna made their way through the maze of shelves, Longarm saw only a few people here and there, intently searching through the thousands of books for the one particular volume they were looking for.

"Here's our map section," said Lorna as they turned a corner. Longarm hoped she planned to stay up here with him. He wasn't sure he could find his way back out of this wilderness of books. The young woman went on, "What were you looking for? Maps of Nevada? I believe you said that's where you're going."

"That's right."

Lorna ran a well-manicured hand along the spines of several tall volumes bound in dark leather. "Perhaps one of these." She pulled one of the books from the shelf. It was so big she had to use both hands to hold it as she gave it to Longarm.

He opened the book and started flipping through the pages. As Lorna had said, these were topographic maps, and each page covered only a small section of the state. It took Longarm a few moments to figure out how the book was arranged and reach the pages that covered the area in which he was interested.

The light up here wasn't particularly good. There weren't enough oil lamps hanging from the high ceiling, and the windows were rather tall and narrow and didn't admit much sunlight. The shelves themselves cast a lot of shadows, and Longarm had to bend his head close over the book of maps to make out the details.

He was pretty intent on what he was doing, but not so much so that he didn't notice when Lorna's fingers began unfastening the buttons on the fly of his trousers. He lifted his head from the book and said, "Uh, just what is it you think you're doing there, gal?"

"Nobody's around," said Lorna, "and you've been gone a long time, Custis. I'm too impatient to wait."

"I saw some folks on this floor—" he began.

"They're not paying any attention to us. They're up here for their own reasons." She had all the buttons undone now, and her hand slid through the opening. "And so am I."

Longarm couldn't help but respond as she began to caress his manhood through his long underwear. The thick shaft began to stiffen as Lorna rubbed harder on it. She opened his underwear to free it, and a moment later she was stroking his erection as it jutted out from his trousers.

"That feels mighty good," said Longarm, his voice hoarse with the arousal she was creating in him. "But I came up here on business . . ."

"So did I," she breathed. "The business of getting this big old thing inside me. But I'll settle for just a taste here and now."

True to her word, she sank down onto her knees in front of him and leaned forward to run the tip of her tongue around the crown of his shaft. She obviously wasn't going to "settle" for just one taste. She kept licking him, sending waves of pleasure through him. His grip on the big book tightened, and he forced himself to hold back the groan that tried to well up his throat.

Lorna took her mouth away from his organ and whispered, "Lean back against the shelf a little."

"You sure about that?" asked Longarm. He could just see the tall shelf tipping over, which would send it crashing against the next one in line, then the next one and the next one after that would fall, and all the shelves on the third floor would come crashing down like a row of dominoes just because this randy little gal was anxious to practice her French lessons on him.

"The shelves are bolted to the floor," Lorna said breathlessly. "They can't turn over."

With that, she leaned forward again and opened her mouth wide to engulf him, taking the head of his shaft and another couple of inches into her mouth.

What she was doing to him felt so good that Longarm had to close his eyes for a moment in sheer bliss. Lorna's tongue circled the crown again and again as she wrapped her hands around the rest of the thick pole of male flesh and stroked it toward her. From time to time she paused in her licking to lap at the juices she milked from the opening at the tip of his manhood. Gradually she swallowed more and more of him until her mouth was stuffed.

Taking one hand from his shaft, she went exploring in his trousers again, finding the heavy sacs and cupping them in her palm. She rolled them gently back and forth.

Longarm knew from experience that Lorna Hammett was mighty good at what she was doing. She withdrew slowly, her lips clinging to his flesh, until only the very tip of his shaft was in her mouth. Then she leaned forward and took it in again, repeating the motion so that her head bobbed up and down over his groin. Longarm withstood this exquisite torture as long as he could, but his climax was building up steadily inside him, creating a pressure that would not be denied for long.

The part of his brain that realized how crazy this was listened for footsteps approaching the part of the library where he and Lorna were. He didn't figure Billy Vail would take it too kindly if he received a report that one of his deputies was cavorting lewdly and indecently in a public place, especially as staid a place as the Denver Public Library.

But no one came near. Lorna had been right about nobody paying attention to them. With a sound that was half-groan, half-sigh, Longarm gave himself over to sensation, surrendering to the thunderous culmination that roared through him like floodwaters breaking through a dam.

With a muffled cry, Lorna pulled back. Longarm knew she liked to take his climax on her face, so he let it fly, erupting with burst after burst of the hot seed. It landed in white ropes across her pretty features. His explosion was so emphatic some of the stuff even got in her hair.

She tipped her head back, closed her eyes, and jerked a little as her own spasms rippled through her. Longarm had known a few women who could achieve a release of their own simply by sucking on a man's talleywhacker, but none of them ever came quite as hard from it as Lorna. As he finished up, she gave a long sigh. Her hand reached into her pocket and came out with a lacy handkerchief, which she began using to clean off her face.

"You, uh, got a little in your hair," said Longarm, feeling vaguely flustered at having to tell her that.

She laughed throatily. "That's all right, Custis. You're worth a bit of a mess."

She got to her feet and quickly cleaned herself up. As

she was doing that, Longarm became aware that he was still clutching that big book of maps. He had forgotten all about it when they got carried away. As Longarm buttoned up his trousers, he asked, "Is there some place in here that's got better light?"

"Yes, there's a table over by one of the windows." She laughed. "But I'm afraid we can't carry on like this over there. It's too much out in the open."

"That's all right," said Longarm hastily. "I reckon it's gonna be a while before I'm up to any more carrying on."

She gave him a squeeze through his clothes. "I could take that as a challenge," she said, "but I won't."

With Lorna leading the way, Longarm carried the book over to the table she had mentioned and spread it open in the light from the nearby window. Now that he could see better, it didn't take him long to find the pages he was looking for. Each one covered a different section of the mountains south of the Humboldt River valley. Longarm flipped through them, studying them intently. He brought out the map he had taken from the dead outlaw, opened it, and flattened it out next to the book. After a moment he leaned over, almost putting his nose on the page of the book that interested him. "Well, what do you know?" he muttered. "Zamora ain't a person. It's a place." Longarm looked up. "There's a town there . . . a ghost town."

Chapter 9

"A ghost town?" Lorna sounded interested and excited as she bent forward to peer over Longarm's shoulder.

He nodded as he rested a fingertip on a spot on the map. "Yep. Right there between Shelburne Peak and Mount Montgomery."

"But how do you know it's a ghost town?"

"Because right under the name is the word *abandoned*, printed in those whatchamacallems . . . parentheticals."

"Parentheses," corrected Lorna. "That *would* seem to indicate that Zamora is a ghost town. Do you know anything about it?"

Longarm shook his head. "Not a blessed thing. I never heard of the place before, at least not that I recollect. I can make a few guesses, though, based on what I know about Nevada. It was probably a mining town, starting out. There are pockets of ore scattered all across the state. Mostly silver. Some of the mines really had a mother lode in them, but a lot of them played out after they'd been worked for a while. That might be what happened in Zamora. Folks heard about the strike and rushed in, a town sprang up almost overnight, and then when the silver was gone they all left and went to chase that shiny metal somewhere else."

"That makes sense," agreed Lorna.

"Besides, there ain't no other good reason for there to be a town right there. That's rugged, desolate country around it. Not much good for ranching or anything else." Longarm leaned back in his chair with a frown. He scraped a thumbnail along the line of his jaw and muttered, as much to himself as to Lorna, "Now why in blazes would a couple of stagecoach bandits down in southern Arizona head for a ghost town in Nevada?"

He started turning the pages of the big leather-bound volume again and asked, "Is there anywhere in this book that tells about the places on the maps?"

"Check the back. Sometimes there's a descriptive listing of the geographic features. I'm not sure if settlements are included, though."

In this case, they were, Longarm discovered a moment later. " 'Zamora'," he read from a page in the back of the book. " 'Established 1863 following the discovery of silver ore in the region.' " He looked up at Lorna. "Yep, that's what I thought." He resumed reading. " 'Named after muleteer Pedro Zamora, who made the original discovery. Several mines located near the settlement were in operation from 1863 to 1869, when a dwindling supply of ore forced them to shut down. The town was abandoned soon after.' "

"So it's been a ghost town for more than ten years," commented Lorna.

"Sounds like it." Longarm tugged at his ear again.

"Which makes it curiouser and curiouser. If there's nothing there but a bunch of run-down old buildings, why go there?"

Lorna leaned over and nuzzled Longarm's ear. "Custis, if I know you—and I do—I have a feeling you're going to find out. But not before we have our night together . . . right?"

He cupped a hand under her chin and smiled into her blue eyes. "Darlin'," he told her, "whatever is in Zamora can wait for one more night, and that's for damned sure."

Longarm boarded the northbound train for Cheyenne at ten thirty the next morning. At Cheyenne he would leave this train and switch to a westbound that would eventually deposit him in Carson City, Nevada, where he could rent a horse and double back to the east, into the rugged mountains where the ghost town of Zamora was located. That was the plan, anyway. Longarm knew quite well that sometimes things didn't go according to plan.

He sat down on one of the benches in the passenger car and stretched out his legs as best he could in the somewhat cramped quarters. He took out one of the three-for-a-nickel cheroots and put it in his mouth, then glanced across the aisle. The sharp-faced, middle-aged woman in a dark traveling outfit who sat there glowered at him. Figuring that she was one of those folks who didn't like the smell of cigar smoke, Longarm left his lucifers in his vest pocket and didn't light the cheroot. He didn't mind just chewing on it for a while, and if he really wanted to set fire to the gasper he could always step out on the platform to do it.

Anyway, not having to worry about ashes and the like made it easier for him to think about the night he had just spent with Lorna Hammett. His lips curved in a faint smile as he recalled all the things they had done to and with each other. Somewhere along the way that Lorna gal must have read some books she didn't find in the library, to learn all the things she knew.

But that encounter, as pleasurable as it had been, was behind him now. He turned his attention to the job facing him. Earlier that morning he had gone to the Federal Building to tell Billy Vail what he had learned about Zamora. The chief marshal had been interested, even though he had tried to a certain extent to conceal that interest.

"Ghost town, eh?" Vail had said. "Wonder what those owlhoots wanted there."

"I'm wondering the same thing, Billy," Longarm had replied. "I'll let you know what I find out as soon as I can. Chances are it'll be a pretty long way to the nearest telegraph office, though. Maybe all the way back in Carson City."

Vail had snorted. "Do what you can. Just try not to bend too many laws or run up too many expenses."

"Aw, Billy . . . When do I ever do those things?"

That had brought another snort, even more emphatic, from Vail.

Now as he sat waiting for the train to pull out, Longarm reached inside his coat and took the folded map from a pocket. He opened it up and looked at it, studying the terrain and trying to figure out the best route from Carson City to Zamora. He thought he could reach the ghost town in a two- or three-day ride.

With his attention focused on the map, Longarm didn't notice the person standing in the aisle next to his seat until a voice asked, "Excuse me, is there room here for me?"

The question was in a well-modulated female voice, which made Longarm look up quickly. The woman who stood there was about twenty-five, with blond curls tucked up under a dark blue hat that matched her traveling outfit. She was very pretty, with some of the warmest brown eyes Longarm had ever seen, and the smile she gave him made him forget all about Nevada for the time being.

"Yes, ma'am, there sure is," he said. He had placed his saddle at his feet, along with his Winchester. He started to slide them over.

"Oh, I can take the seat by the window if you'd like," offered the young woman.

"No, you'd best let me have it," said Longarm. "That way you won't get as much of the soot and cinders from the locomotive."

"That's very kind of you." She sat down beside Longarm as he slid over next to the window. "Mister . . . ?"

"Long, ma'am, Custis Long."

"I'm Amelia Richmond. Miss Amelia Richmond."

Longarm reached up and tugged on the brim of his Stetson. "It's an honor and a pleasure to make your acquaintance, Miss Richmond."

"Oh, no need to be so formal. Call me Amelia."

Longarm was glad to do so and said as much. He didn't know where Amelia Richmond was bound for; probably she wasn't going all the way to Carson City like he was. But for at least part of this trip he would have some pleasant company, maybe more than just pleasant.

Not that he was in much shape to get carried away with such things. Lorna had just about plumb worn him out the night before.

But as Amelia Richmond smiled at him again, Longarm felt a stirring inside him. Maybe he was closer to being recovered than he had thought. One thing that had always worked to his advantage—he had amazing recuperative powers.

Maybe before this trip was over he would put them to the test.

It seemed to Brad Corrigan that he and his brother Tom had been riding forever. Their horses were gaunted, and so were the riders. Men and animals alike had been on short rations for the past few days as they wound their way through these godforsaken mountains. Brad had never been to Nevada before, and as far as he was concerned, if he could leave the place right now he wouldn't care if he never saw it again.

What was really frustrating was that they had passed through several nice little settlements where they could have stopped and laid low for a while, if that was what Tom had in mind. They had plenty of money, so that wasn't a concern.

But no, Tom had to keep going. He had to get to this place up in the mountains he kept talking about, the place he had been told about by an old outlaw named Greevey, one time while they were in a Phoenix whorehouse. Brad hadn't known anything about it, because he'd been busy bedding the Chinese girl he had picked out in the parlor, but evidently Tom and Greevey had spent quite a while talking that evening, trading gossip about various hideouts.

That was when Greevey had brought up Zamora.

Tom hadn't really explained anything about the place to Brad, just said that the old man had talked about it, and that he and Asa had discussed it and decided that it would be a good place for them to go if things got too hot for them in Arizona. Brad had asked if there was a bank or something there that they ought to rob, and Tom had just smiled and said that they wouldn't be holding up any banks or anything like that while they were in Zamora.

That was all right with Brad. To tell the truth, he was getting a mite tired of being a desperado. He didn't like being shot at. And he would never forget the horrible moment when he'd seen that lawman kill Asa and Logan.

"How much farther you reckon it is to the place?" Brad asked now. He and Tom were riding through a narrow canyon with steep-sided walls. Those stone walls rose about fifty feet in the air and were close enough together to make Brad a little nervous. When he glanced up at them, it seemed almost like they were closing in on the two riders.

"How the hell would I know?" snapped Tom. "I've never been here before."

"Are you sure we're even going the right way? I mean, since you don't have the map anymore—"

"We're going the right way," Tom broke in. "Asa and I studied the map I got from that old-timer until I had it memorized."

Something occurred to Brad, and he asked carefully, "Tom, did you have to *pay* the old man for that map . . . ?"

Tom reined in and jerked his horse around so that he could glare at Brad. "Are you sayin' that I got took, that the map was worthless?"

"No, not at all," Brad replied hastily, knowing that his big brother was angry with him. Of course, that was exactly what he had been trying to ask, but clearly, Tom wasn't even going to entertain the notion.

The more Brad thought about it, though, the more sense the idea made. An old man draws a circle on a map, writes some cryptic word on it, and spins a yarn to somebody he meets in a whorehouse about how valuable the map is. . . . It could have happened that way, Brad told himself.

But he didn't tell Tom, because Tom already looked mad enough to knock him out of the saddle or even shoot him. Brad wondered if Tom had reacted so strongly because he was starting to have doubts of his own.

"Let's just keep going," suggested Brad. "I'm sure we'll be there soon."

Tom snorted. "Damn right we will be." He jabbed his heels in his horse's flanks and got the animal moving again.

The canyon twisted and turned. The strip of sky that was visible overhead was leaden with clouds. Brad hadn't heard any thunder, but he began to worry about rain. Did they have flash floods up here in Nevada like sometimes occurred down in Arizona? If a downpour started and a wall of water came roaring through this canyon, he and Tom wouldn't have anywhere to go. The walls were too tall and steep for them to escape.

There was always *something* to worry about, seemed like.

And when they rode around yet another sharp bend in the canyon, that included the rifle muzzles that poked out from behind some rocks on a ledge above them, and the rough voice that called, "Hold it right there, you two! Move a hair and we'll blast you!"

Tom and Brad brought their horses to an abrupt halt. Obviously this canyon wasn't as deserted as it appeared to be at first glance.

Brad lifted anxious eyes to the ledge and saw the muzzles of three rifles trained on him and his brother. He could see only glimpses of the men holding those rifles behind the rocks. The ledge was about twenty feet above the floor of the canyon, and Brad didn't see any way the men could have gotten up there.

"Who the hell are you?" demanded the same voice.

"My name is Tom Corrigan," replied Tom. "This is my brother Brad."

"What are you doin' up here?"

Tom hesitated, then said, "We're looking for a place called Zamora."

"Zamora! Who told you about Zamora?"

"An old man named Greevey. We met him at a whorehouse in Phoenix."

That brought a chuckle from the ledge. "A whorehouse, eh? That sounds like Greevey, all right."

"You know him?" asked Tom. "He said that if I ever made it to Zamora, I should mention his name when I got there."

"Oh, I know him, all right, the damned rascally bastard. Never did trust him any farther'n I could throw him."

Brad's heart sank a little at that. If these men were enemies of Greevey's, the welcome he and Tom would receive probably wouldn't be a friendly one.

"Is he dead yet?" continued the unseen spokesman.

Tom frowned. "Greevey, you mean? No, he was hale and hearty the last time I saw him. He was going upstairs in that whorehouse with two of the girls, in fact, not just one."

"Yeah, that's Greevey, always hoggin' the good things. Drop your guns."

The abrupt order made both Tom and Brad stiffen. They didn't want to give up their weapons.

"Do it," added the gravelly voice in an unmistakably menacing tone.

Tom sighed. "I reckon we'd better do like he says," he told Brad.

They untied and unbuckled their gun belts and lowered the belts to the canyon floor.

"Now the rifles."

When they had complied with that order, the voice said, "Now ride on this way a mite, so that those guns are out of easy reach." When Tom and Brad had moved their horses about twenty feet farther along the canyon, the man told them, "That's far enough."

They reined in again. As they sat there in their saddles, unsure what was going to happen next, the man who had been barking orders at them finally stepped out from behind one of the boulders on the ledge. He was short and thick-bodied, with bowed legs, broad shoulders, and arms like an ape. A battered old hat with a turned-up brim was crammed down on a thatch of rusty hair, and he had long mustaches of the same shade. The rifle he clutched in big hands seemed like an extension of his body, he handled it with such ease.

"Stay right there," he told Tom and Brad. "I'll take you to Zamora."

Brad didn't see how the man was going to get down from the ledge. Then the man kicked at something, and a rope ladder appeared and fell over the edge, unrolling as it dropped toward the canyon floor. The man slung his rifle over his shoulder on a leather strap and then climbed down the rope ladder with ease. Brad was reminded again of an ape.

"Stay there for a minute," commanded the man. He

jerked a thumb at the ledge. "The other guards still have you covered, so don't try anything funny."

With that he vanished around the next bend in the canyon. A moment later Brad heard the clip-clop of hoof-beats. The apelike hombre reappeared leading a saddled mule. He swung up onto the animal's bony back, unslung his rifle, and pointed it at Tom and Brad again.

"All right, let's go," he said.

"What about our guns?" asked Tom.

"They'll be collected and returned to you later . . . that is, if'n you're still alive to need 'em."

The man pulled the mule to the side to let Tom and Brad pass so that he could fall in behind them and cover them with his rifle. As the tense procession moved along the canyon, the man went on, "They call me Yellowstone, on account of I used to do some trappin' up there in that country a long time ago. Name stuck, even though I ain't taken any pelts in years."

"My brother and I are pleased to make your acquaintance, Yellowstone," said Tom.

The man grunted. "Better hold off on bein' friendly until we find out whether or not I got to kill the two o' you."

Brad felt sick at his stomach. He wasn't sure what he and Tom had ridden into, but it was quickly becoming obvious that they might never ride out again.

They followed the canyon for another half-mile or so, and it was one of the longest half-miles Brad had ever ridden—having a gun at your back made everything seem different. The last few hundred yards, the canyon floor rose steeply. They were already fairly high in the mountains. When the canyon ended abruptly at the head of a little valley, the ground dropped away in a precipitous slope. As Yellowstone called out for them to stop, Brad reined in and looked down into the valley. A narrow trail wound its way from the mouth of the canyon all the way down to the little creek that meandered through the valley.

Next to that creek, about a mile away but easily visible in the crystal-clear mountain air, was a settlement. It ran for several blocks on both sides of a main street, and there were other buildings and log cabins on the cross streets and scattered around the fringes of the settlement. Some of the buildings leaned a little funny, and the roof had fallen in on a couple of them, but most of the structures looked to be in pretty good repair.

One of them, a big house at the far end of the main street, was downright elegant, in fact. It was a damned mansion, thought Brad in surprise, and looked more like it ought to be in Denver or San Francisco or somewhere other than where it was.

"Well, there it is," said Yellowstone in his gravelly voice. "Welcome to Zamora. Welcome to the city of thieves."

Chapter 10

The tail end of the Sangre de Cristo Mountains loomed in the distance as Jessie and Ki rode toward the little settlement somewhere along the border between the Texas Panhandle and New Mexico Territory. They were still in Texas, but the clearly visible mountains were across the border. To the northwest was Raton Pass, marking the route of the main trail between New Mexico Territory and Colorado.

"Do you think we'll find them here?" asked Jessie.

Ki shrugged. *"Quién sabe?* We know they rode in this direction."

Almost a week had passed since the theft of Shorty. During that time, Jessie and Ki had ridden over a big chunk of Texas, trailing the four members of the gang who had gotten away. They had stopped at innumerable isolated ranches and little settlements, always asking questions and describing the four riders as best they could. Jessie wished they had gotten a better look at their quarry. The Circle Star hands who had battled the outlaws at the siding had given her and Ki descriptions of the men, but they were sketchy at best.

Despite that, Jessie was confident they were still on the right trail. Not only that, but she felt like she and Ki had cut into the lead the outlaws had on them. Given time, she was sure they would catch up.

And she had all the time in the world. Nothing short of death would stop her from settling the score with those men—and finding out who the hell had paid them to steal Shorty.

"Perhaps if nothing else there will be a store in this town where we can replenish our supplies," said Ki. "They're getting a little low."

"I know," said Jessie. She had been pushing herself and Ki at a hard pace, and they had been traveling light so they could move faster. Eventually, though, that kind of pace wore down both people and horses. Their mounts really needed a few days of rest and plenty of grain. She and Ki could use the rest, too.

But there was no time for that.

The settlement was a typical cow town, Jessie saw as she and Ki rode closer to it. There were several huge ranches up here in the Panhandle, covering millions of acres, and small towns like this had sprung up to service the needs of those vast spreads and the men who worked there. Accordingly, most of the businesses in those settlements were saloons, gambling dens, dance halls, and cribs, along with a scattering of mercantiles, saddle shops, blacksmiths, hardware stores, and things like that. The occasional school or church could be found, too, but those harbingers of civilization were few and far between.

"I'll see about picking up some supplies," said Jessie

as they reached the eastern end of the cow town's single street.

"And I could use a drink," responded Ki with a smile.

Jessie knew what he meant. Ki wasn't really interested in beer or whiskey; he just knew that saloons were usually the best places to pick up information, especially about the sort of men he and Jessie sought. As they had done in previous stops on this trek, Jessie would ask a few subtle questions in the town's general mercantile while Ki did the same in a saloon or two.

They veered their horses toward opposite sides of the street. Jessie's destination was a big building with a high porch on the front of it to facilitate loading supplies in wagons and buckboards. The sign above the door read EGAN'S EMPORIUM.

Ki headed for the Panhandle Saloon, diagonally across the street from the general store.

Jessie brought her horse to a stop in front of the high porch, wearily swung down from the saddle and looped the reins around a hitching post. She climbed the steps to the porch and went into the dim, cavernous interior, which was packed with shelves that were filled with an assortment of goods. A long counter ran across the rear of the store, and a balding man in a storekeeper's apron leaned on the counter, talking to a man in range clothes who stood on the other side of it. Both men turned to look at Jessie when her boot's heels rang on the planks of the hardwood floor.

She was accustomed to men looking at her. She had been ever since she was a girl and her body had started developing. She knew she was attractive, knew that many men considered her beautiful. And men, being men, were going to look; that was all there was to it. Trying to get them to do otherwise was like trying to teach a pig to sing.

The two men in Egan's Emporium looked at her, but they didn't say anything. So she gave them a faint smile, nodded politely to them, and said, "Hello, gentlemen." She was willing to give them the benefit of that much doubt.

"Howdy, ma'am," said the storekeeper as he straightened from his leisurely pose. Jessie supposed he was Egan. "What can I do for you?"

"I need supplies," Jessie told him. "All the staples, plus maybe some salt pork or bacon if you have it."

"We sure do." The storekeeper pulled a pad of paper in front of him and took a stub of pencil from a pocket in the apron. "Lemme just write up a list here. . . ."

The other man, who was evidently a customer, said, "You know, ma'am, we don't often see a lady dressed like that in these parts. Never, in fact."

Jessie knew that her garb was unusual for a woman. The fact that she packed iron in a low-slung holster was odd, too. But she was long past caring whether she shocked people. She thumbed her hat back off her head, letting it dangle behind her on its chin strap. That allowed her thick reddish-gold hair to tumble around her face.

She looked at the man who had just spoken. He was tall and broad-shouldered, with the narrow waist of a natural rider. His denim trousers and jacket showed plenty of wear, but the clothes were clean and fairly neat. The same was true of his boots and hat. He might be a drifting cowboy, but he was no saddle tramp.

And the well-worn walnut grips of the Colt holstered on his hip showed that the gun had been used plenty, too. Still, he didn't look like an outlaw. His face was too rugged to be called handsome, but his blue-gray eyes

110

showed both intelligence and, Jessie was a little surprised to recognize, gentleness.

"I wear what's comfortable for riding," she responded to his comment.

"You must have been doing plenty of it," he said. "You're not from around here."

"Just passing through."

The storekeeper began gathering the supplies Jessie wanted. He said, "Well, we're mighty glad you decided to stop in Cottonwood, ma'am. This ol' cow town'll be a brighter place as long as you're here."

Jessie's smile widened. "What a nice thing to say, Mr. Egan. I suppose you *are* Mr. Egan?"

"Yes, ma'am, Claude Egan, proprietor of this here store. And this tall drink o' water is Rance Scott."

Jessie realized they were waiting for her to introduce herself. She didn't want to admit to being Jessica Starbuck; even up here in the Panhandle, there was a good chance they would have heard of her. So she just said, "I'm called Jessie."

"Pleased to meet you, Jessie," said Rance Scott. "Staying in Cottonwood long?"

"No, like I told you, I'm just passing through." She paused, then said, "Actually, I'm supposed to meet some people here. Maybe you've seen them . . . four men, one of them with white hair, one short and dark, a tall, lanky one, and a Mexican vaquero." Those were the descriptions she and Ki had been given by the Circle Star punchers.

Claude Egan frowned and shook his head. "Can't say as I've seen 'em. How about you, Rance?"

"Nope. And if you don't mind my saying so, Jessie,

they don't really sound like the sort of hombres that a woman like you would be associating with. No offense."

"None taken," she said, but her voice was a little cooler now. She couldn't resist asking, "Just who do you think I *should* be associating with, Mr. Scott?"

"Well . . . me, for one." He grinned, which pushed his rugged face a little further toward the handsome side, although it wasn't quite there yet. "I'd be honored if you'd have supper with me at the café down the street."

Just as she was accustomed to having men look at her with admiration and often outright lust, so too was she used to them wanting to spend time with her. Usually she had no interest in doing so.

But she sensed that there might be something a little different about Rance Scott, so she said, "I'll think about it, Mr. Scott. Will you be around town for the rest of the day?"

"Plan to. I'm not heading back to my ranch until tomorrow."

"Rance owns the Box RS," supplied Egan. "It's a mighty fine little spread. Maybe not as big as Charley Goodnight's JA ranch or the XIT—"

"Not as big by a few million acres, he means," put in Scott with a wry grin.

"But it's still a good ranch," continued Egan. "Not just a little greasy sack outfit, no, sir."

Jessie had the feeling that the storekeeper was touting Scott because he had an interest in playing Cupid. That effort was doomed to failure; Jessie had no intention of staying around here long enough to get mixed up in a romance with anybody.

But she didn't see any harm in having supper with Rance Scott, so she smiled at him and said, "I'll let you know about that invitation later."

"I'll be around. Claude and I were about to set up the checkerboard."

Jessie nodded and said to the storekeeper, "I'll be back later to pick up those supplies."

Egan bobbed his head in agreement. "Yes'm. I'll have 'em ready for you."

Jessie left the store, aware that the men's eyes were following her as she walked out. She didn't mind. In fact, the idea that Rance Scott's gaze was lingering on her made a slight surge of warmth go through her. Even though she wouldn't be in Cottonwood for long—she and Ki would be gone tomorrow, if not sooner, depending on whether or not they found a lead to the men they were after—that might be long enough for a little pleasant diversion. . . .

She forced her mind off that subject and wondered what, if anything, Ki had discovered in the Panhandle Saloon.

At first nobody paid much attention to Ki when he walked into the saloon. It was late in the afternoon and business was picking up in the place. Half a dozen cowboys stood at the bar, drinking, while card games were going on at two of the tables. At a table in a rear corner, two men were drinking, one of them with his back to Ki, the other leaning against the wall with his hat tipped down over his eyes. Every so often he lifted a glass of whiskey to his lips and sipped from it.

Ki's dark eyes narrowed slightly as he looked at the two men sitting at the rear table. He could see everyone else in the room clearly enough to know that none of them were the men he and Jessie were after. But he couldn't be sure about those two, and the uncertainty bothered him.

As he walked toward the bar, several of the men standing there looked briefly at him then returned their attention to their drinking. At first glance he seemed like just another cowboy, since he wore the same sort of hat, shirt, vest, and trousers that many of them did.

But there were several things that stood out about him—his skin color, the shape of his eyes, the fact that he didn't wear a gun, the sandals on his feet—and gradually the men at the bar turned their heads to look more closely at him.

Ki ignored their scrutiny. When the bartender came over to him and inquisitively raised bushy eyebrows, Ki said, "Beer, please." If anybody expected some sort of Oriental singsong, he was disappointed. His voice was calm and quiet, with hints of power.

The bartender drew the beer and slid it across the hardwood. "That'll be six bits," he said.

The price was a little high, especially considering the unprepossessing surroundings, but Ki made no complaint. He took three coins from his pocket and placed them on the bar. The drink juggler scooped them up and dropped them in a cash box.

Soft footsteps made him glance toward a door at the end of the bar. It had just opened, and a woman emerged from it, followed by a young cowboy who was buttoning up his fly. That made it pretty obvious what they had been doing, as did the neckline of the woman's blouse, which scooped low enough to reveal the upper halves of full, soft breasts. She was probably around thirty years old, with a well-used but not worn-out look about her. Her auburn hair was cut fairly short, and the lines on her face had been put there not only by time and hardship but also by laughter, as if she fully recognized the travails of the world but found them occasionally amusing.

114

Ki felt an instinctive liking for the woman. Most *nymphs du prairie* were rather pathetic souls, lacking in emotional strength or some other vital spiritual component so that they were used up and discarded at a relatively early age, often wracked by disease and drink. From time to time, though, one ran across a soiled dove like this one appeared to be, a woman of fortitude who happened to earn her living on her back.

She looked along the bar and her eyes found Ki at the opposite end, and suddenly he could tell that she was as interested in him as he was in her. Ki's reaction was, to a certain extent, pragmatic. Whores probably knew more about what was going on in a settlement than anybody else because men, no matter who they were, tended to talk more freely after they'd been with a woman. If the outlaws Ki and Jessie were following had been through here, chances were this woman had either seen them herself or talked to somebody who had.

So when she started sauntering along the bar toward him, Ki was encouraged. If he could get her alone, he could ask a few questions without everybody else in the saloon having to know his business.

One of the men the woman passed put out a hand to stop her. "Howdy, Clarissa," he said. "How 'bout givin' me a chance next?"

"Later, Rollie," she said. "There's a stranger in town, and you know how partial I am to strangers."

Ki smiled at her as she came up to him. "Hello."

"Hello yourself, mister." Now that she was closer he could see the big brown nipples that crowned her ample breasts. "Just ride into Cottonwood?"

Ki nodded. "That's right. I was thirsty, so I stopped here."

115

"You came to the right place. Coldest beer in town."

"And the most attractive woman."

She laughed, and he saw that she wasn't the least bit taken in by his comment.

"Flattery's always nice, but as the old saying goes, actions speak louder than words." She moved closer to him, so that the soft warmth of her breasts pressed against his arm. "You want to go down the hall with me?"

No cowboy would accept an invitation like that without inquiring about the price first, so Ki did so. "How much?"

She took his arm, squeezing it lightly so that she could feel the muscles through his sleeve. "Three dollars . . . and I think you'll find that it's worth every penny."

If she was able to tell him something about those outlaws, it certainly would be. He said, "All right. Let me finish my beer—"

"You can take it with you."

"Are you sure?"

"Certain. I own this place, after all, so I make the rules."

Ki's eyebrows rose slightly. He hadn't expected to find that the woman was the proprietor of the saloon. Picking up the still half-full mug, he started to follow her toward the door at the end of the bar.

One of the men standing with his foot on the brass rail had been glancing at Ki and Clarissa out of the corner of his eye, and now he turned to glare directly at them. "Damn it, Clarissa, look at him!" he burst out. "He's a Chink, for Christ's sake! You haven't sunk low enough to take a damn Chinaman to your bed, have you?"

Crisply and coolly, Clarissa answered, "Who I take to

my bed is no concern of yours, Amos. Just because you've been there a heap of times yourself doesn't give you any say over what I do."

"I never said it did," protested the man called Amos. "But he's a Chinaman!"

"Actually," said Ki, making an effort to rein in his temper, "my ancestry is a mixture of American and Japanese. I have no Chinese blood."

One of the other men at the bar chuckled. "He talks like a reg'lar person, don't he?"

Ki gritted his teeth. He wanted to get Clarissa alone so he could ask her some questions and perhaps spend a sensuous interlude with her, and dealing with these bigoted bumpkins was just delaying him. Maybe he could smooth things over and be done with it.

"When I get back," he said, "I'd like to buy all of you gentlemen a drink."

Several of the cowboys licked their lips and looked appreciative of that offer, but Amos just glared more darkly.

"If you think I'd drink liquor that a dirty Chinaman paid for, you're dead wrong, boy."

Sharply, Clarissa said, "You've had too much to drink, Amos. Maybe you'd better leave—"

Amos stepped away from the bar to block the path Ki and Clarissa had been taking. "I'm not goin' anywhere," he said. He reached for Clarissa's arm. "And neither are you if it's with a yellow bastard like this!"

Before Amos could grab hold of Clarissa, Ki's hand suddenly shot out and closed around the man's wrist. Ki didn't appear to be holding the wrist tightly, but Amos suddenly gasped and went pale. He stiffened as if pain had frozen every muscle in his body.

Smiling slightly, Ki said, "The lady and I would like to get past. Excuse us, please."

Amos sagged, as if he were about to fall to his knees. Ki relaxed the pressure on his wrist, and he was able to move again. He reached out with his other hand and fumblingly grabbed the bar to steady himself. Ki let go of his wrist entirely, and Amos turned and leaned against the bar, breathing heavily.

Clarissa looked at Ki and raised her eyebrows. "You seem to have unexpected talents, mister. Just what else can you do?"

"I will show you," said Ki as he took her arm and started to lead her past the shaken Amos. The other men along the bar and at the poker tables were staring at him, but he ignored them.

Instinct warned him of danger in plenty of time, because when Amos made his move, he wasn't very fast about it. Even on his best day, it probably would have seemed to Ki that he was moving in slow motion. He grabbed up a half-empty whiskey bottle from the bar and turned toward Ki, raising the bottle and then swinging it at the back of Ki's head.

Without turning around or even glancing over his shoulder, Ki reached back with his free hand and blocked the blow, snapping the side of his hand against Amos's wrist. Amos cried out in pain as his hand went numb and the bottle slipped from his fingers. The bartender reached across the hardwood and caught the bottle before it could fall to the floor and smash.

In a continuation of the same move that had disarmed Amos, Ki slashed a side-hand blow against the man's neck. Amos folded up, and no one tried to catch *him* as he fell. He dropped to the floor, out cold but not badly injured because Ki had been careful not to hit him too hard. The blow would have been fatal if Ki had struck with all his strength, instead of only a fraction of it.

"Sorry," he murmured to Clarissa as they continued on toward the door, leaving the unconscious Amos sprawled behind them.

"Don't worry about it," she assured him. "Amos had it coming. He's really not a bad hombre when he's not drunk. I'm the one who should be apologizing to you for the ruckus he caused."

"That's not necessary. It was nothing."

Ki glanced toward the table in the rear corner where the two men had been sitting. He had hoped to get a better look at them as he left the main room with Clarissa, but he saw now that they were gone.

That worried Ki, but not too much. Chances were, they were just a pair of local cowpokes, like the other men in the Panhandle Saloon.

And he had other things to occupy his attention right now, most notably the woman called Clarissa, who leaned against him once more as they entered a hallway lit by a candle at the far end, next to another door. The warm pressure of her breasts against his arm urged him on, and he put the two men out of his mind for the moment.

"I told you it was him," Blue Atkinson said to Simon Jarvis as they hurried along behind the saloon, through the last fading light of day. "I told you it was that damned Chinaman or whatever he is!"

"Settle down," growled Jarvis. "We figured him and the Starbuck woman might come after us. It don't matter.

We'll just find Nick and tell him." The stocky outlaw snorted contemptuously. "Hell, we were likely gonna have to kill them sooner or later anyway. Might as well be here and now."

Chapter 11

Nick Darrow perched on a keg in the shed where they kept their mounts and watched Montoya brushing and combing the horses. That Mexican sure liked those animals, thought Nick, probably more than he liked most human beings. Nick could understand that. Most of the time he thought humans were a pretty sorry lot himself.

But not that girl from the train. She was special. Nick had never known anyone like her. She had haunted his thoughts and even his dreams ever since that day at the railroad siding.

He slipped a couple of fingers inside his vest pocket and brought out the thing she had given him that day, just before the train pulled out. It was a coin, a heavy silver coin with writing on it that Nick couldn't read and an engraving of a distinguished-looking gent with a mustache and long curly hair on the front and a crown of some sort on the back. He might have been tempted to melt it down for the silver, since it was unlikely that any business would accept such a foreign coin, if not for the fact that somebody had taken a knife to it and carved two words on it, one on the front and one on the back. Nick looked at them now, as he had on numerous occasions, and mused aloud to himself, "Zamora . . . Nevada. What in the hell does that mean?"

Of course, Nevada was obvious. Was Zamora somebody who lived in Nevada? Or was it a place, too? It almost had to be, he decided, because the woman had made it sound like he could find her there.

"You ever know anybody named Zamora, Sonny?" he asked Montoya.

The vaquero grunted incuriously and said, "No."

Darrow put the coin back in his pocket. Ever since the gunfight at the siding, they had been traveling in a generally northwestward direction. Darrow intended to continue that way, until they eventually reached Nevada. He hadn't explained to the others why they were going there or even told them that Nevada was their ultimate destination. Figuring that they were well ahead of anybody following them, they had stopped here in this little cow town to rest their horses for a few days, but Darrow intended to push on when morning came.

Darrow was trying to decide whether to go to the café for supper or just head for one of the saloons instead, when he saw Blue Atkinson and Simon Jarvis hurrying toward him. The sense of urgency about their movements told Darrow that something was wrong.

He came to his feet. "What is it?"

"We saw that Chinaman who works for the Starbuck woman," said Blue excitedly. "He's down there in the Panhandle Saloon."

"Doing what?" Darrow asked sharply.

Blue's usual nature reasserted itself. "Well, he went down the hall with that gal Clarissa who runs the place, so I imagine he's gettin' himself a poke right about now."

"Be a good time to go down there, bust in on 'em, and shoot the slant-eyed son of a bitch," suggested Jarvis.

That sounded like a fine idea, but instinct warned Darrow not to rush into anything until he knew exactly what was going on and how big the threat really was.

"Did you see the Starbuck woman?" he demanded.

Blue and Jarvis shook their heads. "Just the Chinaman," said Blue. "He got in a little scuffle with one o' the hombres in the saloon. The fella grabbed up a whiskey bottle and tried to knock the Chinaman's brains out, but the Chinaman stopped him and put him down cold without even seemin' to pay much attention to what he was doin'." Blue rubbed his arm, which was still a little sore sometimes from getting stuck with that star-shaped thingamabob. "I don't like that Chinaman."

"So he was alone, as far as you could tell?" Darrow asked.

"Yeah." Blue scratched ruefully at his jaw. "But we slipped out the back door of the saloon when he wasn't lookin', and we, uh, didn't check the street to see if any more of the Circle Star hands were with him."

"We figured we'd better find you and tell you what was going on as fast as we could, Nick," put in Jarvis.

Darrow's jaw clenched so that a little muscle jumped in his cheek. He wished Blue and Jarvis had thought a little faster and had a look in the street, but what was done, was done, he supposed.

"We can't just bushwhack him," he decided. "Not without knowing if anybody else rode in with him. Everybody spread out and keep an eye peeled for the

Starbuck woman or any of her other hands. Once we've figured out just what we're dealing with . . . *then* maybe we'll kill the Chinaman."

"How'll we know where to find him?" Blue wanted to know.

Darrow grinned tautly. "I've ridden that Clarissa gal a few times myself," he said. "I expect she'll keep him busy for a while."

Ki would have preferred to ask his questions first and then indulge in the pleasures of the flesh, but Clarissa was insistent on doing things the other way around. Since she might have information that he needed, Ki didn't see that he had any choice other than to go along with her wishes.

Once they were in her room she started kissing him. She wrapped her arms around his neck, pressed that large bosom against his chest, and slid her tongue into his mouth. The approach was a bit brazen and unsophisticated for Ki's taste—but he had to admit that it was effective. His manhood began to stiffen with arousal.

Clarissa felt it poking against her soft, gently rounded belly and reached down to caress him through his trousers. She broke the kiss and said, "That feels like some pretty impressive equipment you got there, uh . . . what *is* your name, anyway?"

"I am called Ki."

"Well, Ki, I think I want to get that thing out in the fresh air so I can see just what it is I'm going to have inside me pretty soon."

With a deft ease born of much practice, she flipped open the buttons of his fly and then reached in to free his shaft, which was almost fully erect by now. "Lord have mercy!" she exclaimed as she realized that it took both hands to encircle the thick pole. She slid her palms along it and murmured, "It's long, too."

Ki reached into the neckline of her blouse and lifted first one breast and then the other free from the garment's confines. He cupped the large, fleshy globes and stroked the hard nipples with his thumbs. Clarissa made a noise of pleasure deep in her throat. As she continued to stroke his organ, he lowered his head and ran his tongue around her nipples.

She closed her eyes and began to breathe harder as he sucked each nipple. "Damn it, let's get the rest of these clothes off and get to bed!" she gasped.

Ki complied, undressing her first. He lifted the blouse over her head and arms and dropped it on a nearby ladderback chair, then pushed the long skirt she wore down past her hips so that it fell around her feet. She wore no stockings under it, or anything else, for that matter. She stepped out of the skirt and caught hold of his hand, bringing it between her soft thighs so his fingers touched her moist opening.

"Feel how wet you made me already," she said. "And don't worry, I cleaned up real good after that other fella was through, so what you're feeling all came from me."

Somewhat indelicately phrased, but good information to have, thought Ki. While he had his hand there, he slipped a finger into her, delving between the fleshy folds and probing her femininity. Clarissa ground her pelvis against the base of Ki's hand.

"Here I am naked, and you've still got all those blasted clothes on!" she said breathlessly. She pulled at his belt. "We've got to do something about that!"

Ki dropped his hat on the chair and then took off his vest and shirt while she unfastened his trousers. He stepped out of his sandals. Some men thought he was crazy for wearing that sort of footgear instead of boots, but they just weren't thinking things through properly. At moments like this, sandals were a lot quicker and easier to get off than the tight, high-topped horseman's boots that were so common on the frontier.

Working with a decided sense of urgency, Clarissa finished getting Ki out of his clothes and then started pumping her hands up and down his erection again. After a moment, she stopped and said, "What the hell am I doing? As nice as that is to look at and touch, it'll feel even better inside me." She lay back on the bed and spread her legs wide in invitation. "Come on, Ki. I'm ready for you."

He climbed onto the bed with her and moved directly between her legs. He felt some urgency of his own now. As he positioned himself above her, she grabbed his shaft and brought the head of it to her wet, heated core.

"Now!" she hissed. "Don't make me wait!"

Ki didn't. His hips surged forward smoothly, and his organ slipped in easily. He sheathed himself inside her with a powerful thrust. She gave a low, throaty cry as he penetrated her. Her arms went around his neck, and she lifted her knees high and locked her ankles together over his buttocks.

As might have been expected, she was not especially tight, but her insides were as smooth and warm and slippery as melted butter. Ki liked women of all shapes and sizes and had an appreciation of female beauty in all its myriad forms, so he didn't mind the fact that Clarissa had perhaps a few extra pounds on her bones. As he launched into a steady rhythm and began to pump in and out of her, he was struck by how incredibly *comfortable* it was making love to her.

She was receptive, too, thrusting up at him each time he drove his full length into her. She climaxed quickly, crying out and shuddering and clutching at him, and he was ready to loose his own culmination when she grabbed at him and urged desperately, "Don't stop, Ki, don't stop! Oh, God, you've got to keep going for a while!"

Ki was willing, although he *was* slightly impatient to get to the questions about the outlaws and whether or not she had seen them. Still, he never entered into the physical act of love with a woman without intending to pleasure her to the best of his ability, so he used his finely honed willpower and concentration to postpone his own climax and continued thrusting into her.

What seemed like an hour later but surely wasn't, he was still at it, gritting his teeth now. Clarissa had climaxed at least four times and didn't seem any closer to being ready to stop. Ki had used just about every trick he knew to keep going, but there were limits to everything. The throbbing ache of passion had spread from his shaft seemingly all through his body, until he was just one big need to come.

And finally—*finally!*—she seemed to be ready for him to do so. Her fingernails dug into his buttocks as she urged him deeper, ever deeper, into her. She cried, "Now, Ki, now!"

Like an explosion, his climax roared through him. His juices burst from him, splashing, gushing, streaming out with a force and intensity and volume seldom matched even in his amorously adventurous life.

Spasm after spasm shook him. She slid a hand up behind his head and pulled his face down to hers so that their mouths came together as the last jetting spurts of his fluid shot from his organ. It was as total a climax as Ki had ever experienced in his life.

When it was over it left him breathless and drained, barely able to draw air into his lungs, let alone think coherently.

But that didn't last long, and the real reason he was here soon reasserted itself in his brain.

Clarissa wasn't ready to let go of him yet. She kept her arms and legs around him as his shaft began to soften within her. Ki was still a little breathless, so he took advantage of the opportunity to rest for a few moments and think about what he was going to say to her.

Finally, he was soft enough so that he slid liquidly out of her, prompting her to make a small noise of disappointment in her throat. "One of these days they got to come up with a way of getting a man to stay hard all night," she said.

"Surely such a thing would be a boon to women everywhere," commented Ki.

"You're damn tootin' it would." She sighed. "Ah, well. I guess I shouldn't be greedy. That was some of the best lovin' I've had in a long time, Ki."

"And the same is true for me," he said as he rolled off of her and stretched out at her side. If she was like most whores, she would try to get him dressed and out of here in a hurry as soon as she had collected her money, so that she could move on to the next customer. He was hoping he had pleased her enough, however, so that she would be willing to linger and talk for a spell.

She stretched languidly, like a big cat, seemingly in no rush to get up. Her hand strayed over and massaged his smooth chest, then slid down his flat, muscular belly to his groin. She trailed her fingers through the black hair around his organ, then cupped the shaft itself in her palm.

"Even soft, that's a mighty impressive piece of work," she said. "How long before you reckon you could go again?"

"A man must have control of both his mind and his body to achieve balance and satisfaction in life. My body does what I instruct it to, not the other way around."

"Are you saying you could get it up again *now*?"

"Balance *does* sometimes require patience."

Clarissa laughed. "After the way you just rode me hard and put me up wet, I'm willing to wait . . . for a little while."

She was playing into his hands, but he didn't congratulate himself on achieving his ends, not just yet. Instead he said, "I imagine in your line of work you see most of the men who pass through this settlement."

"My line of work?" She raised herself on an elbow. "You mean being a whore? Or running a saloon?"

"Both," said Ki. "Although I would never refer to you by such a crude term."

Clarissa laughed and said, "Oh, hell, I don't mind being called a whore. You are what you are, I always say. And it's true enough that just about everybody who passes through Cottonwood stops by for either a drink or some loving, or both." Her eyes suddenly narrowed in suspicion. "You're looking for somebody, aren't you, Ki?"

Since she had asked the question, and since he figured that she was too cunning to be fooled by a lie, he answered her honestly. "Yes, I seek four men who may have ridden through here." He described them briefly.

Clarissa listened with an intent frown on her face, and

when Ki was finished, she said, "They didn't ride through here."

Ki felt a surge of disappointment. He and Jessie must have gotten off the trail somehow.

But then Clarissa went on, "I say they didn't ride through because they haven't left yet. As far as I know, they're still here in town."

Ki stiffened. "You have seen them today? You know this for sure?"

"Hell, yes. Two of them were in the saloon when you came in, the ones called Blue and Simon."

"The men sitting at that rear table," guessed Ki.

"That's right. So Nick and the Mexican must still be around somewhere, too."

"Do you know their last names?"

She shook her head. "I just know what they called each other. And none of them called the Mexican by name while I was around, so I don't even know his first name."

Ki wasn't disappointed. He knew quite a bit more than he had when he came back here with the woman, and the most important piece of information was that the outlaws were probably still here in the settlement. Of course, there was a chance that the two who had been in the saloon had recognized him, and they might have hurried back to the others and sent the whole gang scurrying out of town.

He had to tell Jessie.

Clarissa clutched at him as he sat up in the bed. "Hey!" she exclaimed. "Where do you think you're going?"

"There is something I must do," he told her as he swung his legs out of bed and his feet to the floor.

"Damn right there is! You've got to come back here and make love to me again!"

Ki pulled away and reached for his trousers. "I am truly sorry, Clarissa," he said, "but I cannot."

"Oh, hell," she pouted. "I knew I shouldn't have told you the truth about those hombres."

"It is a matter of life and death," said Ki as he picked up his shirt.

"And making a poor gal come *isn't*?"

Ki had no answer for that. Truly, the universe was full of mysteries.

Chapter 12

There was only the one mercantile in town, so Jessie took her horse down to the saddle shop to have a minor repair made on the saddle, a repair that either she or Ki could have done easily themselves, and then she visited the blacksmith to have the man check her mount's shoes. That wasn't really necessary, either, but in both cases Jessie had an excuse for standing around and asking a few seemingly casual questions.

She struck paydirt at the blacksmith's.

"Oh, yeah, those fellas rode in a couple of days ago," the man said. He was tall, muscular, and balding, with a potbelly. "One of them had a horse about to throw a shoe. I put a new shoe on for him yesterday."

"Did they ride out after you were finished with that chore?" asked Jessie, trying not to appear too interested or eager. It was possible she and Ki were only a day behind the outlaws.

The blacksmith shrugged broad shoulders. "I'm not

sure. I don't really pay that much attention to strangers comin' and goin'. But I don't recall seeing them leave town."

Even better, thought Jessie, still concealing her growing excitement.

The blacksmith pointed down the street. "I'd check the hotel. It ain't much, but it's the only one Cottonwood's got. There's a shed out back where guests can stable their horses. Take a gander in there and you oughta be able to tell if those hombres are still in town."

Jessie nodded. "I'll do that. Thanks."

"Sure." The blacksmith seemed totally unconcerned with finding out what Jessie's interest in the four men was. Some people just knew how to mind their own business.

"I'll drop back by for my horse later."

The blacksmith just nodded.

Jessie walked along the street toward the hotel. As the blacksmith had said, it wasn't much, but it *was* the settlement's only two-story structure. Jessie kept her hand near the butt of her Colt as she approached the front door. If the outlaws were still there, it was possible she could walk in on them and take them by surprise. She didn't know whether they would recognize her, but it seemed likely that they might.

And she didn't expect them to just meekly surrender when she confronted them and tell her what she wanted to know. They would put up a fight. She told herself that she should have found Ki before she headed for this possible showdown. She was too impatient to wait, though.

Jessie went up the two steps onto the porch and was about to reach for the doorknob when it turned and the door opened. The tall, powerful figure of a man blocked the doorway. Jessie stopped short, as did the man who had just stepped outside.

"Well, I almost ran into you again, looks like," said Rance Scott with a smile.

Jessie was surprised to see the ranch owner. "I thought you and Mr. Egan were playing checkers."

"We were for a while, but then the store got a mite busy." Scott chuckled. "Claude would rather make money than play checkers, and I can't say as I blame him for that."

"No, neither can I," said Jessie. She wanted to get around Scott and go into the hotel, but he was big enough to block her path and didn't seem to be in any hurry to get out of the way.

"It's getting dark," he went on. "How about that supper?"

"In a minute," said Jessie, not knowing if she was really going to share a meal with him or not. It would depend on what she found in the hotel. She asked, "Are you staying here?"

"That's right. Only place in Cottonwood to stay."

She hurried on, "Those four men I was asking about in the general store, could they be staying here?"

"They could be," admitted Scott, "but I haven't seen them. That doesn't really mean anything, though. I've been spending most of my time talking to folks around town, in the places where I do business. Don't get into town very often, since I've only got a couple of ranch hands and have to stay pretty close to the spread, so I see several people while I'm here."

Jessie understood. She still wanted to have a look around the hotel. She said, "Give me a few minutes, Rance, and then I'll join you at the café."

"I'll wait for you right here, and we'll walk down there together. How's that?"

"Fine," she said, anxious to get inside. He finally stepped aside, and she hurried through the door into the lobby of the hotel.

There was nothing special about the place; it looked like dozens of other hotels Jessie had seen in other little cow towns. There were a few armchairs scattered around, a writing table, a couple of potted plants, and a registration desk on the other side of the lobby with cubbyholes for each room on the wall behind it. A sleeve-gaitered clerk stood behind the desk. The man raised pale eyebrows as Jessie strode toward him. He probably didn't see very many women who looked like her in this place—or any.

"Howdy, ma'am," he greeted her. "What can I do for you? Need a place to stay?"

"That depends," replied Jessie. "I'm looking for some men."

The clerk pursed his lips in disapproval. "This isn't really that sort of establishment . . ." he began.

Jessie put her hand on the ivory-handled Colt. That shut him up in a hurry. "Listen," she said, and then she described the four outlaws.

"Yes, they're here," said the clerk. He licked his lips nervously. "Or rather, they're registered here, but I believe they're out at the moment." He glanced over his shoulder at the cubbyholes. "Yes, all their keys are in the boxes. Is there, ah, is there going to be trouble?"

"Could well be," snapped Jessie. "Do you know where they went?"

The man shook his head. "I'm sorry, ma'am. I have no idea. I assume they're around town somewhere. And Cottonwood isn't that big a place. You should be able to find them."

"Thanks." Jessie started to turn away from the desk.

"Will you be wanting a room?" asked the clerk.

"Don't know yet," she told him over her shoulder.

That would depend on whether or not she found the men she was looking for—and whether she survived the meeting.

Rance Scott was still on the porch, leaning a hip against the railing along the edge. He straightened from his casual pose as Jessie emerged from the hotel.

"Get everything settled?" he asked.

"Not really," said Jessie. "I have to find those four men."

Scott frowned. "Look, Miss Starbuck, what's really going on here?"

Jessie caught her breath and looked intently at him. Her hand moved closer to her gun again, of its own volition. "How do you know who I am?" she demanded. "I didn't tell you my full name in the general store."

"You think I wouldn't recognize the famous Jessica Starbuck of the Circle Star Ranch?" Scott smiled. "Besides, I saw you once in San Antonio. One of the fellas I was with pointed you out to me in the lobby of the Menger Hotel. I've never forgotten you." A faintly wistful tone crept into his voice. "A man doesn't forget a woman as beautiful as you, Jessie."

The compliment touched her, but she really didn't have time for such things right now. Scott had the look of a tough, competent hombre. Jessie didn't really want to get anybody else mixed up in this, but the rancher might make a valuable ally.

"All right," she said, making a decision. "Those men I'm looking for killed a couple of people on my ranch and stole a prize bull from me. They delivered the bull to somebody else. I want to make sure they get what's coming to them, and also to find out who in blazes has my bull."

Scott's rugged face settled in grim lines as Jessie spoke. When she was finished, he said, "Does the law know about this?"

Jessie waved a hand at the vast Texas–New Mexico border country around them. "Just how far is it to the nearest law from here?" she asked.

Scott grunted. "You've got a point there, Miss Starbuck . . . or can I still call you Jessie?"

"Call me Jessie," she agreed. "This is none of your affair, Mr. Scott—"

"Rance."

"Rance. So if you want to forget about that supper and just walk away, I'll understand."

"Not hardly. I'm going to give you a hand looking for those men. You don't need to be going up against hombres like that by yourself."

"I'm not alone," she told him. "My friend Ki is somewhere around town. I want to find him and let him know what's going on, and then we'll split up and start searching."

"I'm going with you," said Scott firmly.

"That's fine. The first thing I want to do, before I locate Ki, is to check the shed behind the hotel and see if the horses belonging to those men are still there. They could have left town without checking out of the hotel."

Side by side, they walked down the alley to the rear of the building. Jessie was tense as they rounded the corner. Night had fallen, so it was dark back here except for a small oil lamp that burned over the rear door of the hotel.

It gave off enough light for Jessie to be able to see the shed. There were half a dozen horses inside the flimsy structure.

"One of those mounts is mine," said Scott. "Not many people are staying in the hotel, so some of the others must belong to the men you're looking for."

"Let's see if we can find one with a new shoe," suggested Jessie, remembering what the blacksmith had told her.

They opened the gate into the shed, and Jessie lit a match and held it while Scott checked the hooves of the horses one by one. It took only a couple of minutes to find one with a shoe that had been freshly tacked onto one of its hooves.

"That's it," said Jessie. "They're still here."

"But where?"

"Probably in one of the saloons. We'll start at the Panhandle. That's where Ki was going." Jessie dropped the match and ground it out in the dirt with her boot.

"What sort of name is Ki?" asked Scott as they started toward the main street again.

"His father was an American sea captain, and his mother was a Japanese lady. He worked for my father."

"Alex Starbuck," said Scott.

"You've heard of him?"

The rancher shrugged. "I imagine everybody in Texas has heard of Alex Starbuck. So now this fella Ki works for you?"

"Well . . . not really. He's my friend."

"Oh." Scott's tone was guarded as he went on, "A close friend, is he?"

Despite the seriousness of the situation, Jessie laughed softly. "Not like that. Ki thinks of himself as my protector. My guardian angel, you could say."

"I see." Scott sounded a little relieved. He didn't have to deal with Ki being a rival for Jessie's affections.

They reached the street and started across it diagonally, heading for the Panhandle Saloon. They hadn't quite reached the opposite boardwalk when Ki came quickly through the batwings.

"There he is now," said Jessie. "And he looks like he's found out something."

They met in the street, Ki casting a curious glance toward Scott before saying, "Jessie, those four men are still here in town."

She nodded. "I know. Their horses are in the shed behind the hotel. Do you have any idea where they are?"

"Two of them were in the saloon when I first entered, but I did not know them at the time," said Ki, a note of self-recrimination in his voice. "I did not discover their identity until after they were gone." He shook his head. "And now I have no idea where they or the other two are."

"Well, we'll just have to find them." Jessie glanced at the rancher beside her and went on, "Ki, this is Rance Scott. He's a friend."

Ki nodded politely to Scott but didn't offer to shake hands. Nor did he ask if Jessie was sure she could trust the man, whom she had met only an hour or so earlier, after all. Ki still trusted Jessie's judgment when it came to people, even though Jonas Gibson had taken her in. That failure on her part still bothered Jessie.

But that was in the past now. She forged ahead, saying, "We'll split up and look for them."

"And if we find them?"

"Come straight back here. We'll all check here every so often." Jessie paused. "Ki, did the men who were in the saloon see you and recognize you?"

"They couldn't help but see me," answered Ki. "There was a bit of trouble, nothing serious, just an annoyance. As to whether or not they recognized me . . . I don't know."

Jessie glanced around. Suddenly the shadows between the buildings along Cottonwood's main street seemed much more menacing. "So they may know we're here and looking for them," she said.

Ki nodded. "They could be waiting to ambush us right now."

Jessie looked at Scott and asked again, "Are you sure you want to take a hand in this game, Rance?"

"Deal me in," he said with an emphatic nod. His hand rested on the walnut grip of his gun. "It sounds like the sort of game that I like."

"In that case," said Ki, "I'll take this side of the street."

"And we'll take the other," agreed Jessie. "Come on, Rance."

They recrossed the street and walked quickly down to Egan's store, which was still open and lit up inside. As they walked in, Egan greeted them from behind the counter. "I got those supplies ready for you, ma'am—" he began.

"I won't need them tonight, Mr. Egan," said Jessie. "I'm still looking for those four men I mentioned earlier."

Egan shook his head. "Ain't seen hide nor hair of 'em, I'm afraid. You givin' the lady a hand, Rance?"

"That's right," said Scott. "We'll be somewhere up the street, Claude. If you happen to see those hombres, come tell us, will you?"

"Sure." Egan frowned, obviously sensing the serious-ness of the mission Jessie and Scott were on. "Is there gonna be trouble, Rance?"

"Could be. If you hear any loud noises, better keep your head down."

Egan swallowed. "Loud noises? Like gunshots?"

"That's probably what they'll be."

Jessie and Scott left the store and began making their way up the street. Some of the businesses were already closed, but others were still open, including the café and a couple more saloons. They looked inside each one, and as Jessie stood by the front window of the café and looked in at the tables covered with neat, red-checked tablecloths, she wished momentarily that she and Rance Scott were sitting in there enjoying a meal and each other's company, instead of prowling through the town in search of a gang of killers.

"They're not there," she said.

"No, but they've got to be somewhere. All we can do is keep looking." Jessie glanced toward the front of the Panhandle Saloon on the other side of the street. No sign of Ki. That came as no surprise. She said, "Let's go."

They walked on, toward the mouth of an alley that loomed darkly on their right.

Inside that stygian gloom, Nick Darrow, Simon Jarvis, Blue Atkinson, and Sonny Montoya all waited, guns in hand. Darrow had no idea who the hombre with Jessica Starbuck might be, but he didn't care. The man was obviously accompanying her on her search for the four outlaws, and that meant he had to die, too.

"Get ready," breathed Darrow to the others. "As soon as they step in front of the alley, gun 'em down!"

Colts lifted in the darkness, ready to spout flame and death from their unforgiving muzzles.

Chapter 13

With no warning, a whirlwind exploded among the lurking bushwhackers. Before any of the outlaws could pull their triggers, Ki leaped high in the air and slammed his sandaled feet into the backs of two of the men, driving them forward. At the same time he smashed his left elbow into the side of another man's head and slashed with his right hand at the fourth man's neck.

That outlaw reacted too quickly, though, jerking aside just enough so that the hardened edge of Ki's hand struck him on the left arm, rather than the more vulnerable point where neck met shoulder. The man yelled in pain, and Ki knew his left arm was probably numb and useless—

But the man still had his right arm, and his right hand was the one that held his gun. He twisted toward the warrior and jerked the trigger, slamming out three shots in quick succession. The flashes lit up the alley garishly, revealing the three men sprawled there.

Ki's left foot struck the ground and then he was up in the air again, leaping and twisting, somersaulting out of the path of the slugs that sizzled through the space he had occupied only a heartbeat earlier. He turned in midair and lashed out with a foot. The kick caught the gunman in the body and threw him back against the wall of the building behind him.

As Ki landed agilely on the floor of the alley like a cat, one of the men he had knocked down earlier surprised him by tackling him. He had thought that all of them would be out of the fight longer than that, but clearly at least one of them was unexpectedly tough. The impact of the tackle knocked Ki off his feet.

Suddenly he didn't have the room to move that he needed. Speed and skill would always defeat brute force, but only if the one wielding that speed and skill had the space to operate. Ki's arms were trapped at his sides, and the outlaw's weight pinned him to the ground. The man lowered his head and butted Ki painfully in the face. Stars exploded behind Ki's eyes.

As Jessie and Scott approached the alley, they heard the sudden commotion and then the blare of shots. Both of them slapped leather, drawing their guns and rushing forward. Colt flame bloomed in the darkness as Jessie reached the mouth of the alley. She heard the wind-rip of a bullet's passage right beside her ear and flung herself to the side. Her finger was on the trigger of the ivory-handled revolver, but she held her fire. It was likely that Ki was somewhere in the middle of that melee, and she didn't want to hit him.

But she and Scott couldn't just stand there and make themselves targets, either. "Rance, get down!" she called to him. She hit the ground and rolled. Scott went the other way. He must have instinctively known that it would be better for them to split up. Jessie came to a stop behind a water trough. Slugs thudded into the thick wood but didn't penetrate.

In the alley, Ki ignored the pain from the head-butt and returned the tactic, lifting his head and driving it into the face of the man who had him in that bone-crushing grip. He felt blood spurt hotly as the top of his head pulped the man's nose. The outlaw howled in pain and turned loose, unable to maintain his hold on Ki any longer.

Twisting free like an eel, Ki flipped up onto his feet. Someone rushed him from behind. He bent forward at the waist and struck backward with a swift kick. His heel drove into a man's midsection, sinking into the belly and doubling the man over. The man's momentum kept him stumbling forward, though, and he blundered into Ki. The warrior lost a couple of seconds as he thrust the man aside.

The world suddenly seemed to explode in his face with a brightness brighter than that of a thousand suns and the roar of a million thunderclaps. Something struck him a heavy blow on the head and sent him flying backward.

Jessie lifted her head above the level of the water trough in time to see the muzzle flash that illuminated Ki's face as a gun went off only inches from it. She screamed his name as the bullet threw him against a wall. Since she knew now where Ki was, Jessie didn't hesitate to trigger several shots. She aimed at the spot where orange flame had just gouted from the barrel of a gun.

She didn't know if she had hit the man who shot Ki. All she knew was that her best friend was down, maybe hurt badly, maybe even dead, although she didn't want to allow herself to think about that. Instead she kept pulling the trigger of the ivory-handled Colt as she rose to her feet, filling the alley with lead. A few yards away, as he crouched at the corner of a building next to the alley, Rance Scott followed Jessie's example and fired into the darkness. Booted feet thudded heavily in the shadows. The bushwhackers were giving up, heading for the tall and uncut.

Or maybe it was a trick. Jessie dropped behind the water trough again even though she wanted to rush to Ki's side and find out how badly he was wounded. As she lay there she fumbled out fresh cartridges and thumbed them into the Colt, replacing the empties. She lifted her head and called to Scott, "Stay back, Rance! It could be a trap!"

"I hear you, Jessie," he replied as he pressed his back against the front wall of the building and reloaded, too.

Tense seconds ticked by. Jessie listened intently for the scrape of a foot or a harshly indrawn breath. She didn't hear anything.

Then the sound of hoofbeats drifted to her ears. It came from down the street, toward the hotel. As the hoofbeats began to recede in the distance, she realized that the outlaws must have run down there to the shed, grabbed their horses, and ridden out of Cottonwood as fast as they could.

Jessie knew she was still taking a chance, but she came up on hands and knees and then surged to her feet. Holding the gun in front of her with both hands, she stalked into the alley. Scott followed closely behind her, also poised for more trouble.

When nothing happened Jessie lowered the Colt and said, "I'm going to strike a match, Rance. Be ready."

"Go ahead," he told her in a taut voice.

Jessie kept the revolver in her right hand while with her left she dug out a lucifer and snapped it into life with her thumbnail, a trick taught to her by Custis Long. As the match flared up, Jessie squinted against the glare and looked around the alley. She saw Ki lying in a huddled heap next to the wall of the building and quickly dropped to a knee beside him.

"Ki," she breathed as she holstered her gun. She reached out and rested a hand on his chest. Relief flooded through her as she felt it rising and falling steadily. He was alive.

The light from the sputtering sulfur match revealed a bloody furrow on the side of Ki's head, in the raven-black hair above his right ear. The wound was shallow. Unfortunately, even a bullet graze on the head packed enough punch to knock a man into the middle of next week. Ki was out cold.

But he would live, Jessie told herself. She knew how strong he was. With a few days of rest, he would be just fine.

"How is he?" asked Scott.

"He'll be all right," replied Jessie. "The slug just nicked him and knocked him out."

"Lucky. A couple of inches the other way and it would have blown his brains out."

"Yes, I know."

"What about those men you were after?"

"I'll catch up to them later," said Jessie without any hesitation. "Right now I'm just worried about Ki."

"You won't have to catch up to one of them. Looks like he's a goner."

Jessie lifted her head as the match began to flicker out. She saw the sprawled shape on the ground at the far end of the alley. Coming smoothly to her feet, she lit another match and stalked toward the man, her hand on the butt of her gun. Scott came with her, covering the fallen outlaw.

The man lay facedown. The back of the short jacket he wore was soaked with blood. At least two slugs must have torn through his body during the brief fracas, maybe more. Scott leaned down, took hold of the man's shoulder, and rolled him onto his back.

"The Mexican," said Jessie. "We never knew his name."

And he was undoubtedly dead, too. Even so, his face showed little expression.

"Damn it, I wish I could have asked him a few questions," Jessie went on. "Maybe he could have told me where the others were headed."

Scott holstered his gun since the threat was obviously over. "He doesn't look like a fella who would have talked easily, even if Apaches had hold of him."

"Well, I could have tried, anyway." Jessie sighed. "Can you search his pockets, Rance, while I see about getting some help for Ki?"

Scott grimaced at the idea of going through a dead man's pockets, but he nodded. "Sure. You go right ahead."

Jessie turned and retreated up the alley toward the spot where Ki still lay senseless. Before she got there, several figures appeared at the alley mouth, silhouetted against the faint glow from windows in the buildings along the main street. Claude Egan's voice asked worriedly, "Rance? You down there, boy?"

"Rance is here, and he's fine, Mr. Egan," Jessie told him. "But we've got a wounded man here."

"Miss Jessie? Is that you?" Egan came closer, trailed

by a couple of townspeople, and Jessie could see now that the storekeeper had a shotgun in his hands. "Sounded like you folks were fightin' the battle of the Alamo all over again down here. Who's that?"

"A friend of mine," replied Jessie as she knelt once more beside Ki. "Is there a doctor here in town?"

"Yeah, Doc Mitchell." Egan turned his head and addressed the men with him. "One of you fellas run fetch the doc."

"I'll get him," offered one of the townies. "Although he probably heard the shots and is already on his way here."

That proved to be the case. The local sawbones, who turned out to be a stocky man with a drooping gray mustache, arrived in the alley only moments later, carrying a lantern. He grunted as he looked at Ki and then asked, "What happened to him?"

"A bullet grazed the side of his head," explained Jessie.

"Doesn't look too bad." Dr. Mitchell put the lantern on the ground and leaned over to study Ki's injury more closely. After a moment he straightened and ordered, "Get him into the hotel and in a bed. I'll clean the wound and bandage it. After that he'll need some rest. Quite a bit of it, I'd say."

Jessie knew that might be a problem. Once Ki woke up, he would be eager to start after the outlaws again. Jessie would have her hands full making sure he recuperated enough before they took up the trail again.

She knew that in the meantime the three owlhoots who had gotten away would be able to build up a big lead again. That was a damned shame, but there was nothing that could be done about it. Ki's welfare had to come first.

Several of the townsmen, including Egan, carefully picked up Ki to carry him into the hotel. Jessie turned toward Scott to tell him where they were going, and as she did so, the toe of her boot kicked something that lay in the dust of the alley. It rolled a foot or so. Some instinct made her reach down and pick it up. The thing was a coin, she realized. One of the outlaws must have dropped it during the fight. She slipped it into a vest pocket, telling herself she would look at it later.

Scott strode toward her, saying, "That fella didn't have anything in his pockets except a little money and makin's."

"No letters or anything else to tell us who he was or where the others might have been going?"

Scott shook his head. "Sorry. We can search his room at the hotel, and maybe his saddlebags if the others didn't take them."

They followed the grim procession to the hotel, where the shocked-looking clerk told the men to take Ki upstairs to Room Seven. "And try not to get too much blood on the sheets!" he added.

"Don't worry about that," Jessie told him coldly. "I'll pay for anything that gets ruined."

The clerk didn't argue. The expression on Jessie's face must have told him that it wouldn't be wise to do so.

Over the next fifteen minutes, Ki was settled in the bed in Room Seven and Dr. Mitchell cleaned and bandaged the wound as he had promised. When Mitchell finally straightened from the bed and turned toward Jessie, he said, "I think the patient will make a full recovery, miss. But with a head injury, it's always difficult to tell the full extent of the damage, especially while the patient is still unconscious. He'll need to be watched closely for several days."

"I can do that," said Jessie. "We're old friends. I'll take care of him."

"I'm sure you will. When he does wake up, he'll probably have a devil of a headache. Keep cool cloths on his forehead. That'll help a little."

Jessie nodded. "All right. Thank you, Doctor."

Mitchell grunted. "Just doing my job."

He picked up his medical bag and left the room. Jessie and Scott were alone now with the unconscious Ki. Jessie pulled a rocking chair over closer to the bed and sat down. She smiled wearily at the rancher.

"I'm sorry we missed out on that supper, Rance," she said.

"You still have to eat," he told her. "I'll go down to the café and get something for you, bring it back up here."

"That would be nice. Thank you."

Scott left the room. Jessie sat there and looked at Ki, watched the rising and falling of his chest under the sheet that had been pulled up over him. The two of them had ridden many dangerous trails over the years and were well aware of the risks involved in the sort of life they had, at times, chosen to lead. But it still left her shaken to know how close he had come to dying. She offered up a silent prayer of thanks that the bullet hadn't been a couple of inches to the right.

Was vengeance worth it? she asked herself. It wouldn't bring back the men who had died on the Circle Star. Was that bull worth risking her life, and Ki's life? And tonight Rance Scott had fought at her side and could have been killed, too. He had no stake in this. What gave her the right to get him involved in it?

Jessie couldn't answer any of those questions. All she knew was that she was who she was, and even though she was relatively young in years, her life had been so packed with action and danger that she could never live as a normal woman did. She had done too much, seen too much death, traveled to the depths of hell and back too many times. Killed too many men herself.

She knew that when Ki was well enough to ride, they would take up the trail again. There was nothing else they could do.

Rance Scott brought Jessie a bowl of stew from the café and sat with her while she ate it. Then he said, "My room's right across the hall. I'd be glad to sit with Ki while you go over there and get some sleep. No offense, but you look about done in, Jessie."

She shook her head. "No, I'll stay here. You go ahead, though, Rance."

"You're going to be stubborn about this, aren't you?" he asked with a sigh.

Jessie smiled faintly. "I'm afraid so."

He stood up and said, "All right. But like I said, I'm right across the hall, so if you need anything, just holler."

"Thank you. You've been a big help already, especially considering you didn't even know me a few hours ago."

"With some people, it doesn't take a long time to know how you feel about them."

She smiled at him again as he went out, then she turned her attention back to Ki. There was no telling how long he would be unconscious. All Jessie knew was that she wanted to be there when he woke up.

Despite her firm intention to stay awake, the long hours in the saddle plus the hectic events of the evening took a toll on her, and she finally dozed off in the rocking chair. When she came awake, she didn't have any idea how many hours had passed. All she knew for sure was that she had been sleeping in an awkward position and her neck hurt. Wincing, she turned her head from side to side and rolled her shoulders.

The creak of a floorboard made her forget all about her aches and pains for the moment. Her hand went to the holster on her hip and slipped out the Colt as she stood up and turned toward the door.

The knob turned and the door eased open an inch or two. Jessie bounded forward, grabbed the door, and flung it open. Her gun came up, and her finger was taut on the trigger.

Rance Scott took a hurried step backward, saying, "Don't shoot, Jessie! It's just me."

"Good Lord, Rance! That's a good way to get yourself killed!"

His face had gone a little pale under its tan. "I can see that," he said. "I'm sorry, Jessie. I just wanted to see how you were doing. I thought maybe you were asleep, so I figured I'd just poke my head in for a quick peek."

Jessie lowered the Colt and slipped it back in its holster. "I *was* asleep just a minute ago," she admitted. She rubbed her eyes. "What time is it, anyway?"

"About three o'clock in the morning."

Jessie turned toward the bed. Ki hadn't moved, and there was no sign that he had regained consciousness.

"The offer I made earlier is still open," said Rance. "I'll be glad to sit up with him while you go across the hall and get some sleep."

Jessie shook her head as she sank back into the rocker. "No . . . no, I need to stay here."

There was another chair in the room, a ladderback with a padded seat. Scott picked it up, turned it around, and straddled it, resting his arms on the back.

"I'm going to stay and keep you company, then," he declared. "Unless you plan on running me out at gunpoint."

"No," said Jessie with a smile. "I don't think I'll do that. Thank you, Rance."

"What was Ki doing in that alley where those bushwhackers were, anyway? I thought he was looking for them on the other side of the street."

"I wasn't surprised to see him," said Jessie. "Ki acted like he was going to search on the other side of the street, then circled around and got behind the buildings on our side. That way anybody who was keeping an eye on us— like those outlaws—would think that nobody was covering our backs."

"In other words, you and I were decoys to draw them out?"

"You could look at it like that."

"Well, it worked, I reckon," said Scott with a shake of his head. "You found the men you were looking for, and one of them is dead now. But Ki's wounded and the other three got away."

"I never said it always works."

Scott thought that over and nodded. "What now?"

"I wait for Ki to wake up and get well enough to travel. Then we'll go after the ones who got away."

"Need any help? I could ride with you. . . ."

Jessie smiled. "I couldn't ask that of you, Rance."

"You're not asking. I'm volunteering."

"You have a ranch to run," she pointed out. "You can't just ride off and abandon it."

"I've got a couple of good hands—"

"It's not your fight," she said softly but firmly. "I'm touched that you want to help, but this is a job for Ki and me to do."

"Well, if you change your mind . . ."

"I won't."

He shrugged, reluctantly accepting that he wasn't going to be able to persuade her.

As they talked quietly, Jessie moved her head around, trying to find some position where that damned crick in her neck didn't hurt so much. Scott noticed what she was doing and asked, "Is something wrong?"

"Oh, when I dozed off earlier, I must've slept on my neck wrong. I've got a crick in it now."

He stood up. "I can fix that."

"What do you mean?" asked Jessie with a slight frown.

"I mean I can fix your neck. I can get rid of that crick."

"How can you do that?"

He moved behind her chair and rested his hands lightly on her shoulders. "Just relax and watch," he said.

He began to rub gently on her shoulders, using just his fingertips. They were very strong, and even though the pressure he applied was light, she felt it beginning to penetrate her muscles. It was a relaxing feeling. Jessie closed her eyes and gave herself over to his touch, enjoying what he was doing.

His hands moved along her shoulders and up the sides of her neck. Despite the fact that his hands were roughened from hard work, his touch was incredibly tender.

She tensed a little when he reached the part of her neck that was so sore, but he sensed it and made a quiet, calming noise, the sort of sound a cowboy would make to calm a skittish horse. It worked with Jessie, too, and as she relaxed again she felt his fingers prodding the muscle and working the stiffness out of it. She sighed in relief as the pain eased.

He was leaning over her as he massaged her neck. She felt his warm breath against her ear. Without thinking about what she was doing, she turned and lifted her face to his. Their mouths met. The kiss was just as gentle as the rubbing he had been doing on her shoulders and neck. But it soon grew in heat and urgency. Jessie lifted a hand and stroked the strong line of his jaw.

When she pulled back she smiled at him, knowing that before she and Ki left Cottonwood, she would have to find a chance to get to know Rance Scott a lot better. But not tonight, of course. Not with Ki possibly still in danger from that bullet graze.

"Thank you, Rance," she whispered.

"Any time," he told her. He reached down, caught hold of Jessie's hand, squeezed it for a moment, and then went back to the other chair and sat down.

Feeling much better now, Jessie turned back toward the bed and watched Ki, waiting for him to regain consciousness. Her hand strayed idly into her vest pocket, and as it touched the hard, round item there, she remembered picking up that coin in the alley after the outlaws fled. Frowning a little in curiosity, she pulled it out, expecting from the weight of it to find a double eagle or something like that.

But instead of gold, the coin was made of silver. Jessie caught her breath in surprise as she saw that the words engraved on it were in German rather than English. She couldn't read them, even though she recognized the language. And she saw one word she knew, the name *Herzog*. It brought back bad memories, although in a much different context.

"What have you got there?" asked Scott, noticing her reaction.

"It's a coin that I found in the alley. I thought one of the outlaws must have dropped it during the fight, but now I'm not so sure."

"Why not?"

"It's not an American coin."

"Mexican?"

She shook her head. "German. Prussian, more than likely."

"Anybody could have dropped it there, sometime before tonight," Scott pointed out. "Although I don't know why anybody in Cottonwood would have a coin like that. There aren't any German settlers in these parts, as far as I know."

The German words weren't the only ones on the coin, Jessie saw. She lifted it closer to her eyes and studied it in the lamplight. Somebody had taken a knife or some other sharp instrument and scratched two words into the silver, one on each side of the coin. The one on the back was *Nevada*.

And on the front, etched across the cheek of the hombre whose likeness adorned the coin, was the name *Zamora*.

Chapter 14

As it turned out, Amelia Richmond was on her way to Carson City, too, so she switched to the westbound at Cheyenne just like Longarm. He was pleased by that development, because it meant that they got to continue their acquaintance.

And on the second night, he found himself in the sleeping compartment Miss Richmond had engaged in one of the train's Pullman cars, naked and flat on his back in the bunk while Miss Richmond her own self straddled him. She slid down his erection until she hit bottom, and then as she gasped in passion, her hips began to pump back and forth.

Longarm hoped she wasn't the sort to get carried away and start yelling and screaming. Trains were noisy conveyances to start with and the continuous clacking and rumbling would cover up a lot of racket, but the partitions between the sleeping berths weren't all that thick.

"Oh! Oh, Custis!" she said. "I can't believe I'm doing this!"

Longarm could believe it. In fact, he believed this was exactly what she'd had in mind when she approached him that first day and asked if she could sit next to him. Her father ran a newspaper in Carson City, she had explained, and for the past three years she'd been back east in St. Louis at a school for young ladies. Now she was on her way home, where she expected to marry a young fella who worked in the state government at Carson City. That was a surefire recipe for some carrying on like this.

Longarm cupped her firm, pear-shaped breasts and thumbed the pink nipples. That made Amelia ride him even harder. She leaned back so that he could penetrate even more deeply within her, and Longarm gladly obliged.

At a time such as this, it was difficult to think about his job, but that was exactly what Longarm tried to do. He wanted to postpone his climax as long as he could so that Amelia would get the most out of this encounter. He asked himself again what could be in the ghost town of Zamora, Nevada, to make those Arizona owlhoots head for it.

Safe haven, of course. The answer was so blindingly simple that Longarm was shocked he hadn't thought of it before now. That shock manifested itself in an extra little bounce that made Amelia Richmond say, "Oh! Oh, my!" She drove her hips down hard.

That distracted Longarm even more, but the part of his brain that was still functioning turned the theory over, examining it to see whether or not it might hold water. One thing outlaws were always in search of—besides ill-gotten loot—was a good hideout. After losing two of their number, the surviving stagecoach bandits might have thought it would be a good idea to get out of Arizona. Like rabbits, owlhoots always headed for a hole when they felt threatened.

Maybe Zamora was such a place. It was isolated enough, and with the silver mines played out, normal folks wouldn't have any reason to go up there. Far from the law the way it was, desperadoes would be pretty safe from arrest.

That was one possible answer, but Longarm told himself he had no way of knowing if it was the *right* answer. He was convinced more than ever that if he could reach Zamora, there was a good chance he would find the men he was looking for.

"Oh, yes, Custis, yes!" said Amelia. She lay forward, stretching out on his broad, muscular chest with its thick mat of brown hair. Her hips bounced wildly up and down as she kissed him.

Yeah, that young fella in Carson City was in for some fine times. Longarm thought briefly that he ought to feel a little guilty for getting there first—but he didn't.

And as he began to empty his juices inside Amelia, he wondered fleetingly who was going to get to Zamora first, him or those two owlhoots from Arizona.

The past six hours or so had been some of the most bizarre of Brad Corrigan's life. All he had to do was look at Tom to see that his older brother was a mite shocked by it all, too. But at least Tom had had some idea of what to expect when they reached Zamora, because he had talked to that old man Greevey.

Imagine, a whole town in the middle of nowhere, set up for the sole purpose of providing sanctuary for outlaws.

As he and Tom had ridden closer to the settlement tucked away in the isolated valley, trailed by the rifle-wielding Yellowstone, Brad had thought at first the place was a ghost town. Judging by the shape some of the buildings were in, Brad surmised they had been abandoned for quite a while.

But there were people around, strolling along the town's boardwalks, so the settlement wasn't deserted. As they drew nearer, Brad noticed that repairs had been carried out on some of the buildings in the recent past. He spotted fresh lumber in the walls and new posts holding up the awnings over the boardwalk. From the looks of things, somebody was rebuilding Zamora bit by bit.

They reached the edge of town and started along the main street. Their arrival drew considerable interest from the citizens, most of whom stopped what they were doing to take a good long look at the newcomers. That was when Brad noticed something else odd.

There didn't seem to be any women or children in Zamora, only grown men. And hard-faced, dangerous-looking men, at that. Brad felt a chill go through him at some of the unfriendly gazes directed toward him and Tom. Some of those hombres looked like they wouldn't have minded at all drawing their guns and blowing holes in the two strangers.

A little way down the street, Brad realized he had been wrong about one thing: there *were* women in Zamora after all. He saw several of them hanging out the second-floor windows of one of the buildings, smiling down at the men who passed below them in the street. Brad couldn't help but stare at them. The women were bare-breasted, with their titties hanging out for all the world to see. They were mighty pretty titties, too.

Brad knew whores when he saw them. Those weren't the only women in the settlement, though. As the three men rode past a saloon, Brad peered in over the batwings and saw several women in short, spangled dresses dancing on a stage. Rinky-tink piano music floated out of the saloon. Men laughed and cheered.

"Tom?" said Brad quietly to his brother. "What *is* this place?"

"What Yellowstone said," replied Tom. "A city of thieves."

"You mean all these hombres—"

"Are outlaws, just like us," said Tom with a nod. "That's what Greevey told me that night in Phoenix. He said somebody had moved into an old ghost town up in the mountains of Nevada and started fixing it up as a hideout for anybody riding the owlhoot trail. The word was out that if you could make it here to Zamora, you'd be safe. There's no law, and no regular citizens to bother you."

"But . . . but I saw those whores, and there have to be bartenders working in those saloons, and I saw a blacksmith shop and a general store back down the street . . ."

"All run by folks who are on the dodge, too. Everybody in Zamora is wanted. That's one reason it's so safe here. Nobody can afford to turn anybody else in to the authorities."

Brad just shook his head in wonderment. He had never heard of such a thing. "Who would ever think of that? Who runs this place?"

"Now that's something I don't know, little brother." Tom looked back over his shoulder. "What about it, Yellowstone? Who's in charge here?"

"As far as you're concerned, right now I am, because I'm the one who's got the gun," rumbled Yellowstone.

"Just keep ridin'. Up ahead on your left is the town hall. You can stop there."

They rode on until they came to the building Yellowstone had indicated. It was one that had had considerable repair work done on it. Now it was a sturdy-looking frame and rock structure. Following Yellowstone's orders, Tom and Brad reined to a halt in front of it, dismounted, and tied their horses to a hitch rail. Yellowstone did likewise, managing to continue covering them with his rifle as he did so.

"Inside with you," he said, jerking the weapon's barrel toward the door.

The Corrigan brothers stepped up onto the boardwalk. Tom opened the door and walked inside, followed by Brad. They found themselves in a neatly furnished room that looked like an assayer's office, or something like that. A low railing divided the front part of the room from several desks.

Only one of the desks had a man sitting at it. He wore a suit and tie and a shirt with a stiff collar. Rimless spectacles perched on his thin nose. He looked up, ran a hand over his graying blond hair, and said, "Hello, Yellowstone. New arrivals, eh?"

"They rode up the canyon, big as brass," said Yellowstone. "Acted like they knew what they'd find."

The man got to his feet and came to the railing, opening a gate in it and saying, "Come in, gentlemen. Welcome to Zamora. My name is Wade Abernathy. I'm the mayor of our little community."

"You mean *you're* the fella who set all this up?" asked Tom, sounding as if he found that difficult to believe. Brad felt the same way. Wade Abernathy looked more like a clerk of some sort than the leader of an outlaw stronghold.

Abernathy chuckled. "Goodness, no," he said in reply to Tom's question. "I'm merely an administrator."

"Don't let him fool you," put in Yellowstone. "He's a damned slick crook, too. How much was it you stole back east, Wade?"

"Two hundred thousand dollars," Abernathy said proudly. "That's why the Empress approached me about investing in Zamora and helping to run it."

The Empress? thought Brad. What the hell?

"Who's the Empress?" asked Tom.

"All in good time, my friend, all in good time." Abernathy waved at a couple of chairs in front of his desk. "Sit down, sit down." He went behind the desk, sat, and steepled his fingers together as he propped his elbows on the desk. Yellowstone remained just outside the railing, his rifle pointed in the general direction of Tom and Brad. "Now then," continued Abernathy with a smile, "tell me just why it is I shouldn't instruct our friend Yellowstone here to shoot both of you and dump your bodies in a convenient ravine?"

The casually phrased question made Brad open and close his mouth and then swallow hard. Tom didn't like it, either, but he didn't show it as much.

"We didn't come here to cause trouble," he said. "We're like everybody else in this town. We're wanted by the law, and we need a place to lie low for a while."

"I see. And how do we know that you're telling the truth? You could be lawmen yourselves, working undercover."

Tom gave a curt laugh. "Not hardly. We've been holding up stagecoaches down in Arizona for the past few months. Made a pretty good haul off some silver shipments."

"Can you prove that?"

"We've got the cash we traded the silver for."

Brad frowned. He wasn't sure Tom should have admitted that. There was nothing stopping these men from killing them and taking the loot. Of course, they could have done that anyway, whether Tom said anything about the money or not.

"You know the standard terms?" asked Abernathy. "One quarter of whatever loot you have?"

Tom nodded. "That's what Greevey said. Seems a mite high to me."

"You're welcome to find sanctuary at a cheaper price." Abernathy paused. "Well, actually you're not . . ."

"What the mayor means," said Yellowstone, "is now that you're here, you can't just ride on. You either agree to the terms, or I dump your bodies in that ravine he was talkin' about."

Brad leaned closer to his brother. "Maybe a quarter of the loot isn't really so bad, Tom."

Tom grunted. "Yeah, I reckon so." He addressed Abernathy again. "What does that buy us?"

Abernathy spread his hands and smiled. "Safety. No lawman will disturb you here. And a number of amenities are included, such as women, liquor, food—"

"We don't have to pay for any of that stuff?"

"Not for the next month. If you decide to stay longer than that, there will be reasonable charges for whatever you use."

"Well . . ." Tom looked over at Brad. "What do you think?"

Brad wasn't sure what surprised him more, the situation in which they found themselves or the fact that Tom was actually asking his opinion about something. He said, "I don't reckon we've really got much choice."

"I suppose not." Tom looked across the desk at Abernathy. "You've got a deal, mister."

"Of course. You have the cash with you?"

Tom hesitated, then told the truth. "Yeah. It's, uh, in our saddlebags. We probably shouldn't have left them outside."

"Oh, no need to worry about that," said Abernathy. "Honor among thieves and all, you know."

"You mean that's really true?"

Abernathy frowned and leaned forward, his voice hardening as he said, "It is in Zamora. When I said there was no law here, that wasn't exactly the case. We have our own laws, and they're strictly enforced. There's no stealing and no killing. The women who work in the saloons and the whorehouses are not to be abused. And you don't leave without proper authorization."

"You mean we're prisoners here?" demanded Tom.

"Oh, no. Permission to leave won't be withheld unreasonably. We just don't want anyone slipping away without us knowing about it. You see, it's not impossible that the authorities might try to get a man in here in an attempt to find out what's going on."

"Yeah, I suppose so." Tom nodded. "All right, like I said, we've got a deal. You want the money now?"

"Please."

As they left the building with Yellowstone trailing them, Tom asked, "What about our guns? You said we'd get them back."

"You will. Let me know where you'll be after you finish your business with the mayor, and I'll bring 'em to you later."

167

Tom looked at Brad. "What do you want to do first, little brother? Get a drink? A woman?"

"Well . . . I'd really like a hot bath and something to eat," said Brad.

"Bathhouse is down yonder," said Yellowstone, pointing. "And there's two or three different cafés and hash houses. Take your pick. I'll find you when I've got your guns."

Tom and Brad took the saddlebags off their horses and carried them into the town hall. Abernathy counted the money and carefully separated out one-fourth of it.

Tom said, "Those laws you were talking about . . . what happens if somebody breaks them?"

"Then they're dealt with, swiftly and efficiently," said Abernathy. "The Empress's men take care of things like that."

"Just who in blazes is this Empress you keep talking about?" Tom asked again.

"You'll meet her, gentlemen . . . when and if she sends for you. Otherwise . . . well, it's best not to pry."

Brad could tell that Tom was frustrated by that answer, but nothing more was said about the subject of the Empress.

Abernathy went on, "We have an excellent safe here, if you'd like to leave the rest of your money with me. I'll write you a receipt for it, of course."

"We'll need some walkin' around money . . ."

"Of course." Abernathy slid a small stack of bills across the desk. "There you are. I'll start an account for you, and you can draw on the rest of your funds whenever you like."

"You mean it's like a damn bank," said Tom. "A bank for outlaws, in a town for outlaws."

Yellowstone chuckled and said, "Now you're gettin' it."

They got it, all right, but it was still mighty strange. Brad figured he could get used to it, though. After soaking the trail dust off in a galvanized tub full of steaming hot water, the brothers had a good meal in one of the cafés—a meal they didn't have to pay for—and then strolled through the town, stopping at several of the saloons. Getting the lay of the land, Brad supposed you could call it. Yellowstone had found them and returned their guns, as promised, and told them that there was a room waiting for them over at the hotel. It was quite a setup, thought Brad. Just about everything an owlhoot on the run could want.

He still wondered about that so-called Empress, though. That was like a queen or something, wasn't it?

And just what sort of woman would it take to come up with the idea of turning an old ghost town into a hideout for wanted men?

Maybe if they stayed here long enough they would find out, thought Brad.

If the Empress sent for them.

He wasn't sure if he wanted that or not. There was something a little worrisome about the idea. The queens in all those old fairy-tale books sometimes ordered men's heads chopped off. . . .

Chapter 15

Longarm woke up as he felt the train give a little extra lurch. He heard the squealing of the brakes. Nothing unusual about the train coming to a stop, he told himself. Maybe the locomotive needed to take on water, or the flag might have been out at some lonely depot. There wasn't much of a reason to stop up here in the barren Humboldt River valley otherwise.

Amelia Richmond stirred sleepily as she nestled against him. They were both naked, lying spoon-fashion in the narrow sleeping berth. Still half-asleep, Amelia wiggled her hips against Longarm's groin. The tip of his rapidly stiffening manhood nudged into her rump.

"Oh, Custis," she murmured, "that's such a naughty idea that it's positively intriguing. But I'm afraid you're too big for me to take you there, dear."

His hand trailed from her breast down over her flat belly to the little mound at the juncture of her thighs. Amelia began to breathe harder, and her hips started to rotate enticingly. Longarm was fully erect now. The thick pole of male flesh slipped between Amelia's thighs and rubbed along the crease between her legs, which was swiftly becoming damp with the juices of arousal.

The train jerked again, harder this time.

That made Longarm and Amelia shift a little in the bunk, and while the extra movement added to the pleasurable sensations going through both of them, it also made Longarm lift his head and frown slightly. Either the engineer had a rough hand on the throttle and brake, which he hadn't demonstrated so far during this trip, or he'd been forced to stop unexpectedly.

And unexpected stops were seldom good.

"Custis, where are you going?" asked Amelia with an almost frantic edge in her voice as Longarm pulled back from her.

"I got to check on some things," he told her. He sat up, swinging his long legs out of the bunk.

"You have to get back here and pleasure me," she said. "That's what you have to do."

"Sorry, darlin'." He stood up, pulled on his trousers, and reached for his shirt. "My guts tell me something's wrong, and I been packing a star too long to ignore a feeling like that."

He finished getting dressed, settled his Stetson on his head, and quietly stepped out into the dimly lit corridor that ran past the sleeping compartments.

There were windows on the other side of the corridor, so Longarm could see that it was still dark outside. He didn't take the time to look at his watch, but he knew it was the middle of the night. Crouching low to avoid anyone seeing him if he was looking in from outside, he moved quickly to the door at the front of the sleeping car. He opened it and slipped out onto the platform.

He heard men shouting somewhere, and as he leaned out and looked toward the engine, he saw a flickering red glare beyond the locomotive. That told him all he needed to know.

The train was being held up.

Outlaws had piled rocks on the tracks so that the train couldn't get by, then stacked brush behind the rocks and set it on fire as the locomotive approached. It was a common tactic among train robbers. The trick was to time the blaze properly. The owlhoots wanted the engineer to be able to bring the train to a halt without crashing into the stone barrier, but it had to stop close enough so that the members of the gang could then swarm aboard and take over the train.

Longarm figured some of the bandits were already in the cab by now. The others would be spreading out through the cars, taking sleepy passengers by surprise. Some of the outlaws would target the express car, too.

Longarm stepped across the gap onto the rear platform of the next car and turned quickly to the grab irons that led to the roof. He climbed them agilely and pulled himself onto the top of the car. He sprawled there, where the outlaws wouldn't be likely to see him. Staying low, he began crawling toward the front of the car.

The shouts came closer as he did so. Just as he had thought, the gang was working its way along the train. When he reached the front of the car he raised his head enough to see that no riders were alongside at the moment. Moving as fast as he could, he dropped to the platform, stepped across to the next car, and climbed to its roof.

He repeated that process twice more as he worked his way toward the engine. That was the place to start, he decided. Probably wouldn't be more than two men holding the engineer and the fireman captive. If he could take them it would cut down the odds a little. He had to do it quietly, though, with no gunplay. Shots would warn the rest of the outlaws.

He reached the coal tender, with the engine right in front of it. Now things got a little more tricky. He couldn't climb over the coal, because the chunks of black mineral would make too much noise shifting around under his weight. He had to swing onto the outside of the car and make his way along the narrow ledge that ran there. He kept moving as silently as possible.

When he reached the front of the coal tender, he snuck a glance around and saw pretty much what he expected to see. Two men with hats pulled low and bandannas over the bottom halves of their faces covered the engineer and the fireman with six-guns. The two members of the train crew looked more angry than they did scared, which was good. Longarm didn't doubt that they would fight if they got the chance. The fireman's shovel lay at his feet, where he had probably dropped it when ordered to by one of the bandits.

Longarm reached as high as he could, got a hand over the edge of the tender's side wall, and took hold of a chunk of coal. He brought it down, carefully transferred it to his other hand, and then leaned out, hanging on with his free hand while he drew a bead.

Then he launched the coal with the same swift, sidearm motion that had sent many a rock skipping across a pond when he was a boy back in West-by-God Virginia.

Longarm's aim was true. The piece of coal thudded into the side of the nearest outlaw's head. He cursed and staggered and blundered into the man beside him. Both men inadvertently lowered their guns for a second.

That was long enough. Longarm swung around into the cab, palming out his Colt as he did so. The gun rose and fell, crashing against the skull of the man he had just hit with the coal. The outlaw's knees unhinged.

At the same time, the fireman snatched up his shovel, as Longarm had thought that he might, and swung the tool with a strength born of shoveling tons of coal over the years. The blade of the shovel clanged off the head of the second outlaw, who dropped like a poleaxed steer to join the man Longarm had just knocked unconscious.

The fireman whirled toward Longarm and lifted the shovel to strike again, but before the blow could fall, the big lawman said hastily, "Hold on, old son! I'm on your side!"

That declaration, plus the gun that Longarm held, made the fireman hesitate. "Are you a lawman?" he asked.

"Deputy U.S. marshal," confirmed Longarm.

"Thank God!" exclaimed the engineer. "We thought those bastards were gonna get away with it."

"They may yet," warned Longarm. "Do you know how many of them there are?"

"I saw eight, I think."

Longarm gestured toward the two unconscious owlhoots on the floor of the cab. "Counting these two?"

"Yeah."

"So, there's half a dozen more. At least." Bending, Longarm picked up the guns that the outlaws had dropped. "Against three of us. I reckon those odds ain't too bad."

The engineer and fireman looked like they weren't too sure about that. They hesitated before they took the pistols from Longarm.

"Are there any more deputies on board?" asked the engineer.

"If there are, I don't know about it," said Longarm. "I'm traveling alone." Well, except for Amelia Richmond, he added to himself—but chances were she wouldn't be much help in fighting train robbers.

"Cal and me ain't, uh, gunfighters or anything like that," said the fireman. But his anger won out over hesitancy. "Just point me at those damned desperadoes, though. We'll teach 'em that they can't hold up our train."

"That's the spirit," said Longarm with a grin. "We'll tie these two up nice an' tight, and then we'll see about taking care of their partners."

Tying the unconscious outlaws with their own belts took only moments. Longarm wasn't any too gentle about it. He also stuffed the men's bandannas in their mouths to act as gags, too.

Then he dropped from the cab to the gravelly roadbed and called quietly to the engineer and fireman, "Come on!"

The three men hurried alongside the train. As they came to the first passenger car, Longarm spotted a man on horseback, holding the reins of half a dozen or more riderless mounts. Somebody always had to hold the horses.

Longarm motioned the engineer and fireman back, then stole forward as they remained in the thick shadows beside the train. The outlaw was looking in the other direction, toward the back of the train. He probably didn't expect any trouble from the direction of the cab, since as far as he knew, two members of the gang were holding their guns on the engineer and fireman.

The hombre was about to find out what a mistake he was making.

Longarm leaped out of the darkness, tackling the outlaw and driving him out of the saddle. The man yelped in surprise and alarm as he fell, but Longarm didn't know if the sound would be enough to warn the others. He hoped not. He and the outlaw hit the ground, the impact knocking them apart. Longarm rolled over and came up onto his feet first. His fist lashed out and caught the other man, who was just starting to rise. Longarm followed the blow with a kick, figuring that at the moment he couldn't afford such niceties as not kicking a man while he was down. As far as he was concerned, that was the best time to kick an outlaw.

The man stretched out on the ground and lay motionless, knocked as cold as the two men Longarm had taken by surprise in the cab.

The horses had scattered a little when the fallen outlaw let go of their reins, but none of the robbers on board the train appeared to have noticed. Longarm waved his two allies forward and stepped up onto the platform of the first passenger car, followed closely by the engineer and the fireman.

The door into the car stood ajar, and through the opening Longarm could see two outlaws collecting loot at gunpoint from the passengers who had been startled out of sleep. This wasn't a Pullman car, so the passengers rode sitting up, even at night. None of them appeared to be particularly well-to-do, but that didn't stop the outlaws from taking whatever they could—money, watches, rings, anything of value. Longarm felt anger burn inside him as he saw one of the owlhoots rip a jeweled brooch off the dress of an elderly woman. The piece of cheap jewelry couldn't be worth much, but that didn't stop the bastards from stealing it.

Longarm stepped into the coach, moving so quickly that the outlaw barely had a chance to realize he was there before the gun in the big lawman's fist jerked up and chopped down to land with a solid smash. The outlaw crumpled. The man's partner heard the commotion and whirled around, only to find himself facing three leveled guns in the hands of Longarm, the engineer, and the fireman.

"Go ahead and try it, old son," grated Longarm as the robber hesitated. "It'd almost be worth warning the others to blow a few holes in your worthless hide."

A tense second ticked by, and then the man let out a curse and dropped his gun to the floor of the car. As soon as he was disarmed, several passengers swarmed him and wrestled him to the floor.

"Hang on to him, but don't hurt him," Longarm told them as he hurried past, bound for the next car in line. "He's headed behind bars where he belongs."

That made five of the outlaws taken care of, he thought. But there had to be more than the remaining three that the engineer had mentioned. From the number of horses he had seen, Longarm suspected that at least half a dozen of the robbers were still loose somewhere on the train.

A couple of passengers stood up and drew their guns. "We'll go with you," offered one of the men, and Longarm nodded curt agreement. The odds were getting better all the time.

Luck couldn't stay with them forever, though, and as

Longarm and his makeshift posse stepped out of the car onto its rear platform, good fortune abruptly deserted them. Three of the outlaws emerged from the next car at the same time, and as they spotted Longarm and the other men, they jerked their guns up and began to fire. Flame jetted from the weapons, lighting up the night.

"Get down!" shouted Longarm as he dropped to a knee and returned the shots. The Colt in his hand bucked heavily against his palm as he triggered it twice. The reports crashed out. He thought he saw one of the outlaws stagger.

Then the three badmen turned and disappeared back into the car, fleeing.

Longarm snapped over his shoulder, "Stay after them, but be careful!" Then he dropped to the ground and raced alongside the train, the gravel of the roadbed crunching under his boots. He figured he could move faster out here in the open than the outlaws could inside the car. Sure enough, he reached the far end of the car just as the door burst open and the three men rushed out. Screams came from inside the car as the outlaws fired wildly behind them, forcing the passengers to scramble for cover and drop to the floor to get out of the line of fire.

"Hold it!" yelled Longarm as he skidded to a stop.

Taken by surprise, the three outlaws tried to whirl toward him and bring their guns to bear on the deputy. A couple of them actually got shots off before Longarm's bullets scythed into them, driving them off their feet.

But then Longarm's Colt was empty and one of the outlaws was still upright. In the moonlight, his face split in an ugly grin as he brought his gun up, ready to kill.

The derringer Longarm had palmed out of his pocket with his left hand cracked wickedly before the third outlaw could pull his trigger. Flame lanced from the muzzle of the little gun. The bandit grunted in shock and pain and doubled over as the slug punched into his belly. He toppled off the platform to lie bleeding his life out in the gravel of the roadbed.

Longarm dropped the derringer back in his pocket and pivoted toward the rear of the train. The express car was back there, and not surprisingly, the rest of the gang leaped out from it with guns blazing, aware now that their carefully planned holdup had gone awry. Longarm leaned back against the train as he thumbed fresh cartridges from the loops on his belt into the empty chambers of the Colt. Slugs sizzled and ricocheted around him.

More gunfire erupted as the engineer, the fireman, and the volunteers who had come with them emerged from the car and joined the fight. The outlaws cut and ran, trying to reach their scattered horses. Longarm dropped to a knee, drew a bead in the uncertain light, and squeezed off three shots. He saw one of the fleeing owlhoots spin wildly off his feet. Another one bent over, managed to run a few more steps as his momentum carried him ahead, and then pitched forward onto his face in the loose sprawl that signified death.

That left only one of the outlaws, and despite the storm of lead that clawed the night around him, he reached one of the horses, vaulted into the saddle, and kicked the animal into a frenzied gallop. Longarm sent a couple of shots after him as the man thundered off into the night, but he had no idea if either of the bullets found its mark.

The engineer and the fireman hurried up to him as he came to his feet. "Are you all right, Marshal?" asked the engineer anxiously.

"Yeah, I'm fine," said Longarm. "How about you boys?"

"One of the passengers got nicked, but he ain't hurt bad. The rest of us didn't even get nominated!"

The fireman was so excited he danced a little jig. "A dozen of the no-good bastards, and we got all but one of 'em!" he crowed. "Lord, there ain't never been a gun battle like that in all the history of the West!"

Longarm knew that was a mite of an exaggeration—more than a mite, actually—but let the man have his celebration, he decided. They had saved the train from being held up, after all.

The conductor and the express messenger hurried up, both of them gripping guns in their fists. "Any of 'em left?" asked the conductor. "If they need shootin', I'm ready!"

"We've got five prisoners," said Longarm. "I think the shooting's over."

"Who are you, mister?" demanded the conductor.

"Deputy U.S. Marshal Custis Long, out of the Denver office," Longarm identified himself.

"Oh." The conductor, so fierce a moment earlier, was somewhat abashed. "I didn't mean I'd murder those scalawags in cold blood, Marshal."

"I know that," Longarm assured him. "Let's just round up the prisoners and the horses and see what we've got."

The two outlaws in the cab had regained consciousness, but all they could do was squirm around a little and make angry noises behind their gags. The other three who had been knocked unconscious were still out cold. Of the five who had been shot, four were already dead and the other one probably wouldn't live out the hour.

The wounded man was awake, lying on his back on

one of the platforms as he suffered incredible pain from the bullet hole in his belly. "You . . . you gotta help me!" he gasped as Longarm knelt beside him. "It hurts so much!"

"That's too bad, old son, but you're gut-shot," Longarm told him bluntly. "I don't reckon there's much anybody can do for you now."

"Wh-whiskey . . ."

"It won't help," warned Longarm.

"I want it . . . anyway!"

Longarm shrugged and looked around. One of the passengers offered a flask. Longarm took it and held it to the wounded outlaw's lips. He trickled some of the fiery liquor into the man's mouth.

As Longarm had predicted, the whiskey just made the pain worse. The man gasped and groaned and cursed, then said, "N-never should've listened . . . to Rawlings . . . said it'd be easy to . . . hold up the train . . ."

"This Rawlings was the leader of your bunch?" asked Longarm.

"Y-yeah." Cords stood out in the man's neck as he battled futilely against the pain. "S-said we'd pull just one more . . . just one more job . . . then head for . . . Zamora . . ."

Longarm leaned forward, suddenly intensely interested in this owlhoot's dying words. "Zamora," he repeated. "What's that?"

The man was almost out of his head with the pain. He wasn't even thinking about keeping any secrets now. "Old ghost town. Been taken over . . . by outlaws. R-Rawlings said . . . we'd live like kings there. Heard talk about it . . . never should've listened to him . . . Lord, it hurts!"

Longarm knew the man was talking about the owlhoot

trail, the informal line of communication that stretched across the West, wherever men on the dodge from the law encountered each other. Obviously the word was out about Zamora.

And this dying outlaw's babbled statement had confirmed Longarm's earlier theory. Somebody had taken over the old abandoned mining town and turned it into a haven for owlhoots. The whole thing was beginning to make sense now. Those stagecoach bandits down in Arizona had heard about Zamora, and since their operation down there had been broken up by Longarm, they had decided to head for Nevada and lie low for a while.

Longarm was now more determined than ever to pay a visit to Zamora himself.

The wounded outlaw raised a shaking hand and clawed at Longarm's sleeve. "Help me!" he rasped.

"I reckon El Señor Dios is the only one who can do that now, old son," said Longarm.

The outlaw didn't hear him, though. The man's head fell back and a rattling sigh came from his throat. He was gone.

Longarm pushed himself to his feet and looked down at the dead man. He shook his head. The fella had been right about one thing—he never should have listened to the hombre who convinced him to become an outlaw.

The train crew and volunteers from among the passengers got to work clearing the makeshift barrier off the tracks so the train could continue on. Longarm returned to the sleeping car in the meantime and found Amelia sitting up on the bunk, a sheet wrapped around her.

"What in the world happened, Custis?" she demanded. "I heard all sorts of shooting and yelling. I was so frightened."

"Some bad hombres tried to hold up the train," he told

her. "They didn't have much luck." He didn't go into detail about his own part in foiling the holdup.

"Is it all over now?"

"Yeah. We should be moving again in a little while."

"Good." Amelia let the sheet slip down from her shoulders, revealing that she was nude underneath it. "Then you can come back to bed and finish what you started."

Longarm smiled. She was one single-minded gal, that was for sure. But that wasn't necessarily a bad thing.

Chapter 16

Longarm sat across the table from Sheriff Bodic Haines and Captain Thaddeus Mortimer and said, "So that's the story, gents. I wired my boss back in Denver, Chief Marshal Vail, as soon as I got here to Carson City and told him what was going on up in the mountains, and he sent a message back ordering me to talk to you fellas."

Captain Mortimer, who was the image of a spit-'n'-polish military man right down to his narrow little mustache, frowned and said, "I'm not sure this is a matter for the army, Marshal Long. Harboring fugitives and lawbreakers is a criminal offense not a federal offense. What would give either of us jurisdiction to go in there and make arrests?"

"Some of the outlaws holed up there are federal fugitives who broke federal laws," Longarm pointed out. "My badge gives me the right to chase them down wherever they are."

"Yes, but that still doesn't involve the military."

Longarm bit back a curse of frustration and impatience. It had been his bad luck that the commander of the local army post was one of those by-the-book fellas. With some officers, Longarm could have appealed to a sense of one of Uncle Sam's boys doing a favor for another. He could tell that approach wouldn't work with Mortimer, though.

Sheriff Haines, on the other hand, was more down to earth. "I can give you a hand, Marshal, and provide several deputies who'll pitch in," he offered. He was a short, thick-bodied man of middle age, with a mostly bald head and a drooping walrus mustache. He went on, "I don't know if that'll be enough, though. From the sounds of what you've told us, that whole place may be packed to the gills with outlaws, and I don't reckon very many of 'em will be in a surrenderin' mood."

"That's what I thought," agreed Longarm. "That's why Marshal Vail and I figured it might be a good idea to bring the army in on this." He cast a meaningful glance at Mortimer.

The captain said stiffly, "I'll have to communicate with my superiors at the War Department in Washington before I can make any sort of commitment to you, Marshal."

Longarm shrugged, knowing that was probably the best he could hope for where Mortimer was concerned. "Fair enough, Captain," he said. "In the meantime, I'll try to find out some more about what's going on in Zamora."

"How are you gonna do that?" asked Haines.

"The best way I know how . . . I plan to see for myself."

Haines frowned in surprise. "You're goin' in there?"

"Thought I would," Longarm said calmly.

"A lawman wouldn't last five minutes in a place like that!"

"I don't intend to go in with my badge pinned to my shirt. If only outlaws are welcome in Zamora, then I reckon I'll have to be an outlaw."

"What in blazes are you talking about?" asked Mortimer.

Longarm leaned back in his chair and grinned. "Tomorrow I'm going to rob the First State Bank of Carson City."

Longarm had asked the train crew and the officials of the railroad he had met when the train arrived in Carson City to keep quiet about his part in stopping the holdup. The plan that would soon go into effect had already been in the back of his mind even then, and for it to be successful, the fewer folks who knew who he really was, the better.

In fact, as he walked into the First State Bank the next day, he knew he was taking a considerable chance by not revealing his identity to even more people. The president was the only employee of the bank who was aware that the big, deeply tanned, roughly dressed hombre was really a lawman.

Sheriff Haines was standing at one of the high tables in the bank lobby, filling out some sort of paperwork, as Longarm walked in. The sheriff's eyes flicked toward him, but that was the only sign Haines knew he was there. The local star packer continued to pretend that he hadn't even noticed Longarm.

Longarm suspected that there were a few of Haines's deputies in the bank, too, but he didn't know that for sure. If everything went off as planned, Haines was going to look pretty bad. It wasn't good for a sheriff's reputation to let a bank be robbed right under his nose. But he was fully aware of that and was willing to put up with whatever temporary grief it might cause him. Things would look a mite different when the full story came out later on.

Longarm rubbed a finger across his nose as he shuffled past Haines. That was the signal they had agreed on. If everything was all right, Haines would stay where he was. If the plan needed to be called off for any reason, Haines was supposed to turn and leave the bank.

The sheriff didn't budge from where he stood at the table.

That was it, then, thought Longarm. He walked toward the tellers' cages, and as he approached he lifted his left hand to the bandanna tied loosely around his neck. He pulled it up over the lower half of his face as he palmed the Colt from the cross-draw rig with his other hand.

"Don't panic, old son," he said to the teller as he leveled the gun at the man, whose eyes bulged out in shock and fear. Longarm pulled a canvas pouch from under his coat and slid it under the wicket in the teller's cage. "Nobody'll get hurt if you'll just fill that up with cash, and be quick about it."

A female customer saw the gun and screamed. Commotion started to spread through the bank.

"The money, now!" snapped Longarm.

Haines came out from behind the table and hurried toward him. The sheriff clawed at the gun on his hip. Longarm turned smoothly and lashed out with the Colt, laying the barrel against the side of Haines's head in a wicked-looking blow. They had practiced for quite a while in the jail the night before, so Longarm knew that the sheriff's hat cushioned most of the blow. It still had to hurt some, but Haines had assured him that was all right.

"Hell, even if it leaves a welt and bleeds a little, that's fine," Haines had told him. "Might be even better that way."

Longarm kept moving, snaking an arm around

Haines's neck as the sheriff stumbled, apparently from being pistol-whipped. Haines dropped his gun. Longarm jerked the man against him and pressed the barrel of the Colt against the side of Haines's head.

Glaring at the teller, Longarm grated, "Do what I told you, you four-eyed son of a bitch"—he sort of just threw that in, since the teller wore spectacles—"or I'll blow this old geezer's brains out and then I'll shoot *you*."

"Take it easy, take it easy, mister," babbled the teller. "I'll get you the money." He started stuffing greenbacks from his cash drawer into the pouch.

When Longarm thought it was full enough, he said, "That'll do. Give it here."

The teller slid the pouch back under the wicket. By this time, everybody in the bank knew what was going on, of course, and they all stood around tensely, afraid to make a move against Longarm because of the gun he held to the sheriff's head.

"Pick up that pouch," Longarm told Haines.

"You're making a big mistake, you no-good bastard." Haines proceeded to turn the air blue with a stream of angry profanities intended to convince anybody that he was really being held hostage by a bank robber. But he picked up the pouch full of money as Longarm had told him to.

Longarm manhandled Haines toward the front door of the bank. "Everybody get back!" he shouted. "Stand clear, damn it!"

His biggest worry was that somebody would try to be a hero and start shooting at him. Getting Haines involved as an apparent hostage was designed to discourage that. The sheriff was well-known and well-liked in Carson City, and he and Longarm were both hoping that because of that, nobody would get trigger-happy. It had worked so far, but Longarm wasn't out of the woods by any means.

He backed through the door, hauling Haines with him and keeping the sheriff's body in front of his as a shield, just like a real outlaw might do. As they reached the boardwalk, Haines said under his breath, "I think we pulled it off, Long!"

"Just remember to keep that posse off my trail as much as you can," muttered Longarm.

Then he lifted the gun and brought it down with a chopping motion on Haines's head. Again, the blow was a practiced one that looked much worse than it really was. Haines reacted like he'd been buffaloed. His knees folded up, and he dropped to the boardwalk in an apparently senseless heap.

This was the single most dangerous moment of the whole thing, Longarm knew. He whirled and leaped to the horse that was tied at the hitch rack, ready to ride. Haines had assured him that the animal was fast and had plenty of sand. Longarm jerked the reins loose, grabbed the saddle horn, got a foot in the stirrup, and had the horse moving even as he swung up into the saddle.

Somewhere behind him, a gun roared. He heard the bullet sing through the air above his head. He hoped that was one of Haines's men firing, so that the fella would know to aim high.

Leaning forward over the horse's neck to make himself a smaller target, Longarm kicked the mount into a gallop. The horse surged away from the bank, dust boiling up from its hooves. Longarm heard more shots, but none of the slugs came near him.

Then he was racing out of Carson City, heading east toward the mountains, for all intents and purposes and as far as most people knew, a bank robber desperately on the run from the law who needed a place to hide out for a while.

Just as he had planned.

Chapter 17

Ki woke up the next morning after he was wounded, and exactly as Jessie had expected, he wanted to get up out of bed right away and go after the men they had been pursuing. That impulse hadn't lasted very long, though, because he had tried to stand up and promptly fell back on the mattress as dizziness overwhelmed him. Ki was more aware of his body and what it needed than just about anybody Jessie knew, so she wasn't surprised when he admitted that he needed to rest. He might not like it, but he accepted it. Just as he accepted Jessie's decision not to go after the outlaws without him. Letting them build up another lead was annoying, but it could be overcome.

After all, Jessie had a possible lead now to their destination.

While Ki was recuperating from his head wound, Jessie rode to the nearest town where a telegraph office was located and burned up the wires for a while. The vast Starbuck business empire had offices in Chicago, Denver, San Francisco, and various other cities, and those offices were full of people who were only too happy to help Jessica Starbuck find out whatever it was she wanted to know.

In this case, what she wanted to know was as much as possible about the words *Zamora* and *Nevada* and whatever connection existed between them.

Rance Scott had ridden with Jessie to the telegraph office. Just to keep her company, he'd said, but Jessie suspected it was more than that. Being a man, Scott wanted to protect her, whether she really needed protecting or not. Jessie was willing to go along with that because she liked him.

"What did you find out?" asked Scott as Jessie emerged from the office carrying a stack of yellow telegraph flimsies. Replies to her messages had come from all over.

"Zamora's a town," she said. "A mining town in Nevada. Or rather, it *was* a mining town. As far as anybody knows, it's been abandoned for more than ten years, ever since the silver deposits petered out and the mines were closed."

"A ghost town," mused Scott. "What's that got to do with those outlaws, and why would anybody scratch the name of a place like that on a German coin?"

Jessie could only shake her head. "I don't know. But I intend to find out."

"You'll be heading for Nevada?"

"As soon as Ki is healthy enough to ride, which ought to be in another three or four days." Jessie smiled. "I'm sure you'll be glad to see us go. We've taken up so much of your time that you've been neglecting your ranch."

"My spread is fine," insisted Scott. "And any time I've

spent with you, Jessie, has been purely my own choice. Fact of the matter is, I'd go with you to Nevada if you'd let me."

"That wouldn't be a good idea. We don't know what we'll find there, but I'm willing to bet that it won't be anything good. And it'll probably be something dangerous." She looked into Scott's eyes. "I won't risk your life again, Rance."

He looked like he wanted to argue, but instead he just said curtly, "Fine. You ready to ride back?"

"Yes, of course."

They mounted up and headed for Cottonwood, some thirty miles away.

They wouldn't make it before nightfall, so both Jessie and Scott kept an eye out for a good place to camp. They found one in a clump of trees along the banks of a twisting, narrow creek. They dismounted and Scott tended to the horses while Jessie began gathering wood. Ten years earlier it wouldn't have been safe to build a fire out here on these plains at night. That would have drawn the attention of roaming bands of Comanche or their Kiowa allies. But ever since the cavalry under the command of Colonel Ranald McKenzie had broken the back of Comanche power at the Battle of Palo Duro Canyon, east of here in the Panhandle, the threat of Indian attacks had vanished . . . much like the Comanches themselves, who were now all on reservations up in Indian territory.

Jessie had known that they might not make it back to Cottonwood before dark, so she had asked Dr. Mitchell to look in on Ki, and Claude Egan had promised to help out, too. She had brought a few supplies with her in case she and Scott had to spend a night on the trail. Now, as soon as she had a fire going, she put coffee on to boil and began frying up some bacon and warming some biscuits she had brought from the café.

Scott sat on the other side of the fire and said, "It's hard to believe that the grand lady I saw at the Menger Hotel in San Antonio can whip up a meal of biscuits and bacon like any grizzled old trail cook."

Jessie glanced up at him and smiled. "You don't think I'm a grand lady anymore?"

"No, that's not it at all," replied Scott hastily. "I still think you're a . . . a fine, fine lady. I just meant—"

"Relax, Rance," she told him, still smiling. "I know what you meant. But most people have more than one side to them. They can look and act one way in one situation, and be completely different in another situation."

"That's true enough. But I can honestly say that I like every side of you that I've seen so far, Jessie."

She liked hearing that. She valued Rance Scott's opinion. He might be just a small rancher in the Texas Panhandle, but he was the sort of solid pioneer stock that had made it possible for the West to be settled in the first place. The job wasn't finished yet, but the fact that it had even gotten started was due in large part to men like Rance Scott.

They ate the food Jessie prepared, and Scott pitched in by cleaning up afterward. Then they spread their bedrolls in the large ring that Scott formed by laying out a horsehair lariat on the ground. Snakes wouldn't crawl over a lariat like that during the night.

Jessie crawled into her blankets and stretched out, using her saddle for a pillow. They let the fire burn down to embers. Scott lay on the other side of the still-glowing coals, and Jessie waited to see if he was going to approach her. She had a hunch he was too much of a gentleman to do that. He would wait for her to make the first move, if a move was going to be made.

She could tell from his breathing that he wasn't asleep. After a few minutes she said softly, "Rance?"

"What is it, Jessie?"

"Why don't you come over here with me?"

"Are you sure?"

"I'm as certain as I can be," she told him honestly. That honesty, to the point of being blunt sometimes, was something she had mixed emotions about, but she was who she was and couldn't help being that way.

Scott stood up, came around the embers of the fire, and slid into her blankets with her. He had taken off his boots and socks and shirt but still wore his denim trousers. Jessie turned toward him and let him take her in an embrace. She welcomed the feel of his strong arms around her and the way his bare, muscular chest felt against her breasts through the fabric of her shirt. Their mouths met in a kiss that rapidly grew more heated and urgent. When he slipped a hand between them and began unbuttoning her shirt, she didn't object. He unfastened several of the buttons and then slid his hand inside her shirt to cup her left breast. His thumb found the hardening nipple in its ring of pebbled brown skin.

Jessie's hands clutched at his shoulders as her arousal heightened. Scott spread her shirt open and lowered his head to her breasts so that he could suck first one nipple and then the other between his lips. His tongue circled them teasingly, and Jessie arched her back as if urging him to take more of the firm, creamy globes into his mouth. As he continued his oral caresses on her breasts, he reached down and insinuated a hand between her thighs, rubbing her mound through the denim. Jessie felt herself growing wetter under his touch.

To keep herself from getting too carried away too quickly, she said huskily, "Your turn," and put her hands on his shoulders to move him back a little. That gave her room to return the favor he had done for her. She gently sucked his nipples in turn, all the while running her fingers through the thick mat of hair on his broad chest. She knew that some men liked that and some didn't. Rance Scott responded with a deep groan of sheer pleasure.

After subjecting him to several minutes of exquisite torture, Jessie began kissing her way down his lean, well-muscled body. She ran a hand over his groin and felt the hardness waiting for her there. She unfastened the buttons of his trousers and began trying to push them down. Scott raised his hips slightly to help her in that task. The trousers slid down over his hips, allowing his erect manhood to spring free. Jessie took hold of the shaft with one hand and squeezed it affectionately. Scott groaned again.

"My God!" gasped the rancher when Jessie lowered her head still further and began to plant kisses around the head of his organ. Then she pressed her lips against it up and down its length. The thick pole of male flesh throbbed in her hand as she began to lick it. Finally, she parted her lips and took the crown into her mouth, sucking on it with an urgency that was intense yet tender.

Scott's strong hands caught at her hips, maneuvering them toward his head. He hooked his fingers in the waistband of her trousers and pulled them down over her thighs. Jessie kicked them off without ever pausing in what she was doing to him. Now wearing only her mostly unbuttoned shirt, she swung around even more, so that she was lying on top of his powerful form with a knee planted on the blanket on each side of his head. He reached up with his hands, found the heated wetness at her core, and used his thumbs to spread open the folds of her sex. He lifted his head, his tongue flicking several times against the sensitive nubbin at the front of her opening. As Jessie cried out in ecstasy, Scott speared his tongue into her. She responded by sucking harder on him and cupping his balls in her hand.

Both of them spiraled higher and higher until Jessie sensed that they were nearing the point of no return. As much as she enjoyed what they were doing, she wanted more. With a passionate gasp she lifted her head from his groin and began trying to shift around again. With seeming reluctance, Scott let her go. That reluctance vanished quickly as she took a new position poised above his hips. She reached down to grasp his shaft and guide it into her as she sank down on him, impaling herself on the iron-hard spike of his manhood.

When he was fully sheathed within her, she began rocking her hips back and forth, occasionally throwing in a circular rotation that made him moan. As she rode him, he stroked her thighs, her belly, her breasts. Jessie leaned forward, and Scott cupped her face and brought it to his so that he could press his lips gently to hers. That gentle kiss soon grew rougher and more demanding on the part of both of them. Jessie's hips bounced harder, making Scott's member slide slickly in and out of her at an even faster pace. He thrust hard into her, giving her the pleasure she demanded from him, and her fingers dug into his shoulders as she gripped him hard and rode him as if racing for her life on a galloping bronco.

Suddenly she shifted her hands to his chest and

pushed herself into an upright position. She threw her head back, closed her eyes, and panted softly as wave after wave of incredible sensation cascaded through her. The spasms shook her to her core and became even stronger as she felt Scott begin to gush inside her, emptying himself in throbbing culmination.

With every muscle in her body going limp, Jessie fell forward on him like a puppet with its strings cut. Scott wrapped his arms around her, cradling her. He kissed her hair as he stroked a hand down her back to the upward sweep of her rump. His fingers dug into the sensitive area at the base of her spine, prompting a deep, heartfelt sigh of satisfaction from Jessie.

"You make it . . . mighty difficult to say . . . that you can't go to Nevada with us," she said.

Scott laughed softly. "Maybe that was what I was after all along."

He was still hard inside her. Jessie squeezed him with her inner muscles and returned the laugh. "Somehow I don't think so," she said, "but I think you've talked me into it anyway."

"Talked?" he asked wryly.

"Well, maybe in a very special language . . ." She kissed him, slipping her tongue between his lips and into his mouth, where it danced sensuously with his. When she came up for air a moment later, she whispered, "We'll see how the conversation goes the rest of the night."

"A ghost town?" asked Ki with a frown.

"That's the best information I could get about the place," replied Jessie. "Zamora was originally a silver mining boomtown, but it's been abandoned for a long time."

They were talking in the hotel room where Ki had been taken to recuperate on the night he was wounded. Ki sat up in bed with a couple of pillows propped behind him, while Jessie was in the rocker and Rance Scott straddled one of the ladderback chairs. Jessie had filled Ki in on everything she had learned from the replies to the telegrams she had sent.

"Let me see that coin again," requested Ki.

Jessie took it out of her vest pocket and flipped it to him. His hand darted out and deftly plucked the spinning coin from the air. Ki knew that by tossing it to him that way, Jessie had been testing his reflexes in what she thought was a subtle manner. He said nothing and allowed her to continue thinking that.

He turned the coin over in his fingers several times as he studied both the front and back of it. Then, like the rising of the sun, an idea burst on his brain. His head lifted sharply.

"What is it?" asked Jessie. "You've figured it out, haven't you, Ki?"

He smiled faintly. "Yes, and so have you, Jessie. You just haven't realized it yet."

"Damn it, don't get all inscrutable on me now," she said with a wicked laugh. "Tell me what you're thinking, Ki."

"Very well." He tossed the coin back to her. She caught it and looked at it intently as Ki continued, "First we must make an assumption, which is always a perilous thing. But in this case I believe it is safe to say that the coin most likely was lost by one of the men we seek."

"I don't have any trouble believing that," put in Scott.

"That's not the sort of thing that anybody around Cottonwood would normally have, and anyway, if somebody had dropped it in that alley earlier, somebody else probably would have come along and found it before the night of that ruckus. It's not like nobody ever goes through that alley."

Ki nodded. "This is my thinking as well. We must accept the most likely explanation, without forgetting that there is no guarantee that explanation is true and correct."

"Get on with it," urged Jessie.

"Of course. If the coin was being carried by one of the outlaws, as we assume it must have been, then it could be a calling card, so to speak."

Jessie frowned. "A calling card?"

"To identify the bearer as being someone who has a right to enter a certain place."

Jessie came to her feet, shocked out of her chair by the realization that had just hit her. "Zamora!"

Ki nodded. "I believe that to be true. Those four men were on their way to this ghost town in Nevada, and the coin would have identified them to someone once they got there."

"But who? And why would they be going to a ghost town?"

Ki shook his head. "This I do not know. What do outlaws want more than anything else?"

"Loot?" suggested Scott.

"No." There was a newfound certainty in Jessie's voice as she went on, "They want a hideout. Someplace they'll be safe from the law."

Ki made a small humming sound as he frowned in thought. After a moment he said, "What you say makes sense, Jessie. And what better place for lawless men to hide from justice than a town that has been abandoned by its law-abiding citizens?"

Scott said, "It sounds like you're talking about an outlaw town."

"That is exactly what I'm talking about," agreed Ki.

"We're getting ahead of ourselves," cautioned Jessie. "We don't *know* that any of this is true."

"We know that the course those men have been following will take them to Nevada if they continue long enough in that direction," said Ki. "And we know that they are days ahead of us because of my carelessness in allowing myself to be injured."

Jessie shook her head. "You can't blame yourself for that, Ki. My God, the way the lead was flying around in that alley, it's a wonder you weren't hurt worse!"

"But there is no denying the fact that we would still be close on their trail if you had not been forced to wait here while I recovered." Ki paused. "Which I am now, by the way."

"Recovered, you mean?"

He nodded. "Fully."

"That'll be up to Doc Mitchell to decide." Jessie smiled and shrugged. "I've got to admit, though, you look to me like you're pretty much back to normal. A little skinnier than usual, maybe, because you haven't been eating as much."

"I can ride. Fresh air and activity will soon restore me to full strength."

"I guess we'll have to put that to the test."

"Now," said Ki, "here is the other question you must consider: Do we find out where this Zamora is and proceed straight there, or do we continue trying to follow the trail of the men we pursued this far?"

"You mean try to get ahead of them, or at least cut their lead way down, by using the railroads instead of traveling the whole distance on horseback?"

"Exactly. It is a gamble. If we're wrong about the coin's meaning and we go to Nevada based on what we surmise, it's possible those men may veer off in another direction entirely, in which case we will probably never find them."

"Oh, we'll find them, all right, because I'm sure they're going to Zamora," said Jessie. She looked around the room at Ki and Scott, then added, "And so are we."

Chapter 18

Nick Darrow was still angry about what had happened back in that jerkwater town on the Texas–New Mexico border. The Starbuck woman and her Chinaman friend ought to be dead by now, he thought. Maybe the Chinaman was; he'd taken a slug to the head at mighty close range. But the woman had been alive when Darrow and the others galloped out of town. There was no doubt about that. And she'd had somebody else fighting on her side, too, some hombre who looked like a cowboy. Maybe she had brought him with her and the Chinaman from the Circle Star.

But the fact that Jessica Starbuck was still alive wasn't the worst of it. The worst thing to come out of that fracas was that Darrow had lost the coin that had been given to him by the beautiful woman on the train.

He told himself it didn't matter. They were in Nevada now, and he had already discovered from asking questions in settlements along the trail that Zamora was the name of an old mining town up in the mountains south of the Humboldt River. A ghost town now, because the ore had played out and the miners had all gone elsewhere. Darrow had no idea what connection the woman on the train had with Zamora, but he damned sure intended to find out.

He wasn't going to stop until he had found her again. He *couldn't* stop. It was like some compulsion that drove him on.

Neither of the others knew about that, and to be honest, they were getting a mite peeved with him. Like now, as the normally cheerful Blue Atkinson asked dourly, "Nick, why in blazes did you drag us up in these godforsaken mountains? There ain't nothin' up here to steal."

"There ain't nothin' up here, period," added Simon Jarvis.

"I know what I'm doing," said Darrow coldly. "If you don't like it, you're welcome to ride away on your own."

Hastily, Blue said, "No need to do that. You've been ramroddin' this outfit for a long time, Nick, and you've always done a mighty fine job. No reason to change now."

Jarvis didn't look as convinced of that. Darrow knew that Jarvis sometimes got some high-and-mighty notions, like the idea that *he* ought to be in charge. Darrow knew he would have to keep an eye on Jarvis.

But once they reached Zamora and found out what was there, everything might change. They wouldn't know until they got there.

Which ought to be soon, thought Darrow. The directions he had gotten from a dangerous-looking old-timer back down the trail had sent them into this winding canyon between a couple of almost sheer stone walls. The old-timer, who by the looks of him had heard the owlhoot on many a lonely nighttime trail, had told Darrow that if they rode through the canyon, they would find what they were looking for.

"Best not let your trigger fingers get itchy, though," the old man had said. "Keep your dew claws away from them smokepoles, elsewise you'll be liable to get ventilated."

Darrow had taken that to mean that there were guards on duty in the canyon. So far he hadn't seen any signs of sentries, but maybe they just hadn't gone far enough yet. They rode around a bend—

And suddenly found themselves with the muzzles of three rifles staring at them from a ledge on one side of the canyon.

"Hold it right there!" bellowed a deep voice that sounded like a wagon rolling over ten miles of bad road.

"Son of a bitch!" yelled Jarvis. His hand started toward the gun on his hip.

Darrow's arm shot out. His fingers clamped tightly around Jarvis's wrist. "Hold it, you fool!" he said. "Can't you see they've got the drop on us?"

"They do now, for sure," groused Jarvis.

"They always did, Simon," put in Blue Atkinson. He looked at Darrow with eyes that were narrowed in suspicion. "And I've got the feelin' that ol' Nick here had a pretty good idea somethin' like this was goin' to happen."

Jarvis glared at Darrow. "Is that true, Nick?"

"What if it is?" Darrow shot back. "You know I do the thinking for this gang, Simon. That's the way it's always been and the way it will always be."

"I'm not so sure about that. It ain't much of a gang anymore, is it? Just the three of us now. We've lost three men since we started out on that job down in Texas."

"You can't blame me for Jonas Gibson."

"You shot him."

"It was his idea to double-cross us."

Jarvis shrugged and started to say something else, but before the words could come out of his mouth, the man who had shouted at them from the ledge spoke up again. "Hey, down there!" he rumbled. "Can't you stop your jaws from flappin' for long enough to realize that you're covered? We could blow you bastards right out of the saddle!"

"Why would you do that?" challenged Darrow. "For all you know, we're welcome here."

The unseen gunman said, "Ain't nobody welcome here except them what was invited."

"How do you know we weren't invited?" Darrow took a chance. "This is the trail to Zamora, isn't it? What if I was to show you a big silver coin with the name of this place scratched on it?"

For a moment there was only silence from the ledge, but then finally the spokesman for the sentries said, "A big silver coin, eh? And just who was it gave you this coin, mister?"

"A blond woman on a private train down in Texas," said Darrow. He added honestly, "The most beautiful woman I've ever seen."

Again silence reigned in the canyon for several tense moments. Then the man on the ledge ordered, "Show me that coin you were talkin' about. Toss it up here."

Darrow hesitated, even though he knew there was no point in trying to lie. "I don't have it," he said at last. "Not anymore. But I did, and the woman gave it to me, just the way I told you."

The snorts of disdain from the hidden sentries were

clearly audible. "Yeah, and just why the hell are we supposed to believe you, mister?"

"If I hadn't had the coin, how could I describe it?" Darrow pointed out. "It was silver, heavy, with a crown on the back and a fella's head on the front. The words engraved on it were in some language I don't savvy, but I know it wasn't English or Mex. And somebody had scratched *Zamora* on the front and *Nevada* on the back."

For the third time, the man on the ledge didn't respond right away. When he finally spoke again, Darrow heard the doubt in his voice.

"I reckon you've *seen* a coin like that . . . but that don't mean it was given to you."

"Then take us to whoever is in charge here," suggested Darrow. "The worst they can do is kill us."

Jarvis and Atkinson shifted nervously in their saddles at that comment.

"The worst they can do to *you*, you mean. Lord knows what they might have in store for me. But I reckon you're right. Somebody else will have to figure out what to do with you. Now, you boys shuck those guns. Just toss 'em on the canyon floor."

Jarvis cursed bitterly. "I don't like givin' up my gun, Nick," he said.

"I don't much like it, either, but I don't see that we've got any choice," Darrow told him. He unbuckled his gun belt and dropped it next to his horse, then followed it with the rifle he pulled from the saddle sheath. Reluctantly, Jarvis and Atkinson discarded their weapons as well.

"All right, ride ahead, well away from them hoglegs," ordered the gravel-voiced man.

As the three riders walked their horses farther along

the canyon, the man emerged from behind the rocks on the ledge. His two companions stayed where they were and kept their rifles trained on the outlaw trio. The man was short and squat, with drooping red mustaches and a battered old hat. He climbed down a rope ladder that was attached somehow to the ledge. He didn't bother gathering up the weapons, but instead fetched a saddled mule from around the next bend in the serpentine canyon. Positioning himself behind Darrow, Jarvis, and Atkinson, he herded them on up the canyon at rifle point.

"They call me Yellowstone," he introduced himself, although none of the newcomers had asked his name. "I reckon you could say I'm sort of in charge o' keepin' folks from gettin' in here who shouldn't't."

"What is this place?" asked Darrow without turning around. "What's so special about an old abandoned ghost town?"

"You mean you really don't know?" Yellowstone sounded surprised.

"All I know is that the woman on the train promised us an extra thousand dollars for doing a job, and she said I could find her here and collect."

Jarvis said, "You didn't tell us anything about an extra grand!"

"We've been headin' for this place all along, haven't we?" asked Blue Atkinson shrewdly. "But are you more interested in collectin' that money, Nick, or in the gal who promised it to you?"

Darrow ignored the question and instead addressed one of his own to their guard. "Who is she, Yellowstone? Who's the woman from the train?"

"You'll find out soon enough," replied Yellowstone. "Most newcomers I take to see the mayor first thing. With you boys, though, I think I'm gonna skip that step." A grim edge came into his voice. "I'm gonna take you straight to the Empress, and Lord help you if you've been lyin' to me."

The Empress! Darrow couldn't get that name out of his mind. The title certainly fit the beautiful blond woman who had been on the train. Despite her youth, she had carried herself with a decidedly regal bearing. She was special, not like the common people.

Zamora itself was impressive enough. Somebody had taken hold of the old ghost town and was rebuilding it into something special. As Darrow, Jarvis, and Atkinson rode along the main street with Yellowstone following on the mule, Darrow looked around at all the signs of recent construction and cleanup. The settlement was busy, too, with quite a few men on the street and others going in and out of the buildings.

They weren't the typical frontier settlers, though. They were all hard-faced and gun-hung, and Darrow even saw some familiar faces that he recognized as belonging to hombres who were regular riders of the owlhoot trail. Yet they strode the streets of Zamora with ease and impunity.

That was when Darrow began to realize what he and his companions had gotten into here. Zamora was an outlaw town, populated solely by men on the dodge.

What a brilliant idea, thought Darrow. Whoever was running things here could charge a steep price for the privilege of being safe from the star packers.

At the far end of the street stood the largest, most impressive building in town, a three-story Victorian mansion surrounded by a carefully tended lawn dotted with flower beds and trees and shrubs. It looked like it could have been lifted whole from the nicest neighborhoods in Denver or San Francisco. Whoever lived there had to be the boss of this place.

The Empress? Darrow couldn't help but wonder, although it was hard to imagine that a young woman, even one as elegant and beautiful and compelling as the blonde he had met, could set up a big operation like this.

Still, she would be right at home in a mansion like that.

As the riders passed one of the buildings in town, a man in a derby hat stepped out and lifted a hand in greeting. "Strangers, Yellowstone?" he said.

"Yeah, but I'm takin' 'em straight to see the Empress, Mayor," rumbled Yellowstone. "That one there"—Darrow knew Yellowstone must have pointed to him—"says he had one of them special coins o' hers."

"Then by all means, take them right on," said the mayor. "Do you need any help?"

"No, I don't reckon. These boys are smart enough to know that if they give me any trouble, I'll blow a damn hole in 'em."

"No trouble," said Darrow over his shoulder. "We want to meet the Empress as much as you want to take us to her."

"Yeah, yeah, just keep movin' up there."

The four men rode on to the mansion. Darrow and his two companions reined in and dismounted when Yellowstone told them to. He prodded them along a flagstone walk to a columned porch. A bellpull hung next to a massive mahogany door with elaborate patterns carved on it.

"Yank on that fancy rope," ordered Yellowstone.

Darrow did so and heard the faint peal of the bell through the thick door. After a moment the panel swung open, revealing one of the tough hombres who had been with the blonde on the train. Darrow couldn't remember which one the man was, Heinrich or Conrad. He was dressed in butler's livery now, and the sober black suit didn't make him look any less grim and dangerous.

The sight of him, though, confirmed Darrow's suspicion that the woman from the train and the Empress were one and the same.

"I reckon she needs to see these fellas," said Yellowstone to the hard-faced butler. "They claim to know her."

Darrow had seen the flicker of recognition in the man's eyes. He said, "This hombre knows us, too. Don't you, Heinrich? Or are you Conrad? I can't quite recall."

"I am Conrad," said the man stiffly. He looked past Darrow, Jarvis, and Atkinson and continued, "Yah, *Herr* Yellowstone, these are the men the Empress hired to steal the bull."

Yellowstone lowered his rifle and got a slightly friendlier look on his rugged face. "Is that right? They rustled ol' Shorty? Well, why the hell didn't you say so?"

"I wanted to see the Empress," said Darrow. "That's where you were bringing us, so I didn't see any point in arguing."

Conrad stepped back and extended a hand. "Gentlemen, if you will come in, please."

Darrow strode confidently into the mansion's foyer. Jarvis and Atkinson followed a bit more tentatively. They were unarmed, after all, and stepping into a place that could turn out to be a lion's den. But for now, at least, they were still willing to follow wherever Darrow led.

Conrad shut the door and moved around them to take the lead again. Yellowstone remained behind them, more relaxed now but still alert, his rifle still clutched in his big hands, ready to use it.

Conrad took the group down a hallway with a thick carpet runner on the polished hardwood floor. Spindly looking side tables graced the walls here and there. They didn't look like much, but Darrow was willing to bet that they were expensive. Paintings hung on the walls, mostly landscapes but a few portraits of dour, well-dressed men. Darrow wondered if they had been in the house to start with or if the Empress had had them hung there.

They came to a set of double doors. Even before Conrad opened them, Darrow heard the strains of piano music coming from the room beyond them. Someone was playing a light, airy melody, and doing a fine job of it, at least as far as Darrow could tell. He supposed his musical tastes weren't the most refined in the world, since most of the piano-playing he'd heard in his life had taken place in various saloons and whorehouses and honky-tonks.

Conrad swung the doors open and ushered them into a large room that was brightly lit by the sunlight washing in through tall windows with gauzy curtains hanging over them. A grand piano sat on one side of the room, not far from a big fireplace with a massive mantel, and perched on the bench at the piano was the young, beautiful blonde from the train. She frowned prettily in concentration as her slender fingers moved almost too fast to be seen on the keys. She didn't look up at the newcomers as she continued playing. The melody, which had been so delicate only a moment earlier, now became stronger, more urgent and aggressive. The chords crashed with newfound power. The song built to a thunderous climax, then died away in a few fragile notes that dissipated like a gossamer web carried away on a breeze.

As the echoes of the music died away, the woman lifted her hands from the keyboard and turned to face the men. With a solemn expression, but seemingly no surprise at seeing Darrow and the others, she said, "Welcome to Zamora, gentlemen. I am Katerina von Blöde."

"The Empress," said Darrow in a hushed voice.

She smiled. "Some call me that, yes. The title is strictly honorary. I am not a member of the nobility."

Katerina von Blöde looked pretty damned noble to Darrow as she stood up and came around the piano to walk toward them. She wore a lightweight gown with a low scooped neck and short, puffy sleeves. Her thick blond hair was swept up in an arrangement of elaborate curls, leaving her smooth, sleek shoulders mostly bare. Darrow wouldn't have thought it possible that she could look more lovely than she had in their previous meeting, but he was wrong. She took his breath away.

"Did you come to collect that additional payment I promised you, Mr. Darrow?" she asked.

"And to see you again," he replied, so strongly affected by her beauty that he didn't even think about playing his cards close to the vest.

"How charming," she said with a smile. "Do you have the coin I gave you?"

His breath hissed between his teeth as his jaw tightened. He wished she hadn't asked about the coin.

"I'm sorry," he said. "It got lost somewhere along the way."

For just an instant her blue eyes turned icy, and the idea that she might be angry with him lashed at Darrow like the cut of a whip. But then the reaction was gone, and she waved an elegant hand casually.

"No matter. I know you and your friends, and all of you are welcome here." She looked past Darrow, Jarvis, and Atkinson. "Is that understood, Conrad? Yellowstone?

These men are welcome in Zamora and are exempt from the usual charges. I owe them a great deal."

Conrad clicked his heels together and bowed his head. "*Jawohl*, Empress," he said.

Yellowstone rumbled, "Whatever you say, ma'am. Reckon I'll be headin' back out to the canyon now."

"Thank you, my friend," Katerina told him.

Darrow got the idea that these men would run through a stone wall if Katerina von Blöde told them to. And he understood exactly why they felt that way.

"A drink, gentlemen?" asked Katerina as she turned back toward the piano.

Jarvis spoke up before Darrow could say anything. "I could use a drink. This place has got me throwed. I never saw anything like it."

Gracefully, Katerina settled herself on the piano bench again. "There is no other place like it in your country. Oh, there are hideouts . . . crude places with few if any comforts, where danger still lurks. But no place other than Zamora, which some call the city of thieves, where men such as yourselves can truly rest and relax without worries. Well-armed men patrol the mountains around this valley. No law officers can get in here without us knowing about it and taking steps to deal with them."

Darrow realized then that they had probably been watched even before they reached the canyon. It bothered him a little that he hadn't figured that out and spotted the watchers, but the Empress's men doubtless knew what they were doing and were highly skilled at it.

"And you're the one who's runnin' all this?" asked Blue Atkinson.

"That is correct. It was my idea to establish such a sanctuary, and I looked around until I found the proper location for it—an abandoned mining town high in the mountains of Nevada. A ghost town, I believe you Americans call it."

"It must have taken quite a bit of money to get started," said Darrow.

"I have money," said Katerina with that gentle but compelling smile of hers. "Although the operation of Zamora has proven to be lucrative, I didn't embark on this enterprise for financial gain."

"Then why?" asked Darrow bluntly. "Why do all this? And why pay us to steal that blasted bull from Jessica Starbuck?"

Her eyes glittered again briefly, and Darrow realized that it was at those moments when she was truly the Empress.

"My motives are my own," she said. "Call Zamora a legacy, if you will, a memorial of sorts. And as for Jessica Starbuck . . . I have my reasons for everything I do that involves her."

Darrow's gaze locked with hers for a second, but then he shrugged. If she said it was none of his business, then it was none of his business. "All right," he said. "What happens now?"

Her smile came back. "You enjoy your stay in Zamora. You're welcome to remain here for as long as you like."

"Here in this mansion?"

Katerina shook her head. "Alas, no. I live here alone save for my trusted servants. But there are several hotels in the town. You can take your pick of rooms. Lodging, food, drink, women . . . all yours for the taking."

Jarvis said, "That reminds me, we never got that drink you promised us, Empress."

Darrow glared at him for being so impolite, but Katerina laughed, clearly not offended. "That's true, Mr. Jarvis. We started talking and I forgot about it. Conrad, brandy for the gentlemen. And if you'd like, you can stay for supper."

"Oh, we'd like that, wouldn't we, boys?" said Darrow. Jarvis and Atkinson nodded.

So did Katerina, and then she swung back around on the bench to face the piano's keyboard once again. Her hands lifted, and her fingers began to caress the keys. Conrad brought snifters of brandy to the three outlaws and told them to make themselves comfortable in the overstuffed armchairs that were arranged around the piano and the fireplace. As Darrow sank onto the cushions, he thought about how damned strange this whole setup was. Here he and Simon and Blue were, three owlhoots who had never known much of anything fancier than a cow town whorehouse, and yet here they were sitting in a luxuriously furnished mansion sipping fine brandy and listening to the most beautiful woman in the world play the piano. Darrow could only sigh and shake his head in amazement.

America was a *great* country!

Chapter 19

Longarm had a good head for directions and the instinctive, innate ability to know where he was most of the time. Plus he had pretty well memorized that map he'd found on the dead outlaw down in Arizona Territory. So he didn't have to pull out the folded piece of paper and study it very often as he made his way through the mountains toward the old ghost town called Zamora.

He felt eyes on him as he rode, and he knew they didn't belong to any of the members of the posse Sheriff Bodie Haines had taken out of Carson City after him. Haines knew exactly where Longarm was going, and he would have led the posse in some other direction, keeping the pursuit off Longarm's trail without being too obvious about what was going on. At least Longarm hoped that was the case.

Actually, the sense of being watched told Longarm that he was on the right track. Anybody smart enough to set up a vulture's sanctuary like Zamora would be smart enough to have plenty of guards around the place.

The map led Longarm to a narrow, twisting canyon. His nerves crawled a mite as he rode through it. This would be a damned good place for an ambush. He could just imagine a nice big target painted right on his chest . . .

"Hold it!"

The voice rang out as Longarm rounded a bend in the canyon. A trio of rifle barrels poked at him from behind some boulders on a ledge to the left of the trail. Without being told to, Longarm reined in and then lifted his hands to shoulder height. "Easy on the trigger, old son," he called back. "I ain't looking for trouble."

"Then what *are* you lookin' for, mister?" asked the spokesman for the sentries.

Longarm took the plunge, saying, "A place called Zamora. I hear tell that if you're on the dodge, it's the best hideout this side o' the Hole in the Wall."

The man on the ledge snorted. "The Hole in the Wall ain't nothin' compared to Zamora. That's like sayin' some snot-nose punk who thinks he's fast with a gun is the same thing as John Wesley Hardin. Now shuck that hogleg, and I'll take you where you want to go."

Longarm had the feeling that what followed in the next few minutes was a well-established pattern. He carefully dropped his Colt and Winchester on the floor of the canyon, then rode a short distance away from them and stopped again on the unseen sentry's orders. Then and only then did the man emerge from behind the rocks on the ledge and climb down a rope ladder, leaving his two fellow guards up there to keep their rifles trained on

Longarm. The spokesman was a short, burly hombre who introduced himself as Yellowstone. Something about him was familiar, and after a moment Longarm realized that he had seen the man's face on reward posters. Yellowstone was wanted for bank robbery and for holding up several trains. Longarm couldn't recall any other charges against him.

Yellowstone had a mule tethered around the next bend. He fetched the jughead, and then he and Longarm rode on, single file, with Yellowstone in the rear keeping his rifle pointed at Longarm's back.

"You know I'll blow your spine in two if you try anything funny," warned the outlaw.

"I ain't feeling the least bit humorous, old son," Longarm assured him.

"What's your name?"

"Parker." Longarm left it at that, not giving any front handle.

"You on the run from a posse?"

"I robbed the bank in Carson City a couple of days ago. What do you think?"

"How much you get?"

Longarm had counted the money in the pouch the first night after the staged robbery. "Nearly eight thousand."

Yellowstone grunted. "Not the biggest haul I've ever heard tell of, but not bad for a few minutes' work, I reckon."

"That's sort of the way I figured it."

"You ready to part with a fourth of it?"

Longarm hipped around in the saddle as he rode so that he could look over his shoulder at the red-mustachioed galoot. "Is that what it costs to visit Zamora?"

"What, you didn't know that? I figured whoever told you about the place mentioned that it ain't free . . . except to certain folks."

Longarm wondered what Yellowstone meant by that, but he didn't want to ask too many questions just yet. Instead he said, "The hombre who told me to light out for this place if I ever found things getting too hot where I was didn't say anything about what it costs. Seems a mite steep."

"You may not think so when you get there and see what you get for your money."

Longarm nodded and faced forward again. He planned to get the bank's money back eventually, anyway, so he supposed it was all right for him to spend some of it. The bank president wouldn't be happy if a couple of grand went astray somehow, though.

Of course, it was possible Longarm would never get back to Carson City with any of the loot—but in that case he'd likely be too dead to worry about it.

A short time later they reached the head of the canyon, and Longarm was impressed but not surprised when he looked down into the little valley spread out before them and saw the settlement of Zamora. He had known that they had to be practically on the ghost town's front doorstep.

"That's the place, eh?" he said to Yellowstone.

"Yep," replied the owlhoot. "Don't let the buildings that ain't been fixed up yet fool you. Give her time, and the Empress will have the whole town lookin' like a showplace."

Longarm shot a glance at him and repeated, "The Empress. Who's that?"

"The lady who's responsible for all this. You'll meet her. Maybe."

Longarm tried not to frown. It seemed hard to believe that a woman could have set up such an elaborate scheme, not to mention her being in charge of the crew of hard-bitten desperadoes that would be necessary to run a place like this. But he had known some mighty capable—and dangerous—females in his life, so he supposed it was possible. It would take a woman as strong as Jessie Star-buck to do this, though, and gals like that were few and far between.

The two riders wound their way back and forth down the twisting trail to the valley floor and then rode on in to Zamora. Longarm's muscles were tense as he and Yellow-stone reached the main street and started along it. With the whole town being full of outlaws, it was possible, even likely, that Longarm might have crossed paths with some of them before. He had let his beard grow for sev-eral days, so his cheeks and chin and jaw were covered with dark stubble, but that might not do enough to alter his appearance. He still might be recognized as a law-man. If that happened, his ruse was ruined and his life would be in deadly danger.

He kept his head tilted forward, and his hat was pulled a little lower than usual in an attempt to obscure his fea-tures. Some of the men he and Yellowstone passed glanced at him curiously, but others paid no attention to him. Longarm was thankful for those gents. The fewer outlaws who looked closely at him, the better.

Yellowstone told him to stop in front of a square build-ing made of stone and thick planks. Accompanied by the burly sentry, Longarm went inside and was introduced to Wade Abernathy, the mayor of Zamora.

"What about this so-called Empress I've been hearing about?" Longarm asked the pasty-faced administrator.

Abernathy reminded him uncomfortably of an older version of Henry, Billy Vail's secretary.

"I'll pass along the news of your arrival to her, Mr. Parker," replied Abernathy. "As our benefactor and the founder of the current incarnation of Zamora, Miss von Blöde takes a keen interest in every new potential citizen of her town."

Only Longarm's iron will kept him from showing the shocked reaction he experienced at Abernathy's words. He felt like a giant fist had just slammed into his guts. He knew the name von Blöde—but he had fully expected never to hear it again.

"Thanks," he forced himself to say. "Now what do I do?"

"You pay a one-fourth share of whatever loot you have, and in return for that you've bought yourself a one-month stay in Zamora. If you want to remain here longer than that, mutually agreeable arrangements can be made."

Longarm nodded. His pulse hammered inside his head, and the wheels of his brain were racing. Now that he knew a von Blöde was involved with Zamora, the whole setup didn't seem so far-fetched.

If this "Empress" was related to old Herzog von Blöde, anything was possible.

"Guess I'll go get the money." Longarm turned toward the door of the mayor's office.

Yellowstone blocked his way. Abernathy said, "Don't worry, our friend Yellowstone can bring it in. If that's all right with you."

Longarm nodded. What else could he do?

"Sure, go right ahead."

Over the next few minutes, Abernathy counted the money in the pouch, separated a fourth of it from the bigger pile, and then put the balance back in the pouch.

"We have a fine safe here, Mr. Parker. I'll put the rest of your money in there, and it will be waiting for you whenever you need it."

"Like a bank, eh?"

Abernathy smiled thinly, not really amused. "Everyone seems to say that. I suppose men in your line of work take a natural interest in banks."

"I reckon. Well, that's all right with me. But how do I pay for grub and drinks and such?"

"You don't," said Abernathy. "Now that you're one of us, so to speak, there are no charges for Zamora's amenities." The mayor leaned back in his chair. "Enjoy yourself, Mr. Parker. You've made your escape."

Not really, thought Longarm a moment later when he stepped out on the building's porch and gazed up and down the street. Any of the couple of dozen men he saw would likely be glad to fill him full of lead if they found out he packed a badge. And in a way he was a prisoner of fortune, because he might be recognized at any moment. Those two stagecoach robbers from Arizona might be here. Even though he hadn't gotten a good look at their unmasked faces during the holdup, they had seen him just fine. He was sure that if he ran into them, they would be more than curious about what he was doing here. They would probably guess, correctly, that he was after them.

This job had turned into more than an attempt to arrest a couple of stagecoach bandits, though. Much more. Longarm still wasn't sure exactly who the Empress really was—Herzog's daughter, more than likely, since Abernathy had called her *Miss* von Blöde—but Longarm was sure of one thing.

If she was anything like Herzog, and if her operation

225

wasn't stopped here and now, by the time she was through, the whole frontier might be in danger.

Ki's senses reached out from him, seeking over the rugged landscape for any sign of potential trouble or peril. Not only his eyes and ears and even his nose sought danger, but also an intangible instinct as well, a questing that would tell Ki if anything was out of place in the desolate mountains around them.

He stiffened in the saddle as that instinct told him something was wrong.

"Jessie," he said quietly, "we're being watched."

She sat calmly on her horse beside him, not outwardly alarmed. "Where?" she asked.

"I don't know yet . . . There, on that hill to the right, about five hundred yards away."

On the other side of Jessie, Rance Scott asked, "How does he do that?"

Jessie's full lips curved in a smile. "When it comes to Ki, I've learned not to ask how. I just believe him."

"Oh, I believe him, all right," said Scott. "It's just a mite spooky, is all."

"Not really," said Ki. "If a man is truly in balance, he can look around him at the rest of the world and see that which is *not* in balance."

"If you say so. I reckon the important thing is, how many of the hombres are up there, and are they fixing to ambush us?"

"One man, I would say, and for now he seems content merely to watch us."

"Has he seen all three of us?" asked Jessie.

"That is likely, but I have no way of knowing for certain."

She thought about it for a moment, then came to a decision. "Rance, you and I will ride straight ahead on this trail. Ki, circle around and see if you can get behind him. If he jumps us—"

"I will jump him," finished Ki with a smile.

Jessie nodded. "Come on," she said to Rance as she heeled her mount into motion again.

They had bought the horses in Winnemucca after getting off the train there instead of going all the way to Carson City. Winnemucca wasn't much of a town—it was pretty much the middle of nowhere, in fact—but there was a livery stable there and Jessie and the two men had been able to pick up some decent mounts. Then they had ridden south into the mountains, following the route Jessie had traced on the map she'd bought in Denver.

While they were in Denver she had gone to the rented room where Custis Long lived, hoping to see her old friend and occasional lover and partner in adventure, but Longarm wasn't there. Jessie had thought about paying a visit to Billy Vail at the Federal Building to ask the chief marshal if he knew where Longarm was or when he was expected back, but there was really no time for that. She wanted to get to Zamora, deal with those bastards who had stolen her bull, and hopefully find out who was behind that bit of wide-looping in the first place. So she and Ki and Scott had gotten back on the train without her talking to Billy Vail.

Now, Jessie estimated that they were within a few miles of the old ghost town. She wasn't surprised that someone was watching them. There were bound to be guards patrolling the area around the formerly abandoned settlement if the theory she and Ki had hatched about it was correct.

"You seem to be in the habit of making a target out of yourself," said Scott in a quiet voice as he and Jessie rode toward the hill where the lookout waited.

"I just adopt whatever tactics seem to have the best chance of being successful," she said.

"You sound like a military officer." Scott grinned. "General Jessie."

"I think I'd prefer General Starbuck." Jessie chuckled. "That doesn't sound bad."

"No, it doesn't," agreed Scott.

Before either of them could say anything else, a rider suddenly spurred out of the trees at the base of the hill. The man leveled a rifle at them and called out sharply, "Hold it, you two!"

Jessie and Scott reined in. The rifleman came closer, saying, "If either of you move, you're dead."

"We're not moving, mister," said Scott. "Take it easy with that repeater."

The man was only about twenty feet from them now. He was an ugly, hatchet-faced hombre, and he got even uglier as a sneer twisted his face. "Don't tell me what to do, mister," he threatened. "I'll part your hair with a bullet. I'll—"

Before he could continue his blustering, Ki suddenly appeared, coming out of the trees behind the man. The warrior was on foot, moving swiftly and silently, the smooth efficiency of his movements testifying that he had indeed completely recovered from the wound suffered back in the Texas Panhandle a couple of weeks earlier. He left his feet in a leap, soaring high in the air behind the man with the rifle. Ki twisted in midair, and his left leg snaked around the man's body so that his foot came up under the barrel of the Winchester and knocked it up to point at the sky. At the same time, Ki's body slammed into the man's back and drove him forward, knocking him completely out of the saddle. He pitched toward the ground with a startled yell. The rifle went spinning away, unfired.

Ki snapped a foot into the back of the man's head as he landed lithely on the ground. The impact smashed the man's face into the dirt, stunning him but not doing any permanent damage. Ki reached down to pluck the man's six-gun from its holster. Then he grasped the man's shoulder and rolled him over onto his back.

"Tell us," said Ki as he knelt next to the man, eared back the pistol's hammer, and placed the muzzle right under his nose, "what we will find in Zamora."

The man was still groggy and didn't seem to understand what was going on at first, but then his eyes widened in fear and crossed a little as he tried to look down at the barrel of the gun.

"It . . . it's a t-town f-full of . . . of outlaws!" stammered the man. "F-fellas come there . . . and pay to b-be s-safe from the l-law!"

Jessie and Scott looked at each other and nodded at this confirmation of their theory. Ki kept his attention focused on the prisoner.

"Who is in charge there?" he asked.

The man opened his mouth, but before he could say anything, hoofbeats sounded somewhere close by, a lot of them. And they were coming closer in a hurry.

"Blast it!" said Jessie. "He must have signaled for help somehow after he spotted us!"

Ki reached inside the prisoner's shirt pocket and pulled out a small mirror. "With this, almost certainly."

"Get him on his feet, and let's get out of here," ordered Jessie. "We've got more questions to ask him."

Ki straightened and started to lift the man to his feet, but for once even the warrior was taken by surprise. Fear and desperation gave the prisoner enough speed and strength to enable him to slam an elbow into Ki's belly, staggering him for a second. The man grabbed hold of his gun and began trying to wrestle it out of Ki's grip.

That was an effort that was doomed to failure. But the man succeeded in wrenching the barrel around and getting his finger on the trigger. The gun roared.

Unfortunately, the barrel was pointed down between the two of them, and the bullet ripped into the man's groin. He screamed as the slug tore through the lowest part of his guts. Ki let go of him, allowing him to double over and collapse as blood flooded from the wound and soaked the man's trousers.

"Come on!" snapped Jessie as she wheeled her horse. From the sound of the hoofbeats there were a lot of riders coming, and she and Ki and Scott couldn't fight a large group. Besides, it had been their hope that they could slip into Zamora undetected and find out what was going on.

Scott was right beside her as she kicked her horse into a gallop. Ki faded back into the trees, intent on reaching his own mount. They could rendezvous later, once they had given their pursuers the slip.

But as Jessie and Scott raced back up the trail, they suddenly heard still more hoofbeats, and as Scott exclaimed, "Damn it!" a second group of riders boiled into view ahead of them. They were caught between two forces now.

Jessie reined in and reached for her rifle. "We'll have to make a fight of it!" she said.

"Fine by me!" responded Scott. He pulled his own Winchester from its saddle boot.

The riders in front of them raced toward them. The ones behind were in sight now, closing in rapidly. With her hands taut on the stock and breech of the rifle, Jessie waited for the shooting to start. She and Scott might not be able to get away, but they would do some damage before they went down, she vowed to herself. And once again, she felt a strong pang of regret for getting Rance Scott involved in this. It wasn't his fight, but from the looks of things, he was going to pay the ultimate price anyway.

But as the two groups of outlaws closed in, they didn't fire. Jessie saw that there were eight men in front of them and six behind. Not good odds, but as long as the bullets weren't flying, they might have a chance.

"Back the other way!" she called to Scott as she jerked her horse around yet again. "We're going to bust through them!"

Scott followed her lead. They galloped straight toward the smaller group of riders, who looked shocked that their quarry would try such a thing. Jessie heard one of the men shout to the others, "Don't shoot! The Empress wants them alive, especially the woman!"

The Empress! Who in blazes was the Empress?

There was no time to ponder that question now. The rifle in Jessie's fists blazed shots at the men. She was aiming high, loathe to shoot them when they were holding their fire, but she hoped the bullets came close enough to make them turn aside and give her and Scott room to get past them. Beside her, Scott followed suit, triggering several rounds.

The maneuver didn't work. The men closed ranks instead of scattering, and Jessie gave voice to an involuntary cry of alarm as one of their horses slammed into her mount. She felt the animal stagger underneath her and struggle to keep its feet. The horse stayed upright, but Jessie didn't. Somebody tackled her, knocking her out of the saddle and dumping her unceremoniously on the ground. She landed hard enough so that all the air was driven out of her lungs, leaving her gasping for breath.

She wouldn't have been able to fight back anyway. Although she was a match physically for most men and could even hold her own in a fight against two of them, she was swarmed under now. Three or four men held her down, pinning her to the ground. A few yards away, Rance Scott had been knocked off his horse, too, and was suffering a similar fate. The riders from the other group arrived and pitched in, and the sheer weight of numbers meant that Jessie and Scott had no chance of battling their way free.

The scuffle was short-lived. Then one of the outlaws stood up and ordered, "Tie 'em up, and do a damned good job of it. I don't know who this fella is, but the woman's Jessica Starbuck, and she's supposed to be mighty tricky."

"Who are you?" gasped Jessie from the ground. "Why are you doing this? Why did you attack us?"

"You know damned well why," replied the owlhoot who seemed to be the boss of this bunch. "You were on your way to Zamora, right? Well, you're gonna get what you wanted, because that's where we're takin' you, soon as we've got you trussed up so you can't get into any mischief."

Another man prodded Scott in the ribs with a boot. "Who's this hombre? I thought the woman traveled with a Chinaman."

"I told you I don't know who he is," said the leader,

"but the rumors I've heard say that the Chinaman got himself killed back in Texas. Reckon Miss Starbuck's got herself a new partner."

Hope sprang to life inside Jessie's breast. They didn't know that Ki was still alive and on the loose somewhere in the vicinity. She looked at Rance Scott. He met her gaze squarely, and she hoped he understood that she wanted him to keep quiet about Ki. The only one of the outlaws who had seen the half-American, half-Japanese warrior had been the first one they encountered, and he was dead. Just before she was knocked off her horse, Jessie had caught a glimpse of his body lying beside the trail in the large pool of blood that had come from the wound in his abdomen. Nobody could lose that much blood and still be alive.

So maybe this wasn't all bad, she told herself. As the boss outlaw had pointed out, they were being taken to Zamora, which was where they had wanted to go all along. And they had a secret weapon in the person of Ki. Jessie was confident that he had seen them being taken prisoner. He would follow along, his characteristic stealth making him almost impossible to spot, and when the time was right he would strike and try to free Jessie and Scott.

The showdown she had been seeking for weeks was coming, thought Jessie. And with it, perhaps, the revelation of the identity of this mysterious Empress.

Chapter 20

Longarm took a cheroot from his pocket, put it in his mouth, and used a lucifer to set fire to the gasper as he strolled, apparently nonchalantly, toward one of Zamora's saloons. Despite his casual appearance, inside he was a roiling mass of thoughts and emotions. Of all the things he might have expected to find in this newly reborn ghost town, a relative of the late Herzog von Blöde would have been mighty low on the list.

Several years earlier, Jessie Starbuck had been involved in a lengthy, violent war against the worldwide crime cartel that had been responsible for the murder of her father. That struggle had been responsible for Longarm and Jessie meeting in the first place, and on nearly a dozen occasions after that he had been drawn into the epic, bloody conflict.

The cartel had been headed by five men, five criminal masterminds from different countries. But its founder, the senior member of that axis of evil, had been the Prussian,

Herzog von Blöde. Von Blöde was dead now and had been for quite some time. Like the other leaders of the cartel, he had been killed in the final showdown with Jessica Starbuck. Longarm had been there, too, and had seen von Blöde die.

Obviously, though, that hadn't been the end of the evil genius's bloodline. Somebody had finally taken up where old Herzog had left off. Longarm found himself wondering if the establishment of Zamora was the first step in setting up a new cartel—or if the conspiracy was already underway and this town full of outlaws was just part of it.

Regardless of the answer, he knew now that he had to get out of Zamora and fetch some help. Once the Justice Department knew about the von Blöde connection, there was no question that senior officials could persuade the War Department to send in the army. The cartel had represented a serious threat not only to the United States government but also to other governments around the world. No one wanted to be faced with such a menace again.

Longarm had a feeling that if he tried to get on his horse and ride out immediately, though, he would be stopped and possibly killed. He had to maintain his pose as the bank robber called Parker for a little while, at least.

To that end, he went into the Oasis Saloon for a drink.

This was one of the buildings where quite a bit of reconstruction already had taken place. The smell of freshly sawn lumber still hung in the air, along with the usual saloon smells of beer and whiskey and tobacco. A hardwood bar with a somewhat tarnished brass rail along the bottom ran down the right side of the room. Longarm walked over to it, aware that he was the object of some scrutiny from the men already in the saloon. Nobody yelled out that he was a lawman, though, and as he ran his eyes quickly over the crowd, he didn't see any familiar faces. He relaxed, but only slightly. This moment's respite could be over without any warning.

A balding bartender with a prominent Adam's apple came over to greet Longarm. "What can I get you, mister?" he asked.

"You wouldn't happen to have any Maryland rye, would you?"

"Tom Moore be all right?"

Longarm smiled. "Better than all right, old son."

The bartender took a bottle off the back bar and poured the drink, slid it across the hardwood with a glass of water on the side. The shot glass and the water glass both looked surprisingly clean, and the label on the bottle was the proper one. Of course, just because the label was right didn't mean that what was inside the bottle was what it purported to be. Longarm had run into instances of the worst sort of panther piss being poured into bottles that had originally contained fine liquor.

So he was a little cautious as he took a sip. That worry proved unfounded. The drink was both smooth and fiery, undoubtedly the real thing. The warmth it imparted to Longarm's belly was genuine, too. Longarm tossed back the rest of the rye and sighed in satisfaction as he placed the empty glass on the bar.

"Another?" asked the bartender.

"Maybe in a bit," Longarm told him. "I'm all right for now."

He leaned his left elbow on the bar and sipped the water. He could see most of the room in the big mirror over the back bar, so he wasn't surprised when a woman sidled up beside him and said, "Hello." He had seen her coming.

Longarm turned his head and nodded pleasantly to her. "Howdy, ma'am," he drawled.

"My name is Sally." She had some years on her, probably around thirty of them, but although her beauty was somewhat faded, it was still beauty. Ash-blond hair fell around her face and shoulders. She wore a low-cut gown that revealed a goodly portion of hard little breasts. Her hips were slender almost to the point of being nonexistent. She would make for a bit of a bony ride, but Longarm could tell there was a lot of strength in those slender arms and legs. She could probably wrap them around a man pretty skillfully.

Unfortunately, Longarm didn't really have time to be playing slap-and-tickle with any whore, and that on top of the fact that he really preferred his women with a little more meat on their bones led him to say, "I'm pleased to make your acquaintance, Sally, but I really ain't in much of a mood for company right now."

She leaned against him so that one of her breasts pressed into his arm. "That's a real shame, mister, because I'm mighty good company. What's your name?"

"Parker," said Longarm.

"That's it, just Parker?"

He nodded. "Just Parker."

"Well, that's not very friendly. You could at least offer to buy a girl a drink." She bit her bottom lip suddenly and then said, "No, wait, damn it. I forgot I'm not supposed to say things like that anymore. This place doesn't work the same way that saloons in other towns do."

"Because the hombres who come to Zamora pay up front for the right to be here, then don't have to pay for everything else as they go along, right?"

"Yeah. Drinks are free, food is free, and so are the

pokes." She gave him what was intended to be a sultry smile. "So you don't have any excuse for not takin' me upstairs and givin' me a good ride, cowboy."

She obviously liked his looks, and Longarm saw that she wasn't going to take no for an answer. He was about to decide that he was going to have to accommodate her, whether he really wanted to or not, when a sudden commotion broke out in the street outside the saloon. Longarm heard several excited shouts.

"Maybe in a few minutes," he told Sally. "I want to see what's going on out there." He wasn't the only one; several men in the saloon were headed for the batwings. Hombres on the dodge from the law soon learned to be cautious and not ignore any potential warning signs of trouble.

Sally sighed and grimaced disappointedly. "All right, but don't you forget about me, Parker," she said.

Longarm flashed a grin at her. "I could never do that," he said.

He joined the exodus from the saloon, pushing through the batwings and stepping out onto the porch that ran along the front of the building. He saw a large group of riders making their way along the street toward the mansion that rose at the far end. Longarm had already taken note of that big fancy house and figured that was where the Empress lived. If she was related to Herzog von Blöde, that made sense. Nothing but the best had ever been good enough for old Herzog.

Longarm stood there at the porch railing with the cheroot clamped between his teeth and watched as the group of riders approached. There were more than a dozen men on horseback, and they were clustered around a couple of riders in the center. Those two were prisoners, Longarm realized, and the men surrounding them were taking no chances on them getting away. He hadn't quite been able to get a good look at the two captives yet . . .

But then, as the group moved past the Oasis, a gap appeared in the ring of heavily armed outlaws, opening for a moment and then closing again almost as quickly.

And that was long enough for the big lawman to see the faces of the two prisoners. One of them was a man in range clothes who Longarm had never seen before.

But the other captive was a woman, and as Longarm saw her beautiful face and the thick, reddish-gold hair that tumbled around her shoulders, he got the second huge surprise of this eventful day. This one was even more shocking than the revelation of the Empress's identity.

The second prisoner was Jessie Starbuck!

Jessie didn't bother asking questions of the men who had taken her and Rance Scott captive. She figured she would get the answers to most, if not all, of her questions once they reached Zamora.

They rode through a narrow, twisting, steep-sided canyon that was guarded by three riflemen crouched behind some boulders on a ledge, and then came out at the head of the small, surprisingly verdant valley where the settlement was located. There was no chance to get away as the group of riders wound its way down the trail into the valley; their captors were much too careful for that. Besides, Jessie didn't want to get away.

She wasn't surprised that their arrival in Zamora created quite a stir. It was obvious that she and Scott were prisoners, and the sort of men who populated this place would be curious about their identities. Hard-faced gents of all shapes and sizes emerged from the various saloons and brothels and hash houses as the newcomers rode past. Jessie didn't pay much attention to them. She kept her gaze focused straight ahead.

But then something tickled her instincts and made her frown. She glanced to the side, toward a momentary gap in the ring of gunmen surrounding her and Scott, but her reaction came too late. The outlaws had closed ranks again, and Jessie couldn't get a good look at the men standing in front of the buildings, watching the riders.

She didn't understand what had just happened. It was almost like someone had made a sort of connection with her, a link born of familiarity and surprise. If Ki had been here, he would have said that all people are connected in one way or another, but that in some the connection is strong enough to be felt like a physical entity.

But Ki wasn't here—or if he was, Jessie hadn't seen him. It was highly likely he was somewhere nearby, though, waiting for the proper moment to strike.

What could one man do against a whole town full of outlaws, though? Jessie wasn't sure, but if she was going to bet on anyone in a perilous situation like that, it would have been Ki.

A fair-haired, bespectacled man with the look of a bank teller came out of one of the buildings and called to the leader of the outlaws, "Is that who I think it is, Sloan?"

"It's her, all right," replied the man. "I'm taking her straight to the Empress, Mayor."

The mayor—an outlaw town had a mayor? thought Jessie—nodded and said, "Exactly right. She's been waiting a long time for this."

That comment just deepened Jessie's puzzlement.

When the riders came to the wrought-iron fence that

formed a boundary around the well-kept lawn, they dismounted and hauled Jessie and Scott out of their saddles. The two of them were shoved ahead roughly but not brutally, through a gate and up a flagstone path to the big house's impressive entrance.

Their arrival was expected. A tall, grim-faced man in butler's livery opened the door and ushered in Jessie, Scott, the outlaw called Sloan, and a couple more of the gunmen. The other men remained outside. Jessie supposed they thought a few men were enough to handle the two prisoners. She spotted the butt of a gun under the cutaway coat of the butler, and from the look on his lantern-jawed face, he wouldn't hesitate to use it if he needed to.

In a low voice, she said to Scott, "I'm sorry about getting you into this, Rance."

"Don't be," he said. "It was my choice to come along."

"Silence," snapped the butler. "Follow me."

He led the way along a hall to a pair of double doors that opened into a big, airy, well-lighted room. A woman—the Empress—stood there in front of a large fireplace, next to a grand piano, clearly waiting for them. Jessie was surprised to see how young and beautiful she was. She seemed to be calm, but as she looked at the two prisoners, her breasts began to rise and fall more rapidly and her hands clenched into fists, as if she were in the grip of an almost overpowering emotion.

The butler stepped forward and announced formally, "Miss Jessica Starbuck and her companion." He glanced back over his shoulder at them. "I am afraid that I do not know the man's name, Empress."

"That's all right, Conrad," she said. "Thank you." She looked past Jessie and Scott at the three gunmen. "And thank you as well to you and your men, Mr. Sloan. Was anyone injured?"

"Nelson's dead," said Sloan bluntly. "He'd been shot before me and the boys got there."

The imperturbable expression on the Empress's face didn't change, even though she murmured, "I'm sorry to hear that. But there is always a price to be paid, and too often the currency is blood and human suffering."

Jessie couldn't help but speak up. She said, "That's an odd sentiment coming from a woman who offers sanctuary to an entire town full of murderers and thieves."

A faint smile touched the Empress's lips. "The indomitable Starbuck spirit," she said. "My father mentioned it to me, and I see now that it truly exists."

Jessie tried not to show the surprise she felt. Who *was* this woman? Tautly, she asked, "Your father?"

"Herzog von Blöde."

Jessie's nostrils flared and she couldn't help but draw in a deep, stunned breath. She said, "You . . . you're . . ." She was too shocked to finish the thought.

"Katerina von Blöde," supplied the young woman. "Heir to my father's legacy and the new leader of the cartel."

Jessie's head spun. This wasn't possible, she told herself. Herzog von Blöde was dead and the cartel he had headed was destroyed. She and Ki and Longarm had seen to that. It was impossible that that hideous circle of evil was rising again, phoenixlike.

And yet the proof was right here in front of her, living proof in the form of this so-called Empress, Katerina von Blöde. Establishing a town where criminals could hide out from the law—for a high price—was exactly the sort of thing that the cartel would have done in those bad old days when Jessie was at war with them.

"I see that you are surprised," said Katerina. "You thought that my father and everything he had worked for were gone forever, didn't you, Miss Starbuck? Well, my father may be gone, thanks to you, but as you saw if you looked around when you rode in, his legacy lives on."

"A legacy of hatred and lawlessness," said Jessie.

Katerina shrugged. "Your words cannot hurt me. You've already hurt me more than you can ever know by taking my father away from me."

"The way your father took mine away from me?"

"Alex Starbuck was a fool," said Katerina, her lips tightening. "He could have been one of the richest, most powerful men in the world, if only he had cooperated with my father and his friends."

"Alex Starbuck never would have done that," shot back Jessie. "He never would have sunk to that level . . . the level of snakes like the cartel."

Katerina gave an abrupt shake of her head. "Enough! I'll not stand here and trade insults with you, Miss Starbuck. It is enough for both of us to know that you are my prisoner, and that you will never leave Zamora alive." She smiled again. "Just as I planned when I made arrangements to have that prize bull of yours stolen."

"Shorty!" exclaimed Jessie. "You've got him here?"

"Don't worry, the animal is fine. I have a herd of cattle in the hills near here, to provide a steady supply of beef for the town, and your bull is living a very contented and pampered life there, grazing and servicing the cows. I would not try to strike back at you by harming him."

"You knew I'd track down the men who stole him," said Jessie. "You knew the trail would lead here."

"Of course. I heard my father speak many times of what a dogged antagonist you were."

Jessie reached inside her vest pocket. She heard Sloan and the other outlaws stir behind her and knew they had probably put their hands on their guns, just in case.

She drew out the coin she had found in the alley in Cottonwood. "Did you order one of your men to leave this behind as a clue?"

"Ah, the taler!" said Katerina. "So that's what happened to it." She shook her head. "No, I had no idea you had that coin, Miss Starbuck. It was simply luck that placed it in your hands. But if it hadn't led you here, I'm sure something else would have. You see, I have confidence in your abilities. That's why I'm going to take no chances with you." She looked at the butler. "Conrad, see to it that they're locked up."

The man nodded and said, "*Jawohl*, Empress."

"Where does that come from?" Jessie asked quickly. "That 'Empress' business, I mean."

"Zamora is just the beginning of the cartel's new empire," said Katerina, smiling again. "What else would you call a woman who rules an empire?"

"In your case," said Jessie, "insane."

Katerina's smile disappeared as her breath hissed between her teeth. She jerked her head at Conrad. "Take them away."

The butler drew the revolver from under his coat. He and Sloan and the other outlaws prodded Jessie and Scott out of the room at gunpoint. Conrad took them to a door that opened onto a steep, narrow staircase. Darkness lay thickly at the bottom.

"Down there," he said.

Jessie and Scott had no choice but to descend the

stairs. Conrad and the others followed them. The butler had lit a small lantern, and its feeble glow revealed a square, stone-walled chamber. On one side of the room was a narrow opening closed off by a gate of iron bars. It looked much too sturdy to budge.

"All right," said Conrad, "take your clothes off."

Scott finally spoke up, saying angrily, "Now wait just a cotton-pickin' minute—"

Conrad raised his pistol and pointed it between Scott's eyes. "Do as you are told. The Empress does not really care if you are kept alive or not, you fool."

"Do as he says, Rance," said Jessie with a sigh as she reached for the buttons of her shirt. "I don't care. There are a lot worse things than being naked."

Conrad smiled coldly. "Such as being dead. Very wise, Miss Starbuck."

Jessie and Scott stripped off their garments. Jessie tamped down the feelings of anger and humiliation that went through her when she felt the leering gazes of the outlaws playing over her body. She had to be patient, she told herself. Ki was still on the loose somewhere. He would find a way to turn the tables on the Empress.

In the meantime, she and Scott had to stay alive somehow, any way they could. One of the outlaws gathered up their clothes, and then all four of the men began backing up the stairs, their guns still drawn. Conrad took the lantern with him, and with every step he took, the darkness drew in closer around the prisoners.

"Enjoy your captivity," he told them. "No one knows how long it may last . . . no one except the Empress."

With that, he stepped out the door at the top of the stairs and closed it behind him, shutting off the light completely and leaving Jessie and Scott in total darkness.

They heard not only the metallic *click* of a heavy padlock being snapped shut, but also the thud as a thick bar was lowered on the other side of the door. It would take a battering ram to get through there, and at the moment, Jessie and Scott just didn't have one.

"Oh, Rance—" she began.

"Don't say it," he broke in. "Don't apologize for getting me mixed up in this, Jessie. I knew what I was doing. I knew how likely it was that we'd wind up in danger. I don't care. I wanted to be with you."

She moved closer to the sound of his voice. "Thank you, Rance," she said as she reached out in the darkness. Her fingers touched smooth, muscular flesh. "You know, underground like this, with these thick stone walls and us with no clothes, it's going to get a mite chilly in here. We're probably going to have to huddle together for warmth."

"Are you suggestin' we might as well start now? Huddling, that is."

"That's exactly what I'm suggesting," said Jessie.

Chapter 21

Nick Darrow pushed past Conrad as the butler/gunman started to announce him. He was too upset to wait. "I want to talk to you," he said to the Empress.

Katerina sat in one of the comfortable armchairs near the fireplace, an open book in her lap. She looked up calmly at Darrow and then switched her gaze to Conrad, who had come up behind the outlaw.

"No, don't kill him," she ordered. "He may yet prove useful to me."

Conrad shrugged and slipped his gun back under his coat in its shoulder holster. Darrow knew the Prussian son of a bitch still wanted to shoot him. That desire was evident on Conrad's face. But as always, the man followed his Empress's orders.

"Now," said Katerina, "what is it you want of me, Mr. Darrow?"

"Is it true what I heard?"

"I don't know. What did you hear?"

"That Jessica Starbuck is here in Zamora," said Darrow.

Katerina nodded. "It's true. In fact, she is right here in this house."

Darrow tensed even more and glanced around the big room, as if he thought that the Starbuck woman was somehow going to step out of hiding and start shooting at him.

"But she is locked up safely in an underground chamber," continued Katerina. "She and her cowboy friend represent no threat to anyone."

"That may be what you want to believe," said Darrow, "but I ain't convinced. Damn it, I never thought she'd follow us all the way here."

"On the contrary, I always believed that she would. That's why I arranged things as I did."

It took Darrow a few seconds to figure out what the Empress meant by that. When he did, a flash of anger shot through him.

"You used us!" he accused. "You didn't really want that bull. It was just the bait in a trap for Jessica Starbuck. And in a way, so were me and my boys!"

Katerina inclined her head in agreement. "You were well-paid bait," she pointed out. "And it's intelligent of you to have figured it out so quickly. I had a feeling I might be able to make further use of you, Mr. Darrow."

The compliment took the wind out of some of his anger. He still found Katerina to be very compelling, and it was hard to stay mad at such a beautiful woman.

Still, there were some things he couldn't completely forget. "I lost a couple of men," he said. "Pete Malloy and Sonny Montoya were good partners."

"I regret your loss. However, you're engaged in a dangerous business, Mr. Darrow. You know and accept that, and so do the men who ride with you."

He shrugged. "Yeah, I guess."

Katerina smiled and asked, "Would you like to see Miss Starbuck? I can have her brought up here."

"No thanks," said Darrow with a shake of his head. "You can leave her locked up from now on, as far as I'm concerned."

"Only until I decide how exactly I want to take my vengeance on her." Though she was still smiling, Katerina's blue eyes glittered like ice.

"You must really have a score to settle with her."

"The biggest score of all. She was responsible for the death of my father. Her and that assistant of hers, and an American lawman named Long. I'll deal with him next."

Her comment prompted a thought. Darrow asked, "What about that Chinaman?"

"You mean Ki? He's not Chinese."

"Well, what about him?" persisted Darrow. "You didn't say anything about having him locked up in the basement."

Katerina shook her head. "He wasn't with Miss Starbuck when she and her companion were captured. Considering how seldom they've been apart in the past, I have to wonder if something happened to him."

"I think he's dead," declared Darrow. "He was shot in the head when we had that run-in with them down in Texas."

"You know this for a fact?"

Darrow grinned savagely. "I pulled the trigger, saw the muzzle flash light up his face, and saw him go down. That's fact enough for me."

"I suppose even if he was just wounded, she could have been so anxious to follow you and your men that she left him behind," mused Katerina.

"I wouldn't worry too much about him," said Darrow. "He was pretty good at that fancy Chink fighting, but he wouldn't be any real match for all the tough hombres you've got around here."

"No, I suppose not. Would you like a drink?"

The offer took Darrow a little by surprise, but he didn't hesitate in accepting it. "Sure." Any reason that gave him an excuse to spend more time with the Empress was welcome. Since coming to Zamora, he had taken the edge off with several of the local whores, but he still felt a fierce tightening in his guts when he looked at Katerina. Only one thing would ever fully relieve that feeling, and that would be to get her under him, legs spread and screaming with pleasure while he pounded it to her. And that would be just the beginning. . . .

She thought she was pretty smart, the way she pulled everybody's strings and got what she wanted. But she might be too smart for her own good. What she really needed around here was a man to run things, to put her in her place and turn Zamora into a real outlaw empire.

Nick Darrow didn't see any reason in the world why he couldn't be that man.

Brad Corrigan stirred sleepily. When he tried to force his eyes open, his head pounded miserably, so he closed them again and just lay there, trying not to move. Even though the liquor was free—sort of—he wasn't sure why he had tried to drink so much. He told himself he was going to have to settle down and stop all this carousing.

In the week or so that he and Tom had been here in Zamora, Brad had guzzled more whiskey, eaten more fine food, and bedded more gals than he had the rest of his life put together. And all it had gotten him was a pounding head, an uncomfortably stuffed gut, and a talleywhacker that was so worn out it didn't even want to stand up and do its job anymore. Why, just earlier today, he'd been trying to put it to a chubby little redheaded whore named Lily, and damned if he wasn't able to do it, no matter how hard she tried to work him up with her fingers and her mouth. *That* had sure as blazes never happened before. And Brad didn't like it, not one little bit.

Lily had finally dozed off beside him as they lay in the bed in a room above the saloon where she worked. Brad felt her warmth beside him now. He risked moving a hand and found one of her nice plump tits. She made a pleased sound in her sleep as he began to squeeze it. She shifted her hips, and that brought her broad rump against Brad's groin.

Well, son of a bitch, he thought. Obviously, he'd just needed to rest up a mite, because he was getting hard again. He nudged the head of his shaft between the cheeks of her ass.

A moment later, Lily said sleepily, "Brad, what are you . . . you can't. That's not the right—Oh, Lord! Brad, don't . . . don't . . . don't stop now, damn you!" And then, in a few minutes when he was finished, she sighed and said, "What a way for a girl to wake up." She rolled over to face him. "See, I told you that you just needed the right encouragement."

Brad felt vaguely embarrassed by what he'd just done. But it had felt mighty good, so he just smiled and said sort of sheepishly, "Yeah, I guess so."

His headache was gone now, which surprised him. He wouldn't have thought that putting his dick up a whore's ass would cure a headache. But whatever worked, he supposed. He wondered where Tom was.

He sat up and swung his legs off the bed. Lily reached out and touched his bare hip. "Where you goin', honey?"

"Oh, I thought I'd get dressed, maybe go downstairs and play a little poker."

Lily giggled. "I like playing stud poker. Stud-poke-her, get it?"

Brad got it, but he was getting a little tired of her now that he was done. He pulled on his trousers and reached for his shirt.

"Will I be seeing you again later?" she asked, with a wheedling tone in her voice.

"Sure," he lied.

"Good. You're the best fella I've ever had, Brad."

Sure, like he was going to believe that. He stepped over to the window and looked out in idle curiosity as he started to button his shirt.

Then he stiffened and exclaimed, "Shit!"

Lily sat up in bed, her heavy breasts wobbling, and asked, "What is it, darlin'? Something wrong?"

Brad leaned closer to the glass and stared at the man he saw walking along on the opposite side of the street. The hombre was dressed more roughly and had a lot of beard stubble on his face, but Brad recognized the tall, rangy form and the deeply tanned face. It was that bastard from Arizona, the one who had been on the stage and then chased them after the robbery, the one who had killed Asa and Logan. If he had followed them all the way here to Zamora, there was only one explanation that made sense.

The son of a bitch was a lawman!

Brad knew he had to find Tom and warn him as quickly as he could. He stomped into his boots, grabbed his hat, and rushed out of the room, leaving the door open behind him. He ignored Lily when she called his name.

And his headache was back, damn it. It pounded in his head like an imp from hell with a ball-peen hammer.

Longarm was deep in thought as he walked down the street toward the building where he had met Mayor Abernathy earlier in the day. His horse was still tied up at the hitch rack in front of that building. Yellowstone hadn't moved it to the livery stable, so Longarm assumed taking care of that chore was up to him.

Of course, he might not be in Zamora long enough to have to worry about that.

He had planned to take his time about trying to get away and wait for the right moment to slip out of the outlaw haven. The sight of Jessie Starbuck had changed all that, though.

Longarm had no idea what Jessie was doing here in Zamora. He hadn't seen her or talked to her in quite some time, but as far as he had known, she was down in Texas on her Circle Star Ranch, enjoying some well-deserved peaceful days after all the trouble that had plagued her over the years.

He hadn't recognized the fella who was with her, either. He knew Jessie had lots of men friends and had never held that against her. They enjoyed romping with one another whenever they got together, but it wasn't like either had any strings on the other. And despite the fact that the hombre had been a prisoner, just like Jessie, there was still plenty of fire in his eye. Longarm had to like that about him.

And where in blazes was Ki? The warrior was never

far from Jessie. The fact that he hadn't been with her when she was brought into Zamora didn't bode well. Ki might be hurt—or worse.

All in all, it was a sorry situation Longarm was faced with. He had watched, apparently only idly curious, as Jessie and her fellow prisoner were taken up the street and into that mansion. Longarm figured that was where the Empress lived.

Did Katerina von Blöde know who Jessie was? Longarm figured that was certainly possible. And if the Empress recognized Jessie as being one of the folks responsible for Herzog von Blöde's death, would she want revenge?

Longarm rolled an unlit cheroot from one side of his mouth to the other and chewed on it viciously. He sensed that there was still more going on here than he had realized previously. Maybe the Empress had set some sort of trap for Jessie.

Regardless of how it had all come about, the problem remained the same. Longarm had to get Jessie and her friend away from the Empress and out of that mansion, then they all had to give the outlaws the slip and get out of Zamora, so that Longarm could bring back the army and smash this nest full of vipers.

He was busy trying to figure out a way to do that when a man stepped out of a café door in front of him, turned toward him, stopped short, said, "Damn it!" and clawed for the gun on his hip.

Longarm didn't know who the hombre was, but the man sure as hell recognized *him*.

And if he yelled out that Longarm was a lawman, that would probably be the end of it, then and there.

Options flashed through Longarm's brain with the

speed of thought. He considered bounding forward along the boardwalk and trying to coldcock the son of a bitch to shut his mouth. But he realized instantly that he was too far away to do that. The fella would just shoot him before he got there. And it wasn't a permanent solution, anyway. There was only one thing he could do.

Longarm slapped leather.

His hand flashed across his body and palmed out the Colt from the cross-draw rig. He started his move after the other man already had his iron a couple of inches out of leather. Longarm closed that gap in less than the blink of an eye, though, his muscles moving in swift, efficient coordination with his eyes. The barrel of his gun came level, and flame geysered from the muzzle a shaved heartbeat ahead of the blast from the other man's gun. The slug drove into the outlaw's chest, lifting him up and back and slamming him down to the planks of the board-walk. He had managed to pull the trigger, but only after he was falling, so that the bullet went up harmlessly into the wooden awning over the walk.

The pair of shots drew plenty of attention. Most of the men on the street ducked for cover, not knowing how long the fracas was going to go on and not wanting to get hit by a stray slug. But others dashed toward the sound of trouble instead. Longarm had noticed them around town before, hard-faced gents in dark suits and bowler hats, carrying shotguns. They were the Empress's police force, he figured, and that idea was confirmed when several of the greener-wielding hombres ran up and leveled the scatterguns at him. "Put the gun down!" yelled one of them in a European accent.

The last thing Longarm wanted to do was to draw more attention to himself, but it was too late to worry about that now. He bent down and placed his Colt on the boardwalk at his feet. As he straightened, he said, "Take it easy, old son. This was a private fight."

"Killing is not allowed in Zamora."

"Then you hadn't ought to let folks carry guns around," said Longarm. Keeping his hands in plain sight because he didn't want any of the fingers on those shotgun triggers to get itchy, he gestured toward the man he had just killed and said, "Him and me were old enemies. Had a falling-out some years ago over the loot from a job we pulled together. He swore the next time he saw me that he'd kill me. He tried, I reckon. But I didn't know he was here, and I damn sure didn't start this fight. Just ask anybody."

The ruse had come to him out of desperation, but he knew it had a chance of working. The dead man sure as hell couldn't contradict the yarn Longarm had just spun. Now, if nobody else around here had known the fella too well—

"Tom! Oh, my God! Tom!"

Well, hell, thought Longarm. That probably tore it.

Sure enough, a young man with a stricken look on his face dashed up and fell on his knees next to the corpse. Tears welled from his eyes and rolled down his face. "Damn it, Tom," he sobbed. "I was comin' to warn you."

The spokesman for the ginks in the bowler hats said sharply, "Boy, do you know this man? Did he speak the truth when he said that he and this other man had a private score to settle between them?"

The grieving youngster tore his gaze away from the dead man's face and looked up. "Private score, hell! That bastard already killed two more of my brothers down in Arizona, and now he's followed us here! I think he's a lawman!"

Yep. It was torn all to hell now.

The youngster twisted toward Longarm and reached for his gun. The bowler-hatted policeman, or whatever he was, tapped him hard on the point of the shoulder with the double barrels of the greener, making him yelp in pain and stop his draw before it got started.

"We will deal with this matter. Lawlessness is not permitted in Zamora."

Somehow the fella managed to say that with a straight face, as if he meant it. In an odd way, Longarm supposed he did.

The word *lawman* had drawn a lot of attention. Men crowded around, and most of them looked like they would be more than happy to draw their guns and fill Longarm full of lead. The bowler-hatted gents closed in around him, taking him prisoner but at the same time protecting him from the vigilante urges of Zamora's hardbitten citizens. The leader said, "You, boy, come along. We will take this man to the Empress and get to the bottom of this."

He had wanted to get into the Empress's mansion anyway, Longarm told himself—but this was hardly the way he had planned to go about it. Still, he might be able to turn the situation to his advantage. He couldn't give up hope.

Because he didn't have much of anything else left.

Ki waited, waited, motionless in the tree, scarcely breathing, until the man rode beneath him. Then he dropped, his legs scissoring around the outlaw's body, his arm snaking around the man's neck. As the impact drove the outlaw out of the saddle, Ki twisted and felt as much as heard the pop when the man's neck snapped. By the time they hit the ground, the outlaw was dead.

This was the third one Ki had killed this afternoon—and there was still some light left.

The sentries rode a broad circle around Zamora, their routes occasionally overlapping so that they could check in with each other. Ki had started out following one man, and he had been close enough during that man's brief meeting with another sentry to eavesdrop on their conversation and make sure they were part of the force guarding the outlaw town. He didn't want to kill anyone who happened to be riding innocently through these rugged mountains—as unlikely as that was to occur. Once he was certain, he had killed the first man, then gone after the second and disposed of him as well. Now he had found and gotten rid of yet another.

The cold-bloodedness of what he was doing didn't set all that well with him, but he didn't have any choice. From the moment he had seen Jessie and Rance Scott being captured and taken off to Zamora, Ki had known that he would have to go after them and free them. Their chances of escaping from the town and getting away from the pursuit that was sure to come after them would be increased greatly if there were no guards patrolling around the settlement. So he had set out to get rid of as many of them as he could before he ventured into Zamora after dark to find Jessie and Scott. Being a samurai was often a bloody-handed calling, but Ki could not help what he was.

He threw the dead man's pistol and rifle into the brush, dragged the body off the trail so it would be out of sight, took the saddle off the outlaw's horse, and shooed the animal away. It would have to fend for itself. Eventually it might return to the stable in town where it had come from, but by then Ki would either have succeeded in his mission—or he would be dead after suffering the ignominy of failure.

His keen ears suddenly heard the sound of more horses approaching. A group of sentries? He didn't know, but he faded back into the trees where he had left his own horse, determined to wait and find out. He might have to let the riders go on by unmolested, at least for now. He could kill several men in battle, but probably not without at least one of them getting off a shot. He couldn't afford gunfire; it might alert the other members of the outlaw patrol he hadn't caught up with yet.

Crouching unseen in the shadows beneath the trees, Ki watched as three men rode past about twenty yards away. One of them was a burly man in late middle age with a drooping walrus mustache. Ki saw with shock that he wore a badge pinned to his flannel shirt. Next to him was a younger man, also sporting a badge, and the third, to Ki's even greater surprise, wore the uniform of the United States Army.

What were a couple of lawmen and an army officer doing out here?

Before Ki could even think about the answer to that question, the snap of a branch behind him made him spin around. His hand darted inside his vest and came out with one of the *shuriken*, the deadly, razor-edged throwing stars. But instead of sending it spinning across the clearing behind him with a flick of his wrist, he froze because the white-bearded man who stood there pointing a rifle at him also had a lawman's badge pinned to his old buckskin vest.

"I'd 'preciate it if you'd just hold it, son," said the old-timer, "because I don't want to blow a hole in you, and I sure as hell don't want to die, neither."

Chapter 22

Longarm wasn't surprised that the Empress was pretty.
You sort of expected empresses to be good-looking. But
he was a mite taken aback by how young she was, probably not even twenty-five yet.

Her eyes were older than that, though. They were as
cold and hard as flint as she stared at him with a mixture
of surprise and hatred.

"This man," she said when she got her voice back,
"this man, Heinrich, is none other than Custis Long, the
deputy United States marshal of whom I have spoken in
the past."

The bowler-hatted gent who had prodded Longarm
into the big, parlorlike room with the barrels of a scattergun raised his eyebrows. "The man who was to be the
next target of your vengeance, Empress?"

"None other," she replied. She came closer but carefully stayed out of Longarm's reach. "I've seen photo-
graphs of him, and although his appearance is somewhat

different, this man is unmistakably him." Her chin lifted defiantly as she gazed at Longarm. "Do you know who I am, Marshal?"

"If I had to guess," said Longarm, "I'd say you're old Herzog von Blöde's daughter."

She stiffened even more. "You know me?" she asked in amazement. That look was replaced by one of fury. "You came here to assassinate me, as you and that Starbuck bitch killed my father?"

"Your father brought his fate down on his own head," said Longarm, figuring he couldn't make things any worse than they already were by speaking the truth. "Despite the fancy name and the big organization, he was nothing but an owlhoot, and he got what all owlhoots get in the end—justice."

The Empress stepped closer. Her hand flashed up and cracked across Longarm's face in a vicious slap. He had wanted to goad her into being careless, and it had worked. He started to grab her, thinking that he could use her as a hostage to get him and Jessie out of here—

Heinrich was too fast. The barrels of the greener slammed into the back of Longarm's head, dropping him to his knees as the Empress quickly stepped back out of reach again. As Longarm struggled to remain conscious, he heard the shotgun's twin hammers being eared back.

"No, Heinrich!" snapped the Empress. "Do not kill him! As much pleasure as it would give me to see Marshal Long's brains splattered all over the rug, fate has delivered him into my hands at the same time as Jessica Starbuck. There must be a special punishment for them both. Take him downstairs and put him with the other prisoners."

"*Jawohl*, Empress."

264

Rough hands seized Longarm and hauled him back to his feet. With his head spinning from the blow, he was marched out of the room where the Empress stood watching, her eyes blazing with hate.

As Jessie had expected, the huddling together for warmth had soon turned to something else. At this moment, Rance Scott was sitting with his back against the stone wall of their cell and Jessie was straddling his lap. His big shaft was buried deep inside her. She moved slowly, languidly, her hips flexing as she massaged his manhood with her inner muscles. The floor was sort of hard on her knees, and she figured his back was going to be bruised and scraped up a little before they were through, but neither of them really cared about the discomfort, though. All their senses were turned inward, reveling in the wonderful sensations produced by the slippery thrusting of his erect member inside her slick core.

This was actually the third time they had made love since they were locked up in this lightless chamber, and it was the best so far. Jessie wrapped her arms around Scott's neck as she rode him, and her lips found his in the darkness. The kiss they shared was both tender and passionate. Jessie's hips began moving harder, but the pace remained slow and deliberate. When the throbbing of Scott's climax filled her, she tumbled over the brink, too, giving in to the rippling waves of ecstasy that coursed through her.

They had barely caught their breath after the shared culmination when Jessie heard the sound of the bar being lifted and a key rattling in the big padlock on the door at the head of the stairs.

Jessie dismounted quickly from Scott and was sitting

beside him when the door opened and light from above slanted down into the underground chamber. After several hours of darkness, the sudden glare was blinding and almost painful. Jessie slitted her eyes until they began to adjust.

She saw several sets of legs descending the wooden stairs, and the terrible thought that Ki might have been captured crossed her mind. But not in a million years was she expecting to see the person who actually appeared at the bottom of the stairs, being forced down them at gunpoint by Heinrich, Conrad, and a couple more of Katerina von Blöde's henchmen.

"Longarm!" cried Jessie as she leaped to her feet.

Without thinking about what she was doing or the fact that she was stark naked, she threw herself into his arms and hugged him tightly. He patted her back and murmured, "Howdy, Jessie. Wish we could've got together under better circumstances."

"What a touching reunion," said Heinrich with a sneer. "Let go of her, Long."

"Why don't you go to hell?" suggested Longarm.

Heinrich turned his shotgun around and drove the butt of the weapon into the small of Longarm's back. The blow staggered Longarm and made him grunt in pain. Jessie let go of him and stepped back quickly, so Heinrich wouldn't have an excuse to hit him again.

"Get your clothes off, like the other prisoners," commanded Conrad.

Longarm straightened, still grimacing from the pain, and cast a baleful glance at the Empress's men. But he complied with the order and reached for the buttons of his shirt.

Rance Scott had stood up, too. Jessie saw the way he

looked at Heinrich, Conrad, and the other outlaws. She laid a hand on his arm and gave him a tiny shake of her head. The odds against them were still too high. If Scott tried to jump them now, he would just get himself killed. He meant nothing to Katerina von Blöde. If the guards were forced to kill him, she wouldn't mind.

Longarm stripped down to his skin. One of the men gathered his clothes and retreated up the stairs. As they had earlier when Jessie and Scott were placed in this cell, the Empress's men backed up the stairs, keeping their guns trained on the prisoners until the heavy door slammed shut and the padlock and bar were put back in place.

"Well," said Longarm in the stygian gloom, "with it dark like this, at least it ain't quite as embarrassing to be standing around as naked as jaybirds."

Jessie laughed. "I doubt if you've ever been really embarrassed in your life, Custis." She still had one hand on Scott's arm. She reached out and found Longarm's, as well, then she brought their hands together. "Custis, meet Rance Scott. Rance, this is Deputy U.S. Marshal Custis Long, known to some as Longarm."

The two men shook hands awkwardly in the darkness. "This is one hell of a mess, ain't it, Long?" asked Scott.

"You can say that again," agreed Longarm.

"Custis, what are you doing here?" asked Jessie. "You can't have come looking for me, because we were just captured earlier today."

"I was looking for somebody, all right. A couple of owlhoots I trailed up here from Arizona Territory. Along the way I found out about this place and how it's being used as a hideout. I didn't know until I got here, though, that it had any connection to the cartel."

Jessie's voice was cold with anger. "I take it you've met the Empress?"

"Yeah."

"And she knows who you are?"

"That's right. I reckon she would've come after me next, more than likely, if I hadn't sort of fallen right into her lap."

For the next few minutes, Longarm and Jessie filled each other in on everything that had happened to them over the past couple of weeks. It had been an eventful time for both of them. Jessie wasn't surprised that eventually their trails had converged and brought them both here at the same time, delivering them right into the hands of their worst enemy. As Ki might have said, everything in the universe followed its own preordained path. There was no such thing as coincidence.

But neither did people have to accept their destiny, if they were strong enough and determined enough to change it.

Or perhaps, that alternate course was really their destiny all along.

Jessie shook her head. This wasn't the time for philosophy, Eastern or otherwise. She said, "Custis, what are we going to do?"

"Is there any way out of this hole?"

"Not really. There's some sort of opening on the other side of the room, but it's closed off with iron bars."

"Have you checked to see how solidly they're set in the stone?"

Jessie bit back a curse. She hadn't gotten around to that; she and Scott had been too busy making love. She realized now that was one of the first things she should have checked.

Without really answering Longarm's question, she said, "Let's see about that."

Keeping one hand on the wall to guide her, she made her way around the underground chamber until she came to the barred opening. It was about four feet wide and six feet tall, she determined by touch. She wrapped her hands around the bars and tugged and twisted. They didn't move.

Longarm spoke from beside her. "Some sort of tunnel on the other side, ain't there?"

"I think so. That's what it looked like, from the brief glimpse I got of it." Jessie tugged on the bars again, still to no avail.

"Put your face up here," said Longarm quietly. "Feel that."

Jessie leaned closer to the bars and concentrated. After a moment she realized what Longarm was talking about. "There's a draft," she said. "It's very faint, but it's definitely there."

"That means there's an opening at the other end," Scott put in from behind them.

"Yeah," said Longarm, "this is a way out, if we could just get past these bars. I figure this house belonged to one of the fellas who owned silver mines around here. Maybe he had this tunnel put in to connect his house to one of his mines. Don't know why he'd want to be able to go back and forth like that without anybody knowing about it, but you never can tell what an hombre with a lot of money will do. Sometimes they come up with crazy ideas."

"Let's all get hold of the same bar," suggested Jessie. "Maybe between the three of us, we can loosen it."

"Good idea," said Longarm. "Crowd on in here, Scott."

Jessie tightened her hold on the bar. Working by feel, Longarm got his hands on the same bar, and so did Scott. Jessie was between them, with Longarm on her left and Scott on her right. Even though the sensation was definitely strange, Jessie reflected that, under other circumstances, having a naked, muscular, male body pressing against her from both sides might not be such a bad thing. She put that thought out of her head and said, "Ready?"

"Ready," said Longarm, and Scott echoed the response.

"We'll try to turn it clockwise, so we won't be working against each other," said Jessie. "Now."

With grunts of effort, the three of them began trying to twist the iron bar in its moorings. They strained for long, fruitless minutes, their breath hissing between their teeth as they poured all their strength into the attempt. The bar didn't budge.

Then suddenly, with a tiny grating sound, it turned just slightly.

"Everybody stop a minute and catch your breath," said Longarm. When they had done that, he went on, "Let's give 'er another try."

Again the three of them threw all their weight and strength into trying to turn the iron bar. After a moment it shifted some more. The grating sound was like music to the ears of the prisoners.

Once the bar was broken free it took only a few minutes of work before they were able to twist it without much effort. The bar was still set into the floor and ceiling of the tunnel opening, however, so the way was still blocked.

"Work it back and forth," said Jessie. "We've got to get enough play in it to pull it out of there."

With all three of them still holding the bar, they began

pushing it back and forth and from side to side, trying to wallow out the setting enough so that one end of the bar could slip out. They concentrated their efforts on the top of the bar. Mortar dust drifted down around them. Time dragged past as they worked. Jessie had no idea how many hours had gone by, but she was sure night had fallen by now.

Down here in this hole under the mansion, day and night had no real meaning. It was always dark. Jessie's mind began to wander down bizarre paths. She thought that days, perhaps even weeks, must have gone by. Katerina von Blöde was going to leave them in this barren cell to starve. Never again would they see the light of day. Surely they had been working to loosen this bar for at least a month.

Longarm dragged her back to reality by asking, "What happened to Ki?"

"Nothing," said Jessie. "We weren't together when Rance and I were captured, but he was close enough so that I'm sure he knows what happened to us."

"Then he'll be coming to rescue you." There wasn't even a shred of doubt in Longarm's voice when he spoke.

"That's what I've been counting on. But if we can get out, maybe we can find him and all of us together can go after the Empress."

"It'll take more than just the four of us to bust up this rat's nest," said Longarm. "We need a posse, or even the army. Army'd be better."

"Where are you going to find one, though?"

"Oh, you never know," said Longarm cryptically. "Say, I think this bar might be about to come loose! Jessie, stand back for a minute and let me and Scott give it a good yank."

"I can help," protested Jessie.

"Yeah, but if it comes loose all of a sudden, I don't want it snapping back and hurting you."

"Marshal Long is right," put in Scott. "We can do this, Jessie."

"Oh, all right," she muttered. "I'll let you big strong men do it."

She moved away from the tunnel mouth and waited. She heard Longarm say, "Got a good hold on it, Scott?"

"Yeah, I'm ready if you are," replied the rancher.

"On three, then. One, two, *three!*"

Jessie heard them both groan with the strain of what they were doing. With a rasp and a clatter of falling stone and mortar, the bar came loose at the top. "We got it!" said Scott excitedly.

"That's just one," said Longarm. "The gap it left ain't wide enough for you or me to squeeze through it, Scott." He paused. "But you might be able to, Jessie."

Even though they couldn't see her response in the darkness, Jessie immediately shook her head. "The hell with that!" she said. "I'm not going to leave the two of you, so you might as well not ask me to do that, Custis."

"Listen, it makes sense," said Longarm. "With both you and Ki on the loose, Scott and me stand a whole lot better chance of getting out of here alive. You know that, Jessie."

"The marshal's right, Jessie," added Scott. "You've got to go now, while you've got a chance. We don't know how long it'll be before—"

As if waiting for their proper cue, heavy footsteps sounded on the other side of the door at the top of the stairs. They stopped, and again the bar was lifted.

Longarm grabbed Jessie's shoulder and said, "We're out of time! Go on, Jessie. Get out if you can."

"Do it, Jessie!" urged Scott. "Hurry!"

Horribly torn by her emotions, Jessie hesitated, but only for a moment. Then, as the key rattled in the padlock, she moved over to the bars, felt for the gap, and started to slide through it.

"All right," she said to Longarm and Scott. "But don't give up. I'll find Ki, and we'll get you out of here."

"I know that," said Longarm. "Now go!"

The gap was barely large enough for her to fit her body between the remaining bars. She had to suck in her stomach to do so, and the bars scraped roughly on her breasts and hips. For one sickening moment she was afraid that she was stuck, but then she popped on through. The stone floor of the tunnel was the same as inside the cell. She waved her hands around until she found one of the walls, then kept her hand on the stone to guide her as she started moving hurriedly away from the chamber where Longarm and Rance Scott were still imprisoned.

She said a silent prayer that they would be all right until she got back to save them—assuming that this tunnel was even a way out. But she could feel a slight breeze even stronger on her face now. There had to be some sort of opening to the outside world at the end of the tunnel. If there were no other barriers . . . if there were no bottomless pits along the way for her to fall into . . . if she didn't stumble into a den of rattlesnakes or something like that.

Jessie pushed all those thoughts out of her mind and kept moving. She had been in plenty of tight spots in her adventurous life, and she had never given up hope. She wasn't just about to start now.

• • •

Longarm and Scott moved to opposite sides of the cell, instinctively splitting up so they'd have room to move if violence broke out once the men coming down the stairs saw that Jessie was gone. They squinted against the light and clenched their fists. Longarm would have given a lot to have his Colt in his hand at this moment, but that wasn't going to happen.

Heinrich was the first one down the stairs, poking his shotgun in front of him. He stopped short, three or four steps shy of the bottom, and exclaimed angrily, "*Scheiss! The bitch is gone!*"

With a rush of footsteps, he and Conrad came on down the steps, menacing Longarm and Scott with their guns. They held their fire, though, as they stared at the gap in the iron bars.

The light that came from above allowed Longarm to see a short distance along the tunnel, maybe fifty feet or so, and Jessie was out of sight. He couldn't even hear her moving along the stone floor with her bare feet.

Heinrich thrust the barrels of the greener at Longarm's face and snarled, "Where is she? Where did she go?"

"Reckon you can see that for yourself, old son," drawled Longarm. "The important thing is, she ain't here no more, and you're gonna have to go tell that news to your boss, the Empress."

Heinrich's lips drew back from his teeth. "I should kill you now."

"Go ahead. I don't reckon Miss von Blöde'd like it very much, though."

Heinrich backed off. Conrad continued to cover Scott. The third man on the stairs tossed a bundle onto the floor

274

of the cell. Longarm recognized it as his clothes, along with those of another man. He guessed the extra duds belonged to Scott.

"Get dressed," ordered Heinrich. "The Empress is ready to see you again."

Longarm and Scott pulled on their clothes. They didn't get their boots back, or their gun belts, either, of course. With guns trained on them from both directions, they climbed the stairs and emerged from the makeshift dungeon underneath the mansion.

All the lamps in the place seemed to be burning, confirming Longarm's guess that night had fallen. He had lost track of time to a certain extent while he and Jessie and Scott were locked up, but the fact that it was dark outside didn't surprise him. He and Scott were marched to the Empress's parlor, where the draperies were pulled now over the big windows.

Katerina von Blöde waited there for them. She wore a more elaborate gown now, something befitting the title of empress that she had bestowed upon herself. As Longarm and Scott walked in, followed by their guards, Katerina's face tightened with anger.

"I told you to bring all three of them," she snapped at Heinrich and Conrad.

"Empress, the . . . the Starbuck woman is gone," said Heinrich.

Katerina's normally fair face darkened with rage. "Gone?" she repeated. "How is that possible?"

"They broke loose one of the bars that blocked the way into the old tunnel. Even so, I do not see how it was possible for the woman to slip through—"

"Damn it!" Katerina turned and pounded a small fist

275

on the top of the grand piano. "My father told me that Jessica Starbuck seemed able to work miracles, but I didn't really believe him! Damn it!"

Conrad spoke up, saying, "We will send men to find her, Empress, right away."

Katerina straightened and nodded. "Summon Yellow-stone. He knows this area as well or better than anyone. Tell him to take however many men he needs to find the woman and bring her back here."

"I assume she is not to be harmed?"

"That's right. I still have a special fate planned for Jessica Starbuck." The Empress turned again to Longarm and Scott. "For one thing, I was going to force her to watch as I dealt with you two, or rather, as you deal with each other. I believe I will go ahead with that, despite the fact that your woman is not here to see you suffer."

Longarm didn't like the sound of that. Despite her youth and beauty, this woman was crazy enough to come up with just about anything.

"What did you have in mind?" he asked.

Katerina smiled coldly. "From time to time I like to provide entertainment for those who come to Zamora. Tonight will be such an entertainment. You see, Marshal, you and Mr. Scott here are going to fight each other—to the death."

Chapter 23

Jessie felt like she had been trudging along through darkness forever. The tunnel had angled downward for a while, and she had found herself splashing along through puddles of cold water. The stone floor became slippery with moss. Just when Jessie had started to think that she was going to be forced to descend forever, to the dank pits where dwelled the worms of the earth, the tunnel began to slope up again. And as she climbed, the breeze in her face freshened even more. Her feet were numb with cold and goosebumps covered her body, but she kept moving and felt hope leap inside her as she suddenly realized that what she saw in front of her was no longer pitch black. The darkness now had tinges of gray to it.

She was moving so quickly that she grew careless. She ran head-on into a wall, and the impact made her stagger back a couple of steps. She gasped in pain from banging her head against something. After a few moments, the ache subsided and she caught her breath. She reached out in front of her with both hands and moved forward slowly until she touched something. Something different. Not stone, but—wood!

The rungs of a ladder.

Jessie tilted her head back and looked up. She almost cried out for joy when she saw tiny pinpoints of light and realized that they were stars floating in the night sky. The tunnel turned here and went up to the surface. Jessie couldn't tell how far above her the opening was, and she couldn't see if the ladder was complete the entire way. But she grasped the rungs and began to climb anyway.

Up and up she went, tired muscles reenergized now by the nearness of escape. Some of the rungs were indeed missing, and others had rotted until she was afraid to put her weight on them, but each time she was able to reach past the missing or bad ones and find a more secure grip higher up. The starlight grew brighter the higher she climbed. She could see her hands clearly now as they grasped the rungs.

She estimated that she was less than fifteen feet from the top when something suddenly blotted out some of the stars. A voice rasped, "Just keep climbin', ma'am. You're nearly here, and ol' Yellowstone's waitin' for you."

Jessie bit back a wail of despair. To come this far, to nearly get away, only to be recaptured! It just wasn't fair.

But she knew that life was seldom if ever fair, and she quickly discarded the idea that had come to her—to let go of the rungs and plummet to her death. Giving up like that simply wasn't something that it was in her to do. She would fight against her enemies as long as there was breath in her body.

A match flared into life. Jessie ducked her head to shield her eyes from the glare. When they had adjusted, she looked up again and saw Yellowstone peering down at her, match in one hand, rifle in the other. He grinned at her. "Come on, pretty lady. I won't hurt you. I got to take you back to the Empress, but I won't be rough with you."

"She'll kill me," said Jessie.

"Well, if that happens, it'll be a plumb shame, but that's between you an' her, not me." Yellowstone jerked the barrel of his rifle. "Come on now. Don't make me come down there and—"

Jessie heard the thud, saw the burly outlaw stiffen. The rifle and the match both slipped out of his hands and fell down the shaft behind Jessie, the rifle clattering against the walls, the lucifer tumbling so that the light from its flame flickered and shifted wildly before going out. Jessie saw Yellowstone hauled backward out of the opening at the top of the tunnel.

Then another face replaced that of the outlaw, and tears of relief sprang into Jessie's eyes as she recognized it in the starlight.

"Keep climbing," Ki told her as he extended a hand toward her. "You only have a short distance to go."

The Empress must have put the word out to everybody in town. Longarm figured there were close to two hundred men gathered along Zamora's main street, ready for the entertainment that Katerina had promised them. They had left an area clear in the middle of the street, in front of the hotel, and this was where he and Rance Scott were prodded by the Empress's gunmen.

Katerina herself appeared on the hotel porch, overlooking the open area. She was followed by Heinrich and Conrad. Silence fell over the crowd of owlhoots as she moved forward to the edge of the porch and grasped the railing.

279

"Citizens of Zamora," said Katerina into the expectant hush. "Thank you for abandoning your usual pursuits for a short time, so that you may help me celebrate an important occasion—the death of one of my enemies! The death of a man who is a threat to us all! The death of a lawman!"

Cheers and howls of glee went up from the assembled outlaws. Katerina smiled and let the uproar go on for a few minutes before she raised her hands for quiet and got it.

"This man," she said, pointing to Longarm, "is Deputy United States Marshal Custis Long! Some of you already have reason to hate him!"

Longarm looked over and saw the last of the stagecoach bandits from Arizona watching from the front ranks of the crowd. The youngster's eyes glowed with hatred in the glare from the torches positioned along the street.

"I have reason to hate him!" Katerina went on. "He was partially to blame for the death of my father, the man without whose example Zamora would not exist!"

Curses and blasphemies rained down on Longarm. He ignored them. Katerina was trying to work the crowd up into a fever pitch. She was determined that they were going to get a good show tonight.

"Now that blood debt will be settled! These two men will fight to the death!"

More cheers sounded. When they died down, Rance Scott surprised Longarm by calling to the Empress, "Why?"

Katerina frowned at him. "What?"

"Why should I fight him?" Scott waved a hand at Longarm. "I don't have anything against him. I never even met him before today. Same goes for the marshal."

"It's very simple," said Katerina. She nodded to Heinrich and Conrad, both of whom held rifles. They lifted the weapons and trained them on Scott. "You will either fight Marshal Long, Mr. Scott, or my men will kill you right now. Then they will kill Marshal Long. So being stubborn will gain you nothing."

"What will fighting gain me besides a few more minutes of life?"

Katerina smiled. "When faced with death, what can be more precious than a few more minutes of life?" Without waiting for an answer, she went on, "But I'll sweeten the pot for you, Mr. Scott. Kill Marshal Long, and I'll allow you to live. You'll never leave Zamora, of course . . . but you'll be alive."

Scott didn't say anything. He just turned his head and gave Longarm a speculative look.

Longarm said, "What about me? I reckon you plan on me dying either way. Why should I fight? What do I get if I win?"

"A quick death," replied Katerina. "Quick . . . and relatively painless. Which is more than you deserve after what you did."

"You sure know how to make it hard for a fella to turn down your offer," drawled Longarm dryly.

Katerina's face hardened. "There has been enough talk," she said. "The time has come for battle!"

And as soon as the words were out of the Empress's mouth, Rance Scott turned and launched himself at Longarm, swinging a fist in a roundhouse blow at the big lawman's head.

The move took Longarm a little by surprise, but he recovered his wits quickly enough to duck under the wild punch and tackle Scott around the waist. He drove the rancher backward, off his feet. Both men went down, sprawling in the dust of the street as they rolled over and over, grappling with each other.

Scott broke free from Longarm's grip and made it back to his feet first. He swung as Longarm tried to get up. The punch landed on Longarm's jaw and knocked him backward. Scott tried to follow up on his momentary advantage by rushing forward, poised to stomp the life out of Longarm.

But even as Scott's foot started down at Longarm's face, the big lawman reached up, grabbed it, and heaved. With a startled yell, Scott pitched headlong over Longarm, flying through the air and then crashing to the ground. He rolled over a couple of times from the momentum of his fall and was brought up short by the steps leading to the hotel porch.

Longarm scrambled up and went after him. Blood trickled from the corner of the lawman's mouth where Scott had punched him. Longarm cocked a fist and shot it forward as Scott surged up. The blow caught Scott in the face and knocked him backward. He sprawled on the steps. Longarm lunged toward him, hands reaching for Scott's throat, obviously intent on choking the life out of him.

But suddenly, Longarm's hands slapped down on the edge of the porch instead, giving him leverage as he somersaulted over Scott and slammed into Heinrich's legs, bowling over the Empress's man. At the same time Scott leaped up and swung a malletlike fist at Conrad, taking him by surprise. The punch crashed into Conrad's face.

The crowd had been yelling enthusiastically as the two men battled for their lives, but now the tumult took on a surprised note. Longarm moved as fast as he ever had in his life, knowing that he had only split seconds to act. He drove the point of his elbow into Heinrich's throat, crushing his voice box and leaving him gasping futilely for air. In a continuation of the same motion, Longarm snatched the rifle out of the man's hands, rolled over and came up in a crouch. With the Winchester socketed against his shoulder, he lined the sights on the pale, shocked face of Katerina von Blöde.

On the other side of the Empress, Rance Scott had ripped Conrad's rifle away, too, and following Longarm's example he aimed the weapon at Katerina.

Longarm smiled tightly. When he had tackled Scott, he had whispered in the rancher's ear that they should work themselves toward the hotel porch as they battled, and fortunately Scott had picked up immediately on what Longarm had in mind. Once they got close enough to Katerina and her henchmen, they had played it by ear, but things had worked out all right—so far.

They still had to deal with a couple of hundred angry gunmen, any of whom would gladly kill them. But the crowd had fallen into a stunned silence now, too shocked by this sudden turn of events to do anything just yet.

"Better tell your 'loyal subjects' to take it easy, Empress," said Longarm. "Otherwise it'll be *your* brains splattered all over the place."

She stared at him, her lovely face ashen, and gasped, "But . . . but you wouldn't shoot a woman!" Then realization dawned in her eyes, and she laughed coldly. "What a stupid thing to say! Of course you would, if you had to. But you won't."

Longarm didn't like the certainty in her voice. "What makes you think that?"

"Because within seconds of my death, you and Mr. Scott would be filled with hundreds of rounds of ammu-

283

nition." She waved a hand at the outlaws in the street. "These men would shoot you to pieces."

An angry howl of agreement went up from one of the desperadoes.

"Yeah," said Longarm, "but you'd still be dead. All your high and mighty plans would be dust, Empress, just like you. Is that what you want?"

Katerina's lips tightened. "What do *you* want, Marshal Long?"

"For me and Scott to get out of here without getting shot. After that . . ." Longarm shrugged a little, but not enough to throw off his aim.

"After that, all my plans are still ruined. You see, I know you, Marshal. You won't stand aside and let my father's cartel be reborn. You and *that woman* will do your best to smash all my dreams."

Longarm didn't bother denying the charge. He said, "Well, then, I reckon we got us a standoff."

Katerina smiled. "Not really. You see, I'm prepared to die in order to realize my goals." She turned and looked into the crowd of outlaws. "Mr. Darrow!"

One of the owlhoots stepped forward, followed by a couple of other men who were probably his friends. "What is it, Empress?" he asked in a taut, worried voice.

"Mr. Darrow, if anything happens to me, I'm placing you and Mayor Abernathy and Yellowstone in charge of Zamora. I know the three of you will do a good job of running the place."

Darrow, a lantern-jawed man with prematurely white hair, shook his head and said, "Damn it, Empress, don't talk like that. Nothing's gonna happen to you. Nobody will let anything happen to you."

Katerina's smile became wistful. Softly, she said,

"There is always a price to be paid if great things are to be accomplished." She took a deep breath and squared her shoulders, obviously about to say something else, perhaps to give an order.

"Shit," muttered Longarm under his breath.

The Empress's voice lashed out, powerful with command. "Mr. Darrow, kill Marshal Long!"

Darrow's face twisted with the emotions warring inside him, but his hand stabbed toward the gun on his hip.

Longarm pivoted the Winchester and fired, shooting Darrow in the chest. The rifle slug lifted him off his feet and threw him back against his companions.

"Grab her!" Longarm shouted at Scott. "Inside the hotel!"

Scott lunged at Katerina, wrapped an arm around her waist, and jerked her off her feet. Longarm worked the rifle's lever and sprayed the crowd with bullets as Scott darted inside the building, hauling the Empress along with him. Both of Darrow's friends tumbled off their feet, cut down by the lawman's bullets. Longarm whirled around and flung himself headlong at the door of the hotel as bullets began to sizzle around him and chew into the planks of the porch. Miraculously, none of them struck him as he dove through the door and rolled on the floor of the lobby. He kicked the door closed behind him. Slugs thudded into it. A few of them punched all the way through.

Scott had the Empress down, kneeling on her, pinning her to the floor. Longarm crawled to the front window, smashed the glass out with the barrel of the rifle, and raised up long enough to send another couple of shots into the rapidly scattering crowd of owlhoots.

"What the hell do we do now, Long?" asked Scott.

"There's too many of 'em to stand off. They'll either overrun us from the front or get behind the hotel and come in that way."

Longarm nodded grimly. "I know. All we've bought is a few minutes. But like the Empress said, when you're about to die, a few minutes can be mighty important—"

He stopped short as he heard something over the sound of the shots that still peppered the front of the hotel. Something he had never expected to hear in this situation. He listened hard for a moment to make sure that he hadn't imagined it.

Then he said, "You hear that, Scott?"

"Hear what? I don't—" The rancher stopped short, his eyes widening. "Is that . . . ?"

"A bugle," said Longarm. "I ain't sure what they're doing here, but it sounds to me like the cavalry's about to arrive."

Before either man had time to fully wrap their minds around this unexpected development, Katerina suddenly twisted underneath Scott, and her arm flashed up. Scott grunted in pain and fell backward, sitting down hard. He stared in amazement at the handle of the knife protruding from his chest, the knife that the Empress must have had hidden somewhere in her gown.

Meanwhile, Katerina leaped to her feet and dashed toward a door at the back of the lobby. Longarm snapped a shot at her but missed. The bullet knocked plaster from the wall instead. Katerina vanished through the door as Longarm bit back a curse.

It didn't matter that she had gotten away, he told himself. From here on out, she wouldn't make much difference in the fight, one way or the other. She had already

286

done her damage. Longarm crawled across the floor to Scott, who had slumped over onto his side.

"Take it easy, old son," Longarm told him, raising his voice a little to be heard over the crash of gunfire. "You'll be all right."

"Should've . . . known," grated Scott. "Should've known . . . a snake like her . . . would have fangs."

"Just hang on. I'll get help for you as soon as I can."

"Long . . ." Scott's hand caught at Longarm's sleeve. "Take care of . . . Jessie."

"I will," promised Longarm. "But you don't have to worry, Scott." Longarm turned his head toward the sounds of battle that were intensifying outside. "If there's one woman in this world who can take care of herself, it's Jessie Starbuck."

Wearing a shirt and trousers borrowed from one of the members of Sheriff Bodie Haines's posse, Jessie rode at the head of the combined force made up of deputies and cavalrymen, along with Ki, Salty Stevens, Sheriff Haines, and Colonel Mortimer. Both the lawman and the army officer had insisted that she stay well back, all the way behind the group of a hundred and fifty men, if possible.

Jessie had borrowed a Winchester to go along with the clothes and promptly ignored the men's wishes. She had commandeered Yellowstone's horse, too, since he wouldn't be needing it. He was tied up securely and under guard, along with the handful of other outlaws he had brought with him from Zamora when the Empress sent him to find Jessie and bring her back. Ki and Salty had jumped them and taken them prisoner. The warrior and the old-timer, who had explained to Jessie that he had been appointed a temporary federal deputy by Billy Vail, had been scouting out ahead of the main force when they encountered Yellowstone's party waiting at the head of the old tunnel.

Jessie still wasn't exactly sure what was going on, but further explanations could wait. It was enough that these men had come to the mountains to ride into Zamora and smash that vulture's sanctuary.

She just hoped they would be in time to save Longarm and Rance Scott.

They had nearly reached the old ghost town when shots suddenly broke out, a lot of them. Mortimer and Haines exchanged a look, and the sheriff said, "Whatever's goin' on down there, it can't be good."

Mortimer agreed. He raised an arm, called, "Bugler, sound the charge!" and then swept his arm forward in the signal to attack.

One thing about it, thought Jessie, the fact that everybody in Zamora was an owlhoot meant that the posse and the cavalry didn't have to worry quite as much about innocents being hurt. She hoped that the whores and any other noncombatants would hunt a hole and keep their heads down.

In a matter of moments, the riders reached the end of Zamora's main street and thundered into the settlement. Shots roared from both sides of the street, knocking some of the men out of their saddles, but the cavalrymen and deputies returned the fire effectively. Some of them leaped off their horses and plunged into the buildings, guns blazing as they took the battle to Zamora's defenders. The outlaws who were caught out in the open put up a fight, and within minutes the scene in the street had turned into a wild melee.

Jessie stayed mounted and snapped shots from the Winchester. Ki was on one side of her, Salty on the other, both of them wielding rifles as well. Jessie kept an eye open for a familiar face, hoping to see Longarm or Scott, or perhaps both of them. It was possible they were still locked up in the stone cell underneath the Empress's mansion. The rescuers would get there sooner or later.

Longarm would be mighty annoyed at missing all the action, though, thought Jessie as she fired at an owlhoot trying to reach the safety of an alley and sent him tumbling off his feet.

Suddenly she caught sight of another figure running through that alley. Only one woman in Zamora would be wearing a gown that fancy, she realized.

The Empress!

Jessie whirled her horse around and dug her bare heels into the animal's flanks, urging it into a run as she gave chase to Katerina von Blöde.

Brad Corrigan pressed his back to the side wall of the hotel and tried to still the frantic pounding of his heart. His palm was sweaty as he clutched the butt of his gun. Bullets were flying everywhere, and the street was full of cavalrymen and deputies, and everything had gone wrong. Tom had said they would be safe here, and for a while it had seemed that way, but now Tom was dead and the law was here and that big bastard who had killed the other three Corrigan brothers was still alive.

That just wasn't right. No matter what it cost him, Brad knew he had to even that score. He took a couple of deep breaths and felt his wildly racing pulse slow a little.

The son of a bitch had retreated into the hotel. He was probably still there, Brad told himself. All he had to do was get in the back, take the bastard by surprise, and fill him full of lead. Brad swallowed hard and started stealing along the alley toward the rear of the building.

As he reached the back corner, someone dashed past him. In the darkness and confusion, Brad caught only a glimpse of the figure, but he thought it belonged to the Empress. She must have gotten away from Long, he thought.

He didn't care about the Empress, didn't care about anything except avenging the deaths of his brothers. He slipped through the hotel's rear door and catfooted up a hallway toward the lobby, his six-gun extended in front of him, ready to fire.

There! he thought as he stepped through an open door and found himself beside the registration desk. Only a few yards away, Long knelt beside the man he had been fighting earlier. The marshal's back was turned toward Brad. Brad leaned forward, his finger tightening on the trigger . . .

That was when one of the floorboards creaked just a little under his foot. Not much of a noise, but enough of one.

The marshal moved too fast for the eye to follow, spinning around and lifting the rifle in his hands. He and Brad fired at the same instant, but Brad's shot went wild, passing harmlessly over Long's shoulder, while the lawman's bullet smashed into Brad's chest like a blow from a giant fist. Brad was thrown backward by the impact. He caught himself against the registration desk and tried to lift his gun for another shot. He knew he was hurt bad, probably dying, but surprisingly, there was no pain. He was numb from the shock. His fingers fumbled on the gun, losing their grip. He cried out in disappointment as the weapon slipped from his hand and thudded to the floor at his feet.

He followed it, pitching forward, and he seemed to be falling from a great height, so high that he couldn't even see the ground anymore. All he knew was that he was falling, falling, and that he had failed to avenge Tom and Asa and Logan, failed all the way around, and it just wasn't fair, damn it, not fair at all.

He didn't feel it when he landed face-first on the floor, because he was dead by that time.

Jessie closed in rapidly on the Empress. She saw Katerina look around wildly and then try to dart to the side, but the move came too late. Jessie had already left the saddle. She crashed into Katerina in a diving tackle. Both women sprawled on the ground, rolling through the dirt and muck of the alley behind Zamora's buildings.

Katerina fought viciously, savagely, but she was no match for Jessie Starbuck, who had not only packed a lot of adventure into her relatively short life but also worked on a ranch and had always been physically active. Jessie slammed a punch into Katerina's jaw, then drove a knee into her midsection. She hit the Empress in the face again. Katerina went limp.

Jessie pushed herself to her feet, wiped the back of a hand across her mouth, and looked down at the senseless figure. It seemed hard to believe that the pathetic, huddled shape had been responsible for the deaths of so many men, reaching all the way back to Jonas Gibson. Jessie bent, grabbed hold of Katerina's feet, and began dragging her toward Zamora's main street. The gunfire was dying down now. As Jessie emerged from the shadows of the alley, she saw cavalrymen and deputies herding groups of prisoners at gunpoint. The battle was over except for the mopping up.

"Jessie!"

The familiar voice made her jerk her head toward the porch of the hotel. She saw Longarm standing there and cried out, "Custis!"

He hurried over to her, carrying a rifle, and asked anxiously, "Are you all right?"

"Fine," she replied. "What about you?"

"Reckon my hide's still all in one piece." He looked past her at Katerina. "Is that who I think it is?"

Jessie laughed curtly and reached down to roll Katerina onto her back. Her fancy gown was filthy and in tatters now, and her hair had come loose from its elaborate arrangement of curls and hung in dirty tangles around her smudged face.

"The Empress of Zamora," said Jessie caustically. "Doesn't look quite so regal now, does she?"

"Her only empire's gonna be behind bars," said Longarm. "Jessie . . ."

Something about the big lawman's tone alarmed her. "Custis, what is it?" A thought occurred to her. "Oh, my God, where's Rance?"

Longarm nodded toward Katerina. "She stabbed him before she got away from us. He's alive. Colonel Mortimer's company surgeon is working on him inside the hotel lobby."

Jessie's pulse hammered with concern over Scott. She glanced at Katerina and said, "Will you—"

"Don't worry, I'll look after her," Longarm assured her. "She won't get away again. You go see about Rance."

She nodded and broke into a run, heading for the hotel.

When she burst in through the front entrance, she saw Scott lying on the floor with a man in uniform straightening beside him. The officer had a surgeon's bag that he was just closing. Dread gripped Jessie's heart as she saw how still and pale Scott was.

"Doctor," she said as she started forward tentatively.

The surgeon turned and gave her a tired smile. "Miss Starbuck," he said. "Is this man a friend of yours?"

"Yes," she said, choking back tears. "Yes, he's a friend."

"Good, because he was badly hurt. But the knife missed the vital organs, and he's going to be all right if he gets a lot of rest and care. I have a feeling you're just the person to give it to him."

"Oh, yes," she said, gasping with relief as she hurried forward. Now she could see the bandage wrapped tightly around Scott's chest. As she dropped to her knees beside him and grasped his hand, he opened his eyes and looked up at her.

"Jessie . . ." he whispered.

"I'm right here, Rance," she told him. "And you're going to be all right."

"Now . . . I am." His eyes closed again, but his bandaged chest rose and fell steadily.

As she held his hand, Jessie heard footsteps coming into the hotel. She glanced over her shoulder, saw Longarm and Ki, Sheriff Haines and Colonel Mortimer, the old-timer called Salty. Longarm grinned at her.

"It's over, isn't it?" she asked him, aware that silence had fallen over Zamora now.

He nodded. "It's over," said Longarm.

Chapter 24

But it wasn't.

However, Longarm didn't find out about that until much later. First, he had to figure out just what had happened.

"You got Henry to thank for pullin' your irons outta the fire, Custis," explained Salty as they sat in the Oasis Saloon the next day. "He was the one who kept sendin' wires all over the country tryin' to find out more about this place called Zamora. He found out that somebody had been buyin' a bunch of fresh lumber and supplies and havin' 'em shipped in here, and when he traced all the shipments back, he came across the name Katerina von Blöde." The old-timer chuckled. "Once Billy Vail heard about that and realized this business had some connection to that old cartel you once told me about, he started burnin' up the wires and convinced the War Department not to wait to hear from you. They sent Colonel Mortimer and his boys in right away, along with a posse headed by Sheriff Haines. And he appointed me to come along, too,

295

since you and me was in on the start o' this case together, and he wanted the Justice Department to have another representative here."

"So you're a deputy marshal now, too, you old pelican?" asked Longarm with a grin.

"Temporary-like. But I been thinkin' I might try to make it permanent, if you think I ain't too decrepit. My cousin Sleepy works as a range detective, and he's always full o' stories 'bout the adventures him and his pard get into. I wouldn't mind havin' a few yarns to throw back at him."

"You'll have to talk to Billy Vail about that." Longarm shook his head. "Lord, now I'm gonna have to be nice to Henry for a while, I reckon. I don't know if either of us can stand it." He took a sip from the glass of Maryland rye in his hand. "So you led the posse and the army in here?"

Salty nodded. "Yep. Found a way into the valley from a different direction, so we didn't have to go through that bottleneck canyon they kept guarded all the time. First we run into ol' Ki, who'd already wiped out some o' the guards, and then we found Miss Starbuck, and then . . . well, you know what happened after that. We come bustin' in here and cleaned up this buzzard's nest. It was a pretty good fight while it lasted, too."

Movement at the saloon's entrance caught Longarm's eye. He looked over and saw Jessie push through the batwings. She had reclaimed her own clothes and looked like she was back to normal. She smiled at Longarm and Salty as she came toward the table where they sat. Both men stood up to greet her, but she waved them back into their chairs.

"We don't stand on ceremony around here," she said with a laugh. She took one of the empty chairs.

Longarm asked, "How's Rance doing?"

"He's a little stronger today. We'll stay here in Zamora for a while until he's well enough to travel, then head back to the Circle Star for the rest of his recuperation."

"What about Ki?"

"He's going to take Shorty up to the railroad and start back to Texas ahead of us."

Longarm shook his head. "Sure turned out to be a mighty big fuss over a bull."

"The bull was just part of it, a small part. What the Empress really wanted to do was to lure me into a trap."

"Which she succeeded in doing," Longarm pointed out.

Jessie shrugged. "I've been living too tame a life these past few years. I don't spot trouble coming as easily as I used to."

"Well, maybe things will be peaceful for you from now on."

"Maybe," said Jessie. "But I wouldn't count on it." She looked over at the old-timer. "Salty, would you mind if I talked to Custis alone for a minute?"

"Nope." Salty got to his feet. "Talk to the long-legged galoot all you want to. I got to see Ki before he leaves town. He said he'd teach me how to center myself and balance my chi, whatever that is." He slapped the holstered gun on his hip. "I told him I needed balancin', 'cause I been totin' iron for so long I walk a mite slanch-wise!"

Longarm shook his head in amusement as the old-timer stomped out of the saloon. Then he grew more solemn as he looked at Jessie and said, "I'm glad we both came through this all right. I've missed you, gal. We had some high ol' times together, didn't we?"

She reached across the table and clasped one of his hands in both of hers. "We sure did, Custis . . . and that's what I wanted to talk to you about."

"Well, I'm here. Go ahead."

She took a deep breath. "There's nothing I'd like better than to have a reunion with you . . . a *real* reunion, if you know what I mean . . . but under the circumstances, what with Rance being wounded and all, and me taking him back to the ranch to heal up . . ."

"You're saying it'd be a mite awkward for you and me to get together the way we used to."

"That's right. I'm sorry, Custis."

Longarm shook his head. "Nothing to be sorry about. We're still good friends, you and me, and as for what the future might bring, *quién sabe*? Who knows?" He smiled. "I've always said it's best to eat the apple one bite at a time, Jessie. No reason to change now."

She squeezed his hand. "Thank you, Custis. I just didn't want things to get uncomfortable." She hesitated. "Although . . . there was a moment there in that cell under the Empress's mansion, when all three of us were crowded in there together . . . No, never mind. Best not to think about that."

"Yeah," agreed Longarm solemnly. "Best not."

And even though he was sorry to see her go, he was still smiling when she left.

He knew something was wrong as soon as he stepped into the outer office. Henry looked like he'd eaten a whole bushel of prunes.

"What is it?" asked Longarm as he tossed his Stetson on the hat tree.

"Marshal Vail wants to see you right away," replied Henry. "He's had some news from Washington."

Longarm frowned. Any news that came from Wash-

298

ington was usually bad. He went into the inner office without knocking.

Billy Vail looked as upset as Henry did. He jerked a thumb at the red leather chair in front of the desk and said, "Sit down, Custis. I've got something to tell you about Katerina von Blöde."

Longarm settled down on the chair and said, "She's still behind bars, ain't she?"

"She's on a boat bound for Europe," Vail replied bluntly.

Longarm stiffened. "What the hell happened?"

"Officials from the German Empire lodged a protest with the government. Seems that Miss von Blöde really is some sort of Prussian nobility. They claimed that we didn't have any right to hold her or prosecute her, and some jackass in Washington decided they were right. So she was put on a ship and sent home, after being told that she'd never be allowed in this country again."

"But she's loose," said Longarm as he leaned forward angrily. "She got a bunch of men killed, good and bad, and now she's free to go back to Europe and start hatching more mischief."

"Maybe she won't," said Vail. "Maybe she'll settle for the harm she's already done."

Somehow, Longarm didn't think that would be the case. He took out a cheroot and bit the end off it.

"Billy," he said bleakly, "I don't reckon we've seen the last of that new cartel . . . or the Empress."

GIANT-SIZED ADVENTURE FROM AVENGING ANGEL LONGARM.

Longarm and the Undercover Mountie
0-515-14017-1

This all-new, giant-sized adventure in the popular all-action
series puts the "wild" back in the Wild West.

U.S. Marshal Custis Long and Royal Canadian Mountie
Sergeant Foster have an evil town to clean up—where
outlaws indulge their wicked ways. But first, they'll have to
stay ahead of the meanest vigilante committee anybody
ever ran from.